"Are you going to ⟨barcode: W9-AZY-943⟩ hanging out in my backyard?"

"I came by to see you, Riley," Tracy said, "and when no one answered the door, I came back to admire the view. It's better from your yard."

Riley grinned. "You can swing on my swing set anytime, little girl."

Tracy's regard touched on his mouth, then dropped down his torso again. When the blood circled back around to her brain and she homed in on his gleaming eyes, she sighed, resisting another urge to chomp her nails.

"What do you want?" he asked in a voice that was in no way like the one he'd used when she was a child. This was soft, all right, but it was rich with suggestion.

She frowned.

"You said you came to see me," he reminded her.

She gazed at the hair that moved around his head as he shook it. She'd driven over here to ask him to leave, but now the words seemed harsh. "Don't get too comfortable in this town," she said. "And I'm saying that for your own sake. You won't fit in."

His eyes darkened ominously. "You don't think I will?"

"No."

"Then watch me."

Dear Reader,

I love a bad boy–good girl story. Riley Collins, the renegade hero in this novel, was fun to write because he's my favorite kind of bad boy—one who has matured enough to be responsible, but who has kept his adventurous spirit. When I imagine the distant futures of Riley and Tracy, I picture a lifetime of fun and surprises.

In writing this story, I thought a lot about my childhood. I didn't have a counterpart in my life, but Jacque was Riley's female counterpart. She was the little girl from two houses down, and my first best friend. Our family situations were very different, and I admired Jacque for her ability to survive and succeed under difficult circumstances. She moved away during my early teen years, and we didn't keep in touch. I wish we had.

I hope you enjoy Riley and Tracy's story.

Sincerely,

Kaitlyn Rice

THE RENEGADE
Kaitlyn Rice

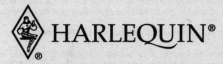

HARLEQUIN®

TORONTO • NEW YORK • LONDON
AMSTERDAM • PARIS • SYDNEY • HAMBURG
STOCKHOLM • ATHENS • TOKYO • MILAN • MADRID
PRAGUE • WARSAW • BUDAPEST • AUCKLAND

ISBN 0-373-75016-1

THE RENEGADE

Copyright © 2004 by Kathy Hagan.

This edition published by arrangement with Harlequin Books S.A.

® and TM are trademarks of the publisher. Trademarks indicated with ® are registered in the United States Patent and Trademark Office, the Canadian Trade Marks Office and in other countries.

Visit us at www.eHarlequin.com

Printed in U.S.A.

This one is for lifelong friends.
To Jacque, wherever you are: I still think about you.
And to Lisa:
I'm so glad we never lost touch.

Chapter One

Tracy Gilbert closed her eyes and lifted her face to the soothing spray of the shower. As she allowed the water to flow through her hair for a final rinse, she calculated the time required to do her morning chores. First, the dry cleaner, then the grocery—the list was already in her purse. An hour should do it. Two at the most. If she told the baby-sitter she'd be home by lunchtime, she might be able to squeeze in a quick trim at Cecilia's shop.

Turning off the tap, Tracy stepped out of the stall. She was just reaching for a towel, when she heard a door slam. Strange—the noise seemed too solid and loud to have come from an interior door. Besides, Hannah should still be asleep and she always left her bedroom door open.

Tracy's mind scrambled to discount the sound. Claus, her cat, might have jumped down from some high perch. A passing car might have backfired. Yet the sound had been a sharp scrape of wood on wood, a span of quiet and then a jarring boom.

Her alarm grew. Neither Claus nor a car could have made that noise. Horrid possibilities flashed through her mind—a home invasion or, worse, a child kidnapped right from bed. A child lost to his or her family for five or ten years. Perhaps never seen again.

Had she locked the door last night? She thought so, but maybe that was the night before last. Was Hannah in her bed? Tracy took off down the hall, wrapping the towel around herself on the way. When she reached the door of her daughter's bedroom and looked in, she breathed a sigh of relief. She stood there a moment, only vaguely aware of the puddle accumulating on the floor at her feet.

Hannah was fine. Her tiny, four-year-old frame was sprawled sideways on the narrow bed. Her glossy black hair fell over one cheek; her feet lay butted against the wall. Most important, her back moved gently up and down as she breathed. Slowly. Deeply. She was still asleep.

Now Tracy wished she'd donned her robe. She needed to investigate that sound right now.

"Yoo-hoo, Tracy. You here?"

Tracy gripped the towel at her chest and whirled around. Even though she recognized the voice immediately, her surprise was enough to keep her heart racing.

Her next door neighbor, Nellie Bell, strolled into the hall wearing a white chenille robe and curlers.

"Lord, Nellie, you scared me to death," Tracy whispered. "What are you doing in here?"

"Sorry," Nellie said, "but I have news. I started to leave a message on your machine, but I knew you were home so I came on over. I rang the doorbell twice."

Tracy grabbed a bony arm to direct Nellie back down the hallway. "I gave you my spare key to use when we're out of town," she hissed, somewhat annoyed. "Not just anytime. I was in the shower."

When they reached the living room, Tracy let go of

Nellie's arm, wondering if her duplex neighbor even noticed that she was dripping wet and covered only by a towel. She considered ushering her right out the front door, but knew she'd only be delaying the inevitable. Usually, the best tack with Nellie was to go along with the drama, then send her away with a polite, but firm, goodbye.

Tracy shook her head. ''Never mind, Nellie. Wait in here for a minute while I dress. And be quiet. Hannah's asleep.''

Tracy padded back toward her bedroom, closing the little girl's door on the way past. While she dressed, she decided that she would ask the landlord to install a dead bolt.

She'd also ask Nellie to return the key. She hoped the news was short and significant. The lovely span of blue sky outside the window made Tracy want to finish her chores early so she could take her little girl to the park.

When she'd brought Hannah home from the central Asian orphanage two years ago, Tracy promised herself that her unmarried status would never be a burden to her child.

Tracy wasn't twenty-nine and single because she was too vacuous or homely to hold a man's interest; she was twenty-nine and single because life was too short for big mistakes. When she married, she'd marry forever.

Adopting a child could never be a mistake, so Tracy had made that commitment. She did her best to provide well for Hannah, and she also tried to be an involved parent. That wasn't always easy. Tracy's office-manager position at Vanderveer Organizing occupied her weekdays, so she sent Hannah to an excellent day-care center that offered preschool activities. Lately, however, Tracy had been bringing work home in the evenings, too.

Hence the need for a diligent handling of weekend chores.

When Tracy returned to the living room, Nellie was sitting on the sofa munching on a doughnut. A white cardboard box containing the rest of the dozen was open on the coffee table in front of her. It looked as if Nellie was settling in. Tracy sighed.

"Here, have a doughnut," Nellie said, nudging the box. "I didn't think to bring drinks. Would you mind?"

Tracy held back a groan and started for the kitchen. "Orange juice?"

"That'd be great."

As she poured the juice, Tracy reminded herself that Nellie was probably just lonely. Besides, this was Kirkwood, Kansas, where major change was generally met with stalwart resistance. Although the student population at Wheatland University caused the town to boom to city size every autumn, permanent residents clung to the ways of their pioneer ancestors. Neighbors talked across fences and borrowed cups of sugar. They lent a hand if a hand was needed. Nellie simply carried that old-fashioned friendliness a step too far.

Make that a few steps. A mile. In fact, she was a total nuisance.

Tracy returned to the living room and set Nellie's glass of juice on the table. "So what's the news?"

Nellie finished chewing her doughnut and blurted, "Riley Collins is back!" Then she scanned Tracy's face with pale, wild eyes.

Tracy's heart started to race again, but she crossed her arms and waited.

"My friend Ruth saw him at the market early this morning, and he was buying a cartful—cereal, bread, cleaners. He bought out the supply of macaroni and cheese. Like he's *staying*."

Tracy drew a deep breath, summoning every ounce of her patience. This was stunning news, absolutely. She still wanted her neighbor out of here. Maybe even more so now.

"He was probably shopping for his grandma," Tracy said as she bent down to close the lid to the doughnut box.

Nellie frowned when Tracy placed the box in her lap, but she didn't stop talking. "Would an old woman use shaving cream and men's razors?"

"Okay, so he's visiting for the weekend." Tracy picked up the full juice glass and walked toward the front door. Just as she expected, Nellie got up and followed her, carrying the box and talking all the way.

"No one would eat a dozen boxes of macaroni and cheese in one weekend. My friend Ruth said he was at the old house all night."

When Nellie noticed that Tracy had opened the door and was handing her the glass of juice, she frowned again.

"I have my own box of doughnuts in the kitchen," Tracy lied. "They'll get stale. You can keep the glass."

Nellie glanced outside and spoke in a louder voice. "We think Riley Collins is hiding out in that old house."

Tracy put a finger to her lips. "The Kirkwood grapevine is thriving, isn't it."

"Aren't you upset?" Nellie asked incredulously.

"Riley is ancient history to me," Tracy said. "And I need to be out the door in twenty minutes."

As Nellie headed toward her own door, she said, sounding put out, "Be that way. I'll bet you another dozen doughnuts that no one else in town has forgotten him.''

Tracy closed the door and drooped against it.

Nor have I.

Riley Collins—the town's most notorious delinquent. The cause of the Gilbert family's biggest heartache. And Tracy's first friend.

Padding back through the living room, Tracy headed down the hall to wake Hannah. The baby-sitter would arrive soon, allowing Tracy to do her away-from-home chores. She'd fit the park visit in after lunch. Later, there was an overflowing laundry basket to contend with, and she'd promised her boss she'd type some reports this weekend. Damn. So little time.

When Tracy noticed her cat sunning on a forbidden windowsill—it was where she displayed a couple of china figurines—she stopped in the middle of the room and glared at him. ''Are you up there again, Claus? Down!''

Other than blinking, the big white tomcat didn't move a muscle. Tracy scooped him up and sank with Claus in her lap into her favorite chair. ''I don't know what he's thinking, coming back here,'' she said. The last time she'd seen Riley, he'd been in some sort of trouble with his father, the equally notorious Otto.

Riley had been out at the curb working on his car that morning, with Otto yelling that he was a good-for-nothing troublemaker from the porch. The next day, Riley had left town in his battered convertible.

That was thirteen years ago. As far as Tracy knew, this was the first time he'd been back.

His leaving town, or rather the *way* he left town and with whom, had proved his father right. Riley was nothing but trouble.

Tracy put Claus on another windowsill and headed for Hannah's room. She wouldn't allow herself to get ruffled. Nellie's informant could be mistaken. The truth would surface eventually, and Tracy could wait to react.

She didn't change her mind until she was strolling down aisle five at Dot's Supermarket. She noticed an entire shelf empty of macaroni-and-cheese boxes, and saw in her mind's eye a tall, blond man tossing them in his cart.

She had to know. She spun around and nearly crashed into an elderly couple conferring over a bottle of olive oil. She retraced her steps, returning the milk to its case and the apples to the stacks, then left the store.

As her car sped north out of town, she thought about what she'd say. Riley's return couldn't be good for anyone but his grandmother, Lydia, and even that was questionable. He had a right to visit Lydia, of course, but he should have no reason to stay. Riley didn't belong here anymore. Tracy had to make sure he knew that.

But when she rang the doorbell at the old house a few minutes later, no one answered. The ugly beige curtains that had always hung over the large front window were open. Tracy would be able to see movement inside, if there was any.

She pressed the bell again. Still receiving no answer, she stepped off the porch to peek through the garage window. The glass was filthy, but she could see there wasn't a car inside. Good. If he'd been here, he was gone now.

Tracy jogged back to her car and grabbed the carafe of green tea she'd left in her cup holder. She'd give herself a few minutes to look around. If she wore an old suit to work on Monday, she could scratch the dry cleaning off today's list and grocery-shop tomorrow.

Hitching up a pant leg, Tracy stepped over the sagging fence to Riley's backyard. It was hard to believe the child's swing set was still back here. The primary stripes that had once painted a falsely optimistic picture of children soaring to the sky had long since mutated to flaking paint and rust. She crossed the lawn quickly and set her drink on the seat of the middle swing. Turning to face the hazy blue hills north of town, she grasped the chains of the swing farthest from the house—always her favorite—and wriggled onto the seat.

The plastic was cold. The weatherman had said it would be warm for late April, but even sixty degrees felt cold through her well-worn ''Saturday jeans''. The swing seemed solid enough to hold her weight, so she pushed off with her feet and swung forward, toward the hills.

''You're trespassing.''

Tracy knew the strange flip of her stomach had nothing to do with the motion of the swing. She skidded to a stop and jumped off the seat, then turned around with her heart in her throat.

It was Riley, standing inside the open storm door at the rear of the house holding a coffee cup. It had to be him. Other men may share a similar combination of smoke-gray eyes and dirty-blond hair, but when you added the teasing smile and dare-me-to-care expression, you had to be looking at Riley.

''Riley?'' she called, in case her thoughts were somehow affecting her eyesight.

''I'm flattered you remember me,'' he said as stepped out and let the door slam behind him.

As if she could have forgotten.

He set his cup on top of a wood box near the door and started across the lawn toward her. As he neared, her throat went dry. Riley had always had a certain heart-wrenching appeal, but he'd improved with age. The eighteen-year-old boy had transformed into every woman's fantasy of confident good looks and muscular build. His hair was longer now, but rather than shaggy and unkempt, it lay smooth, catching the sunlight and making him look sexy. Dangerously so.

Tracy's early-morning stint on her exercise bike had been unnecessary. Her heart had been getting a rather rousing workout ever since her shower. She picked up her tea and took a long swig.

When he reached the swing set, Riley looped an arm over the top beam and ogled her with one side of his mouth tilted up. "Criminy. You've grown up, little girl."

"Guess that happens to everyone." She drank again to wet her throat with the warm liquid, then clutched the carafe against her pounding chest. "I'm not a little girl anymore."

His gaze shot down her body, and back up. "I'll say. What's it been, about a million years?"

The man was too hunky for his own good, and she was tempted to mimic the obvious way he'd checked her out. Instead, she trained her eyes on a lock of hair falling across his forehead. "I was almost sixteen when you left, and I'm twenty-nine now. You were the math whiz."

"My question was purely rhetorical," he said. "I'm perfectly aware of how long it's been. I was the one banished from town, remember?"

"What brings you back now?"

He squinted toward the hills. "There's no reason to stay away now that Otto is gone."

"Are you visiting your grandma?"

"Not exactly." He glanced back over his shoulder.

"I'm renovating her house. I've just come back from the hardware store."

Tracy studied the dilapidated two-story he'd grown up in. For at least half a century, that house had sat next to her parents' limestone cottage. The proximity of the two adjacent, tree-lined lots in the country had fostered strong friendships—and stronger feuds.

For years, Tracy's mom and stepdad had tried to help Otto and Vanessa Collins aspire to better living. Until the night their son had lured Tracy's underage sister away from home, and changed everyone's lives in the process.

"I don't think it'll take too much to make it livable," Riley said, turning around again.

Tracy drank her tea and kept her eyes on the house. It definitely needed work, but she'd thought the Collins family would try to sell it as a fixer upper.

When she realized the significance of what Riley had said, Tracy's tea seemed to curdle in her throat. She choked out, "You aren't planning to live out here, are you?"

Riley's eyes turned dark before he averted them. He began to peel flakes of paint from the top beam. "That makes the most sense to me," he said as he flicked a piece off his thumbnail. "I can work on the place easier if I'm living in it."

"And then?"

At her question, the gaze he aimed in her direction was so intense that she turned her eyes away, pretending interest in a pudgy robin hopping across the yard. In her peripheral vision, Tracy noted that he had crossed his arms over his chest. The seeming force of his will eventually caused her to look up. "And then I'll stop working on it."

"And keep living here?"

He shrugged.

Tracy shook her head. "You think you can waltz back into Kirkwood now and *stay?*"

"I don't see why not."

Tracy sipped her tea once more and realized the last of it was bitter. She unscrewed the thermos lid and poured the liquid onto the grass, then set the container back on the swing seat. Lifting a hand to her mouth, she clamped the nail of her pinkie finger between her teeth.

When he reached out his hand to pull hers from her mouth, she jerked away.

"Don't get all bent out of shape," he said. "I was only trying to stop you from biting your nails."

"Just don't touch me," she said, and her loss of composure sent her eyes careering down his body, over the ribbed white undershirt that clung to a muscled chest and revealed, when his arms were raised to the cross-beam, an inch of enticing bare skin at his flat abdomen, just above the low-slung jeans.

She pulled her shocked eyes up to his glittering ones. The realization that she was drooling over her family's nemesis didn't help at all. Clenching her hands into fists, Tracy said, "Otto wasn't the only one who wanted you gone."

"Oh, really?"

She held his gaze.

"Did you want me gone?" This was said in the same patient voice he'd used when she was a scrawny girl and he was her not-so-secret crush.

"I was a kid. What did I know?"

"You knew me. Did you try to stand up for me?"

She started picking the paint off the swing set, too, thinking back to the day she'd found out Riley was gone.

The phone calls had come first. The high school geometry teacher had called the Gilbert house, looking for Tracy's older sister, Karen. Riley's basketball coach had called his house. Neither teenager had made it to school that day, the teachers reported. And in retrospect, no one in either family could remember seeing them the night before.

Within a half hour, the two families had discovered empty closets, missing personal items and not a word of explanation.

Everyone had looked to Tracy then, of course. Karen had been seeing Riley for a couple of months, but Tracy had been his buddy since days of training wheels and tree houses. None of the parents seemed to know how hurt Tracy had been by the first betrayal—when Karen had sought Riley's attention and he had all too willingly given it.

They didn't know how left out Tracy had felt every time her best friend parked near the train trestle to do who-knew-what with her sister.

They'd expected Tracy to know everything.

She hadn't known anything.

Somehow, that seemed to be the biggest betrayal of all.

"Did you defend me?" Riley prompted, grabbing her hand.

She probably would have if she hadn't been nursing a broken heart. She tried to release her hand again, but he held it firmly, confiscating her attention at the same time.

"How could I?" she asked. "You left with Karen before she finished high school. Otto said—"

"Since when would you believe anything my father said?"

Being close to Riley tangled Tracy's insides like one of Claus's pilfered balls of yarn. She needed to escape. Wiggling her hand loose, she said, "Since you proved him right."

"The people of this never-never land sent me out on the plank before they heard a single word in my defense."

Tracy edged past him, toward the fence. "You had no business taking my sister to California with you."

"Maybe she was ready to leave," Riley said from behind her. "And maybe I was a convenient ticket out."

"People haven't forgotten."

"Then *people* need to enrich their lives."

He sounded closer. Tracy turned her head and saw that he was following her across the grass with her forgotten thermos. She scrambled over the fence and turned around. "My mom's health has been fragile," she said. "I don't want her to be upset."

"Don't worry," Riley said with a smile that seemed too sincere to be believable. "I was planning to walk over and visit your mom and stepdad later this afternoon."

"You can't."

He shifted his weight. "I've been gone for over thirteen years and I haven't seen your sister in just as long. Your parents will listen to reason."

"No, I mean they're not there," Tracy said. "They're on vacation. Dad took Mom to visit relatives."

Riley gave her a long assessing look, followed by a nod. "Gran said your mom had been in the hospital. Is she okay?"

Tracy felt comfort touch her heart as Riley seemed to slide back into his old role as friend. Until she watched him step closer and recognized how easily he could hop the fence and catch her waist between his potent-looking hands.

The thought was provocative in more ways than one.

She stepped back. "Mom had a scare with pneumonia, but she's better now."

"That's good." Riley's crooked smile seemed too open, and he was cupping her tea thermos between his hands with a disturbing familiarity. The last thing she needed was to tie herself up with him again, in friendship or anything else.

He was a stranger now. She wanted him to remain one.

Tracy stared at her thermos, willing him to hand it across so she could leave and sort out her thoughts.

A little more than a year ago, Riley's father had been caught embezzling funds from the company where he worked. Although that particular news hadn't been shocking, other things *had* been.

For one thing, Vanessa had seemed unaffected by her husband's troubles. She'd filed for divorce and headed south to a friend's house in Oklahoma City just two days after Otto's prison term began. For another, Tracy's parents had learned that Riley's grandmother actually owned the house.

Lydia Stephenson was quirky but harmless. Since she was content in her retirement-village apartment, the house had been left vacant. Tracy's mother claimed that sometimes she heard the old place sighing in relief. She'd been looking forward to welcoming new neighbors. It was a good thing she wasn't home this weekend. Tracy could break the news gently.

Riley rested her thermos on top of the fence post and shot a glance down Tracy's body again. "Are you going to tell me why you're hanging out in my backyard?"

"I came to see you," Tracy said. "I rang the doorbell and—"

"It's busted. My father was a slob."

Tracy bit back a retort about Riley having faults of his own. "—And when no one answered, I came back to admire the view. It's better from your yard."

Riley grinned. "You can swing on my swing set anytime, little girl."

Tracy's regard touched on his mouth and dropped down his torso again. When the blood circled back round to her brain and she homed in on his gleaming eyes, she sighed, resisting another urge to chomp her nails.

"What do you want?" he asked in a voice that was in no way like the one he'd used when she was a child. This voice was soft, all right, but it was rich with suggestion.

She frowned.

"You said you came to see me."

She gazed at the hair that moved around his head as he shook it. She'd driven all the way over here to ask him to leave, but now the words seemed harsh. "Don't get comfortable here," she said as she reached up to snatch her thermos from the post. "And I'm saying that for your sake. You won't fit in."

His eyes darkened ominously. "You don't think I will?"

"No."

"Then watch me."

Chapter Two

Riley stood at the fence and watched as Tracy maneuvered her way around the overgrown cedar and across to her parents' driveway. The lady was worth watching. Her faded jeans emphasized a pair of curvy hips and a small waist. She was so feminine now. So alluring. Deep-chestnut hair bounced around her shoulders as she opened the door of a white sedan and folded her trim body inside. Within seconds, she started the car and roared off down the road.

His attraction to her wasn't a complete surprise—he'd always found her enchanting. Full lips and expressive eyes on a well-proportioned face made her classically pretty, but he was charmed by more than her looks. She'd always seemed comfortable with her choices and her world. He'd been pleased that a girl with such winning ways had found something about him to admire. But not anymore. His departure all those years ago had taken care of that.

He returned to the back door and grabbed his coffee cup on the way inside. If he'd learned anything from his reckless youth, it was that running away rarely solved a problem. Way back when, Tracy had been one of few who'd believed in him. Her distrust now was only part of the price he'd paid.

Deciding he didn't need the caffeine, Riley left his full cup of coffee near the kitchen sink and walked through the empty living room. His mother had taken the furniture when she'd moved. She hadn't wanted to live in a house full of bad memories, but she'd wanted her things. And Riley had left his junk in a storage unit out in California. It was hardly worth the cost of moving it, and for now he was content with necessities. He could always send for his things later. If he decided to stay.

When Grandma Lydia had called to request his help, she'd offered to sell him the place—something she'd never done for his parents. And until Riley's arrival yesterday afternoon, he'd laughed heartily at the idea.

It was funny, the way he felt about the old house now. He and his parents had moved here from Topeka when he was six, and he'd always hated the place. For one thing, it was too isolated. The only neighbors within walking distance were Tracy's family. It was said that a community tried to spring to life out here a century ago, but progress had stunted its growth. The dusty rural route in front of the houses had been bisected by a highway curving lazily toward the lake, leaving room for only two.

A bigger factor was the loud and constant criticism he'd received here. Now that his father was gone, the place seemed peaceful. For the first time, it actually seemed like a haven. Maybe he would stay.

He entered the back bedroom, reopened the pail of creamy yellow paint and climbed the ladder to grab his paintbrush. After loosening its bristles against the cleanup rag, he dipped the brush into the pail.

And grinned out the window at the swing. Seeing

Tracy there had erased a whole mess of years and as many bad decisions. It returned Riley to days when he'd come flying out of the house, angry at his father for some cruel taunt, and Tracy would chatter innocently from her perch on that same swing. She'd always manage to cheer him up.

The sexual pull that had been new and mysterious that last winter was still there, but it was different now. He was seeing her through the eyes of an experienced man, and she was just as intriguing.

More intriguing.

Coltish legs had become longer and more shapely, budding breasts had bloomed and she'd become a provocative woman. She'd noticed him today, too, in that way. He'd watched her green eyes trail down his body. He'd felt their heat.

Rough-and-tumble tomboy had grown into sizzling-hot babe. Hot enough to make him forget his good intentions and get into trouble. And new trouble would stack on top of the old, sending the town into towering spirals of gossip.

Hurting Tracy again.

Maybe he should fix up the house and move on.

He applied the paintbrush to the edge of the freshly sanded wood of the windowsill. As he was reaching up to tackle the narrow sliver at the top of the sill, a knock sounded at the front door. Sighing, he balanced the brush across the rim of the can, wondering if he'd ever get his painting chore finished.

But on his way down the ladder, he decided Tracy must have returned. No one else would know to knock, would they? He started a mad dash toward the door, then forced himself to slow. Maybe he could drop the defensive attitude and make a more mature impression.

By the time he reached the living room, the door was opening and his grandmother was backing her way in with a brown paper bag under one arm and a plump text under the other. "It's Gran!" she called in a voice loud enough to carry through the house. "Don't bother coming to the door."

"I'm already here," Riley said from behind her. "If you didn't want me to answer the door, why did you knock?"

She turned around and set the bag in the middle of the floor. "Even if you are my grandson, you're a single adult male with a private life," she said. "I couldn't barge in."

"You did barge in," Riley pointed out as he watched his grandmother pitch the book beside the bag. It was hard to get used to the idea that she was enrolled in college classes, even though he knew she tended to disregard convention.

"My dear grandson, I knocked before I barged," she said primly. "There's a fine but distinct difference."

"Thanks for clarifying that," Riley said. "Next time I'm doing anything adult or private, I'll barricade the door."

"Just like old times," she said with a nod. "Except I'm glad you aren't sucking on those cancer sticks anymore."

Riley grinned. "Same to you, Gran."

"And we thought we had each other fooled," she said, returning his smile. "Want some help today?"

Riley shot a glance at the astronomy text on the floor. "You planning to study while you paint?"

"Nope," she said, lifting her palms. "I figured if I helped you paint and brought you lunch, you might help me cram this afternoon."

Riley chuckled as he imagined his grandmother's silvery locks amongst the hundred assorted freshman styles in the astronomy classroom at the university. "I might remember something," he said. "That class was more interesting than most. I figured I could astound women with my knowledge."

When his grandmother put her hands on her hips and started tapping a foot, Riley chuckled. "Help me paint. We can talk about the stars after lunch."

Two hours and six windowsills later, Riley's grandmother took her bag to the kitchen to pull together lunch. Riley cleaned paintbrushes and hammered lids on cans, then wandered back to check things out.

An open can of pork and beans was waiting on the counter with a plastic spoon stuck inside. Beside it lay several thick slices of bologna, a package of cream-filled cupcakes and two rather shriveled-looking plums. "This is the promised lunch?" Riley asked as he watched his grandmother eat a spoonful of beans from the can.

She nodded. "One of my favorites."

Riley picked up a round of bologna and used it to point toward the can of beans. "Do I just use the same spoon?"

"No." Lydia nudged the brown paper bag a few inches closer. "There's a whole can in here with your name on it."

"How generous." Riley opened the bag and pulled out the beans. When he located the can opener his grandmother had left near the sink, he realized she was drinking coffee out of the cup he'd left there a while ago. "Isn't that mine?"

Lydia scrutinized it. "Possibly."

Riley snorted and opened the cupboard to search for a glass.

"Don't worry," she said. "I wiped the rim first."

"There's no doubt in my mind about which person in the family I take after," Riley said with a grin as he grabbed a wineglass and swooped across to fill it at the sink.

"You could do worse," his grandmother said.

Riley lifted his water, and two of the town's biggest misfits silently toasted the truth: even if no one else recognized their rare form of character, they did.

Honor and propriety were vastly different things.

"The convict my daughter chose for a husband didn't do you any favors," Lydia said. "I can almost hear him bellowing some drivel about women belonging in the kitchen and not out shooting hoops."

She raised her chin and said proudly, "Your grandfather didn't care if I ever set foot in our kitchen. He loved to cook for me."

Riley only grunted. He'd scrounged another spoon from the back of a drawer and was chewing a mouthful of the cold, nearly tasteless beans. Leaning against the counter beside the adult who'd likely saved his sanity, he finished eating lunch with her, grateful for her company. When he'd left town to save his self-respect, he'd lost the opportunity to spend time with Lydia. Well, he was here now. The next few months should be a blast.

"Think I can make it?" his grandmother asked. She was perching her bean can on her open palm and nodding toward the trash can.

Riley laughed. "Those scrawny arms won't lob it halfway."

She held the can in two hands, then gave a cheeky little hop, threw the can and gloated.

"Lucky shot." Riley scooped out his last spoonful and chewed while he wiggled his own can out in front of Lydia's face. Turning his back to the trash can, he tossed it over his shoulder. When he heard the clank of the two cans colliding, he crowed.

And for the next little while, Riley and his sixty-seven-year-old grandmother grabbed cans, plums, spoons and wrappers and performed acrobatic tosses across the room. Most of the time, they each made it. Any misses were met with loud and vigorous hoots from the other. By the time the supply of trash was gone, Riley was ahead by a napkin. Although he didn't say anything, he made sure his preening was obvious enough to catch notice.

Lydia smiled and looked around the room. Her eyes moved from the coffee cup to the wineglass—the only throwable objects left. After a moment's consideration, she picked up the coffee cup and poised.

Riley grabbed the cup and returned it to the sink. "You might have noticed I'm not long on dishes here."

His grandmother cackled as they made their way to the living room. With a limberness belying her years, she scooped the astronomy text from the floor and looked around for a place to sit. "You're not long on furniture, either," she said. "You need to fill this place up—unless you're planning to leave soon."

"I hope to stay a while, although I've already been warned I'm making a mistake." Riley headed to the back bedroom to fetch two unopened gallon paint cans.

"Who told you that?" Lydia hollered.

"Tracy," he hollered back. He paused in the bedroom when he noticed that his grandmother's voice had sounded odd from across the walls. It had a new quality, something not obvious when she was within his sight. As he returned to set the cans a few feet apart in the middle of the living-room floor, he realized what it was—she sounded old.

But she was quiet now, so he picked up a board he'd bought to repair a rotted window and centered it between the cans. "There we have it," he said, directing a tender smile toward his grandmother. "The amazing, instant study desk."

"It's good to know I didn't waste my money on that fancy California university," Lydia said as she sat and stretched out her legs beneath the board. She couldn't be comfortable in that position for long. Criminy, *he* wouldn't be comfortable. He'd have to pick up a table and chairs somewhere.

His grandmother didn't complain, though. She spent a moment perusing a glossy photo of some distant galaxy, then said, "I guess you'll have to convince her she's wrong."

Riley didn't ask who his grandmother was talking about, because his mind hadn't completely left Tracy since he'd seen her. "Convincing that woman of anything would be a pleasure," he said as he attempted to position his legs on the other side of the board. "Is she involved?"

"As in dating?" Lydia flipped through pages until she found the one she'd dog-eared. Then she looked up.

"As in dating, engaged, married, living with…all that brouhaha."

His grandmother shook her head. "Getting involved with the Gilberts' youngest daughter would be a mistake," she said. "You know that, don't you?"

"Who said I was getting involved?" Riley asked. "I asked if *she* was involved."

His grandmother arched an eyebrow. "She's a career

woman and a single mom. She doesn't have time for anything else.''

"Wow, a single mom." Riley pictured a little girl or boy with Tracy's hair and eyes. "What sort of career?"

"She works for Booker Vanderveer. He came here from Chicago a few years ago when his wife took a job as a psychology professor. I'm taking her class next fall.''

"Gran, what kind of business is it?"

"Oh, well, why didn't you ask in the first place? Booker runs an organizing business.'' She chuckled. ''I'll be danged if the idea hasn't caught on. It seems that quite a few college professors and some of the wealthier students are willing to pay through the nose for someone else to clean up their clutter."

"An organizer...that sounds right. She was always a go-getter."

"And despite the fact that tongues will flap faster than a flag in the wind, you're planning to go get 'er?''

Riley snorted at his grandmother's choice of words, but he wasn't surprised by the boldness of the question. He also knew an answer wasn't expected.

He had no idea what he was going to do, but Tracy's words had felt like a dare. He could live anywhere he pleased, and he'd stay around until Tracy admitted that. Or longer.

"Actually, Booker's the consultant," Lydia said, breaking into his thoughts. "I'm pretty sure Tracy just manages the office."

Frowning at the text lying between them, Riley didn't comment. He already had the information he needed, and he was developing a plan. He wasn't sure about the details yet, but he'd find a way to teach Tracy a lesson.

Rotating the astronomy book toward his grandmother, he said, "Is this the section causing you problems?"

Lydia nodded, and the two concentrated on astronomy for the next half hour. They'd just read through a page, when his grandmother said, "I suppose you could use her."

"Use Tracy?" Images invaded Riley's thoughts.

"M'dear grandson, should you decide to stick around, you could use Vanderveer's to get your business up and running."

Riley smiled in response to Lydia's grin, but he tapped his index finger against her book. "We're studying now, Gran," he reminded her. "Besides, I'm a bucket ahead of you."

But when he noticed the snap of her eyes, he knew he'd never truly catch up to the lightning-quick workings of his grandmother's mind. Hadn't she just manipulated him into staying a while?

TRACY STOOD IN LINE at the strip-mall print shop, waiting to pick up a case of forms for Booker. The young woman behind the service desk was working slowly, even for a Monday morning. She'd taken six minutes to fill the first order, and was only now greeting the next customer.

Hannah was beginning to fidget, despite the lemon drop and yo-yo Tracy had found in the depths of her purse and offered as a bribe. The four-year-old bundle of fresh-faced charm and relentless energy was eating the candy with loud smacks, and had just banged the toy into the ankle of the man fifth in line.

Apologizing profusely, Tracy pulled Hannah closer. Even while she swore to herself that tomorrow she'd drop Hannah off at day care before errands, the little girl tried to work the yo-yo again. Of course, she let go of the string and the toy rolled between the legs of the older woman behind them. Hannah dropped to the floor to skitter along after it.

"Hannah, bring me the yo-yo," Tracy said. When she heard the impatience in her voice, she softened her tone. "I'll get you to school soon. You won't miss circle time."

The little girl's dark eyes were solemn as she dropped the yo-yo into Tracy's outstretched hand. Tracy felt a pang of remorse. It wasn't Hannah's fault they were running late. It was hers. She'd overslept, which was something she didn't do. Then again, she hadn't been herself all weekend.

Another employee appeared from a side door to hasten across the shop, so Tracy grabbed Hannah's hand and followed him. "I'm here to pick up a case of forms for Vanderveer's," she announced to a set of pumping elbows.

He was practically running, but after her statement, he glanced over his shoulder and stopped. "I'm just the passport photographer," he said in a voice with a timbre that reminded her of Riley's.

Tracy scowled. Since Saturday morning, Riley's traits were popping up in every man within her path. The knowledge that he was back in town had thrown her for a loop, despite her best efforts to forget about him.

The photographer was staring at Tracy's face, probably wondering about the sudden switch from smile to frown.

Tracy gentled her expression. "I don't mind," she said, once again assuming a calmness she didn't feel. Raising an eyebrow, she pulled Hannah close and waited for the man to get the box. Surely, even a passport photographer could make time for something so simple.

"Yes, ma'am," the man said in a voice that sounded only nervous now. As he hurried around the counter to ask his co-worker where to find the Vanderveer job, Tracy saw a tall, muscular man in hip-hugging jeans pass by the front window.

No. It wasn't Riley. Just a guy who reminded her of Riley, of course.

Still, in a town the size of Kirkwood, Tracy knew she'd run into him eventually. She didn't have to have anything to do with him, though. After all, her parents and his parents had avoided one another for years, and they'd been next door neighbors.

Her behavior this weekend had been flighty, at best. She kept imagining what scintillating thing she might say to Riley, even though she had no intention of speaking to him again. It was as if all those years hadn't passed at all, and she was still a teenager harboring a crush on the boy next door.

Except her imagination had grown up. Instead of substituting herself as the recipient of his kisses down by the train trestle, she was picturing entire weekends spent in bed with him. Heaven knew where Hannah would be during all these misbegotten fantasies.

But Tracy lived in the real world, and Hannah was fine right where she was—at her side.

The little girl had been delighted with the unusual laxity in their routine—especially when she'd been indulged with a three-hour play-clay session yesterday afternoon. Tracy had sat across the table from her, punching a glob of tangerine-colored clay into unrecognizable shapes. Muttering under her breath. Getting up countless times to replay a *Beauty and the Beast* sound track on the stereo.

Several times this weekend, Tracy had picked up the phone to call her sister in San Diego. She wondered if Karen knew about Riley's return. Though she'd married her fourth husband several years ago, Karen might still be in touch with Riley. It seemed to Tracy that her sister had never gotten over him. Either that, or she had horrendous taste in men.

"Here you go, ma'am." The photographer thrust a box against Tracy's midsection. Gripping it under one arm, Tracy was all the way to the door before she remembered to say thanks and instruct the photographer to send the bill to Vanderveer's.

Then to summon her daughter.

After she'd put the box in the trunk and Hannah in her child seat, Tracy got in and started the car. Ten minutes later, she realized that she'd driven past the turn for the day-care center and was heading toward the office. She turned at the next corner.

While she circled around the day-care center parking lot, she glanced toward the seat beside her and suddenly realized she'd forgotten to bring Hannah's little backpack.

Tracy sighed as she pictured it next to the front door of the duplex, with Hannah's lunch card on top. Exactly where Tracy had put them so she wouldn't forget. Most of the time, she didn't. Now she'd have to swing by home and the day care on her lunch break, and the dry cleaning would have to be put off another day.

"I forgot your backpack, Hannah-bean," Tracy said as she parked. "Don't worry. I'll bring it before lunch."

After she'd dropped Hannah off with a hug and a kiss, Tracy returned to her car and tried to shift her mind to her morning's work. Since she hadn't started typing the reports she'd taken home this weekend, she knew she had a tall stack awaiting her. She also had folders to file and phone messages to transcribe, and she wanted to free herself of mundane chores as soon as possible.

Booker had promised to let her sit in on a couple of consultations if she did.

When she passed the Mercedes parked in the first spot in front of Vanderveer's, Tracy made an immediate turn to claim her regular place next to it—and nearly rammed into the motorcycle parked there.

She slammed on her brakes and flinched, waiting for the impact. She was lucky—she'd missed by inches. Her heart pounding, she threw her car into reverse and backed up, slamming on her brakes when she heard a screech and a honk, and glanced in her rearview mirror.

Now she'd nearly been hit from behind. An angry-looking driver jerked his car around hers, and Tracy tried not to lip-read the names he was calling her. She was ready to retrieve Hannah from day care and go home. Today seemed like a good day to camp out on the living-room floor with a game of Candyland, a double batch of fudge and a half dozen of Hannah's favorite videos. Every parent and child needed quality time together.

After the driver she'd nearly hit had disappeared back into the traffic, Tracy shifted her car into gear and crawled on past her spot. There wasn't another vacant space for a couple of blocks.

With a deep sigh, Tracy pulled into it. She wouldn't even attempt to carry the box of forms so far by herself. She'd have to leave them in the trunk until later, and walk to work in her skirt and heels.

She'd told Booker this type of clothing wasn't practical for a glorified messenger, but he had prevailed. His favorite saying was that in business, image was everything. He'd said a woman's femininity was often a viable selling point and had advised Tracy to dress for the job she aspired to rather than the one she had.

Since she had hopes of being promoted to full consultant, she was inclined to bow to his wishes.

The whistle she received from a passing driver as she walked down the busy sidewalk only made her madder. By the time she reached the dusty black motorcycle, she wanted to shove it off its big bad tires. Suddenly, *hog* seemed an appropriate term. She glared at it as she juggled her armful of reports to one hand and whirled around to go inside.

The door to her boss's private office was open, so she called out, "I'm here. Did you see the hairy beast who stole my spot? I nearly ran over his motorcycle."

There was a lengthy pause, then Booker's voice drifted out. "Come in here, Tracy."

Tracy threw the reports on her desk and kicked her shoes under her desk before she headed back. "I had to park two blocks away," she said on the way in. "I'd love to grind my foot into that imbecile's—"

Tracy stopped when she reached Booker's doorway. This time, she wasn't noticing something that reminded her of Riley.

She was seeing Riley, himself.

He was sitting in Booker's plush client's chair with a helmet balanced on his knees. He grinned that wicked, lopsided grin as he stared at her feet. "Where were you planning to put those sassy red toes?"

Tracy looked down at her feet. The polish was not red, it was pink. Rowdy Rouge, to be precise. She stuck her thumbnail between her teeth and grimaced at the taste of the anti-nail-biting cream she'd rubbed in this morning. Drawing her hand back down, she looked across at Riley, whose smile had spread to both sides.

He looked out of place in Booker's office. Even in creased dress pants and a collared shirt, he seemed too dangerous to occupy a space so tame.

Her boss cleared his throat. Tracy dragged her gaze to Booker's most violent frown. He motioned to her feet and mouthed for her to put her shoes on.

She did the only thing she could do.

She walked in three steps farther and sat in the third chair. "It's okay, I know him," she said to Booker.

Then she turned her head slightly and looked down her nose at Riley. "Why are you here?"

Riley's smile revealed an even row of white teeth. Which held her complete attention until a firm grip on her arm wrenched her out of her chair.

"Excuse us, please." This was from Booker, who hauled her out the door and all the way across the office. He didn't stop until they were secluded by the coatrack next to the front door. Leaning close, he said, "What are you doing?"

Tracy tossed her head back toward Booker's office. "He's bad news."

Booker backed up a step and looked at her as if she had a row of Rowdy Rouge toenails growing out of the bridge of her nose. "Oh, really?"

"He probably just came here to torment me."

"Not exactly." Booker stood up straight and cleared his throat. "He came to hire you."

She sniffed. "Why would Riley need a consultant?"

Booker paused, and Tracy finally processed his statement. "You don't mean hire *Vanderveer's*?" she whispered.

Booker had crossed to her desk and was squatting to scavenge around on the floor. "No, I said hire *you*."

"What for?" Tracy scowled across the room at the pair of trousered legs she could see inside Booker's office. Even from this distance, they looked all wrong.

"He's opening a civil engineering firm, and he wants help getting things going," Booker said before he dropped to his knees, pulled back her chair and said, "Aha!"

Tracy had never seen her boss from this angle. The bald spot peeking out of his tidy brown hairstyle was disturbing.

Or maybe it was what he'd just said—Riley, starting a business in Kirkwood. Oh, no!

"Office setup, demographics, personal coaching—the works," Booker said from beneath her desk. He held both of her shoes in one hand and used the seat of her chair to pull himself up.

"But I've never done a full consulting job," Tracy said as she accepted a shoe and bent down to slip it on. "You said it could take another year to work up to that."

"He said that he wants you, and that he'd pay a full month's fees up front if you accept the job."

Tracy stared at the wrinkles in her boss's herringbone jacket. "You'd let me do it?"

"Let's put it this way—if you take on the job and handle it well, you've got your toenails in the door." He handed her the second shoe. "But you'd be wise to keep your shoes on at all times, got it?"

Tracy slumped down in her chair with the leftover shoe still in her hand. "Uh-huh." She peered toward the corner office, oblivious now to the foul taste as she clicked her thumbnail between her teeth. Riley had tucked a leg back beside the chair and was beating his heel against the floor.

Impatiently. Powerfully.

Oh, Lord.

"Tracy, he's waiting."

She knew he was.

She slid out of the seat and walked slowly across the room, dangling one brown pump from her wet fingertip. Up and down all the way she glided, as fluidly as a carousel horse. As she stepped inside Booker's office again, she turned back to her boss and said calmly, "Excuse us, Booker."

And closed his door behind her.

Chapter Three

Remember, image is everything.

Raising her chin, Tracy dropped the shoe in the middle of Booker's cherry-wood desk, then claimed his chair, too. When she found the courage to meet Riley's eyes, she refused to cower. She opened hers wider and said, "My boss is convinced you're starting a civil engineering company."

"I am."

She wasn't completely surprised. She'd always thought Riley would become successful at something. She just wished he wasn't planning to do it within her range of notice.

She forced a puff of air through closed lips and claimed a few seconds to collect her thoughts. "Do you know anything about engineering?"

"I did a two-year stint as associate professor of fluid mechanics and hydrology at the University of California at Berkeley," Riley said with a confidence bordering on boastfulness. "After that, I worked for a couple of firms before I started my own."

"You started your own?" Tracy parroted, studying Riley's crisp blue shirt. His perfectly tailored and expensive-looking shirt. She couldn't remember another man filling one quite so well. "Was it successful?"

He lifted broad shoulders, but she knew the answer.

"If you've already got a firm going, why do you need to hire an organizer?"

There was that smile again. "You told me I wouldn't be accepted here," he said. "So I figured you were just the lady to straighten my image."

Tracy studied the helmet he held in his lap. It was glossy, black and spotless. As far as helmets went, it was stunning. But it didn't fit into the business world.

She moved her eyes up to hair that was a little too long, then looked back into smoke-gray eyes. There was a trace of wildness in them, always had been, even when he was a child.

Riley could never be tamed by anyone.

Least of all her.

"I wouldn't know where to start," she said, searching his face again—this time for the confidant she'd known all those years ago.

"Sure you do. You're a gold-star girl."

Tracy rolled her eyes. After her first day of kindergarten, Riley had taken it upon himself to walk her home from the bus stop. She'd bragged all the way about the shiny stars she'd found pasted on the crayoned pictures she'd drawn that day. Riley had never let her forget it.

"Riley, please," she said, lowering her voice. "Booker's never offered me a chance at promotion before. If I blow it, he may never again. I can't risk my job. I have a little girl at home."

Riley looked pointedly at the shoe she'd left on the desk between them. "How old did you say you were?"

She grabbed the shoe. "I'm twenty-nine, as you very well know."

His eyes returned to hers. "And you're a gofer?"

She sat up straighter. The shoe in her hand dropped to the floor with a clatter. "My title is office manager."

"I see," he said, lifting his eyebrows and nodding as if he was impressed. "You're a *dressed-up* gofer."

Scowling, she busied herself extending her foot to pull her shoe closer and tip it upright so she could slip it on.

"Can you afford *not* to take this chance?" he said next.

That was her problem—she'd been begging for this chance for more than a year. She wanted and deserved a promotion. The adoption had depleted her savings, and now she was working nonstop to pay her monthly bills. If she or Hannah had any kind of emergency, she'd barely land on her feet.

But she could not work with Riley Collins.

She was well versed in Booker's views of business savvy. He wouldn't understand an outright refusal. An opportunity was an opportunity, and you didn't turn down a client because his regard made you uncomfortable.

And since Tracy couldn't explain the history of Riley and her sister without sounding like a whiner with a long memory, she'd have to make an appearance of considering the job. Maybe if she got Riley away from this office, she could figure out his game and let him know he wasn't allowed to make up the rules. It might take a few hours, but the cause was worthwhile. After that, she could work doubly hard to catch up and take a stack of reports home again. If Hannah was allowed to finger paint, she wouldn't care if her mom spent another evening typing.

With as much ice as she could muster, Tracy said, "I guess it wouldn't hurt to assess your situation to see whether there's anything I can do for you.'' When she finished speaking, her heart was racing.

''Great.'' Riley put his motorcycle helmet on the floor, stood up and extended his hand across the desk for a shake.

Tracy looked at his hand, but kept both of hers folded in her lap. She'd taken the same hand in hers often enough in childhood, but that had been a long time ago. Accepting it seemed dangerous now.

She ignored it and stayed seated. ''To be fair, I'll only take the job if I think I can handle it. If you require more expert assistance, Booker will have to handle your needs.''

Finally she stood and pressed her hand into Riley's. Although the handshake was firm, Tracy knew they were solemnizing a deceptive agreement. And not only on Riley's end. She was planning to use the loophole she'd just announced to her full advantage.

Booker may have his sights on the bottom line, but taking the job was her choice. Now that Tracy's toenails were wedged inside the door, she'd find an excuse to send Riley packing and take the *next* opportunity for promotion.

''I think you'll find you and I are a perfect fit,'' Riley said with a warm squeeze.

Tracy's eyes flew to his face, wondering if the double entendre was intentional. But his expression made a grand appearance of innocence.

Grand and obviously false.

One look at the upward curl at one corner of his mouth gave that away. She didn't believe the man had *any* moments of actual innocence. She tugged her hand away. ''Shall we do the initial consult at your office, so I can look around?''

"Absolutely." Riley patted his shirt pocket, then both pants pockets. Finally he reached across the desk and snatched Booker's favorite gold-filigree pen and a business card from their holders.

Typical. Hadn't Riley always taken what he wanted, regardless of the consequences?

He slapped the card blank side up on the desk and scrawled some writing across it. "Here's the address and phone number," he said, handing it to her. "The name is Collins Engineering, but I don't have a sign up yet."

Tracy put the card in her jacket pocket without reading it. "Will a two o'clock appointment work for you?"

"It will if we're talking about this afternoon."

She'd meant this afternoon. She'd meant to get it over with as soon as possible. But suddenly an extra day or two sounded smarter. She'd have time for her stomach to unclench and her heart to slow down. "Oh! No, I meant tomorr— Wednesday. I meant Wednesday."

"I'd prefer earlier in the week," Riley said, his eyes twinkling as if he'd won some sort of challenge. "But any afternoon is fine."

"Then it's settled." Tracy stretched out her hand for Booker's pen. When Riley dropped it in her palm, she opened Booker's appointment book and made an entry. "I'll be there at nine o'clock sharp...Thursday morning." She shot a grin across the desk as she slid the pen back in its holder, and wondered why her little victory felt as false as her smile.

THREE MORNINGS LATER, she knew why.

The delay wasn't a triumph, it was a curse. The few days' respite had been counterproductive, and she'd accomplished little beyond chewing her nails to the quick.

Last night, she'd allowed Hannah to help her make

cupcakes for the day care's spring party. Tracy had lost patience before they'd managed to add even two simple ingredients to the mix. Then, after a half hour struggle with dropped eggs and spilled vegetable oil, Tracy had let the cakes burn in the oven. Hannah had been allowed to eat the candy decorations, and Tracy had promised to buy special treats at the grocery store.

She'd been sluggish at work, too. After three days of misplaced files, cutoff phone conversations and computer crashes, Booker had asked if she was short of sleep. She'd made up a litany of other excuses, mostly relating to single parenthood and moon phases, but she knew they weren't the cause.

She was reminded that first instincts were often best. She should have met Riley at his office ten minutes after he left Booker's.

Now she was in the basement of her parents' home watching her mother transfer another bundle of clothes from her suitcase to her washing machine and add a capful of soap. "What time did you get home last night?" she asked, studying her mother's profile.

Gwen Gilbert had never been less than gorgeous. Even when she was lying in a hospital bed with tubes poking out of absurd places, her blond good looks had seemed graceful. This morning she was stunning, humming under her breath and pink with good cheer. The getaway had worked wonders.

"Matthew and I drove straight through from Cincinnati, so it was well after dark," her mother said, turning on the water and closing the lid. "But I really wasn't paying attention to the time." She began pulling clothes from the dryer.

"Hannah and I came by at dusk," Tracy said. "I watered your gardens." *And kept an eye on your next door neighbor's house. Have you noticed him over there yet?*

Tracy's mother wrapped an arm around Tracy's shoulders, offering a quick squeeze. "Thanks. I don't regret the extra time we took to see the flower show, but I'm sorry we missed you and Hannah."

I wondered where he was, and when he trimmed the bush at the corner of the house. Did you notice that?

Her mother started up the stairs. "Let's take the laundry to the living room," she said. "We can talk and fold."

Tracy picked up the laundry basket and followed her mother upstairs to dump the clothes on the sofa. After they'd sorted for a minute, Tracy said, "You had a good time?"

"You've asked me that three times," her mother said. "I've answered yes every time. It was wonderful." Smiling, she matched a pair of white crew socks and rolled them together. "Is something on your mind?"

Tracy caught the neck band of one of her stepdad's shirts under her chin, folding the arms in. "What do you mean?"

"It's Thursday morning and you're not only dressed for work, you're late for work," her mother said. "You're usually punctual. And we were only gone eight days—you could have brought Hannah to visit this evening."

Tracy smiled as she set the shirt on the arm of the sofa. "I guess you know me."

"Yes, I do. What's wrong?"

Did you notice a new crackle in the air around Kirkwood?

"Have you noticed anything going on next door?"

"Next door?"

Both women glanced up as Matthew Gilbert walked into the living room, jangling his keys in his pocket and whistling.

Tracy had been introduced to Matthew when she was ten. She'd liked him from the start, but he'd been "Matthew my mom's friend" for quite a while. Eventually, he'd married her mother and adopted both girls. He'd been Dad to Tracy ever since.

He paused long enough to plant a kiss atop her mother's head, continuing his tune on his way to the front door. Apparently, the trip had put him in a good mood, too.

"Dad, wait," Tracy said.

Matthew's whistle changed to a grin. "I've got a class to teach this morning, Teacup."

"I have an appointment, too. This'll only take a minute."

With the affability that made him eternally popular with freshman chemistry students at the university, her stepdad returned and gave Tracy his undivided attention. "What'll only take a minute?"

"I wanted to tell you, someone moved into Lydia's old house while you were gone."

"We knew someone would buy it," Matthew said with a frown. "The house needs a little TLC, but it's structurally sound."

Tracy sighed. "Riley's living there."

Her mother seemed vacant for a minute, then she gasped. "Riley Collins?"

Tracy nodded, watching both her mom and Matthew change from happy to thoughtful. "He's planning to open a business in town," she explained.

"I figured Lydia would try to sell the place," Matthew said, frowning across at Tracy's mother.

"Maybe Riley's buying it," her mother said.

No one spoke for a minute. Tracy's green eyes traveled between her mother's blue ones and her stepdad's brown ones, waiting for their reactions. They traded the look they'd always traded when they wanted to discuss something in private. Karen had dubbed it the "worried-parent look," and had compared it to spelling words in front of a toddler.

But Tracy wasn't a child anymore, and she wanted to know their thoughts. Did the night of Karen and Riley's departure still bother them as much as it did her? She swallowed. "You won't mind having him as a neighbor?"

Her mother shrugged.

Tracy shook her head. She'd hoped one of them would say something to help her feel less agitated. If they couldn't do that, she'd wanted them to say something to make refusing the job her only recourse.

"Riley hurt our family once, but he was young," Matthew said as he stood up. "It's ancient history. I've got to scoot, but we can talk when you come to dinner on Sunday."

As her mother walked Matthew out to his car, Tracy checked her watch. Since she was meeting with Riley early, she could go straight to his office in twenty minutes. This morning's cornflakes felt as if they'd sprouted wings. Tracy was reminded that she was not good at procrastinating.

When her mother returned, Tracy said, "I'm glad you're okay with this, because I may be working with Riley."

Her mother blinked. "In what aspect?"

"As an organizer. He went to Booker and asked for me."

"That's good, I guess." Gwen frowned as she tossed another rolled pair of socks onto the done pile.

Tracy frowned, too. "I'm afraid he's got some ulterior motive. People don't request a novice."

"Who knows?" her mother said. "Just be careful, love."

Right. Just be careful. Solid parenting advice, but not a reason for refusal. Tracy looked at her watch again, and felt her heart take off after the cornflakes.

Ten minutes left.

She swallowed. "He flirts with me," she stated softly.

Her mother tilted her head. "How so?"

Tracy sighed. "The way a man flirts with a woman."

Her mother's frown returned as she began to place the folded clothes back in the basket. "Well, he always liked you, but I wouldn't flirt back." She sighed and shook her head. "I'm just glad *you're* here and not your sister."

Right. Tracy was the trustworthy sister. She was the one Riley might tease but would never touch.

"Will Karen care that he's here?" Tracy wondered aloud.

"I doubt it," her mother said. "She told me she's been seeing a marriage counselor. She's trying to change."

"She is." Tracy was skeptical.

"Yes, and as your dad said, it's ancient history."

There it was again. The phrase they were all associating with Riley—ancient history. He couldn't harm her because the harm he'd caused was a long time ago. He shouldn't upset her because everyone deserved a second chance. He wouldn't seduce her because she wasn't the sister he'd seduced before. Tracy knew that's what they were really saying.

But she also knew Riley would affect her in some profound way she didn't want affected. And whether anyone said it or not, Riley Collins wasn't ancient history anymore.

While that worried Tracy plenty, it also pleased some mixed-up inner need in her soul. The fact that he was the hottest man she'd seen in a while was the most troubling realization of all.

Without bothering to check the time, Tracy slipped on her shoes and kissed her mother's cheek. Judging from the sorry state of her nervous system, it was time to go.

KIRKWOOD'S LARGEST employer was the university, and its biggest claim to fame was the man-made lake and campgrounds nestled in the hills near its northern edge. A constantly rotating collection of college students and university staff ensured a steady economy, but most of the businesses had moved away from downtown to the trendier East Side.

Tracy was familiar with the address Riley had given her. The office space was generous, and it was situated between a pet-grooming shop and an insurance agency. The previous occupant had sold holdover items from the sixties—tie-dyed shirts, incense and hand-dipped candles—before packing up and heading to places unknown.

As Tracy pulled into the parking spot closest to the blacked-out door of the vacated Hippie Hut, she wondered at the absence of Riley's motorcycle. A chime announced her arrival as soon as she opened the door, but a large light table three feet inside blocked her path. She couldn't get through unless she got down on her knees and squeezed through a narrow opening underneath the desk.

Even then, successful entry was questionable. Beyond the light table, file cabinets were stacked side by side along the floor. Faint tones of a Pink Floyd song filtered in from somewhere in the background, but Tracy detected no other sounds to give away Riley's whereabouts.

"Anyone here?" she called, keeping one hand on the door. If he didn't greet her within twenty seconds, she'd have her excuse to leave. She could explain to Booker that the client was obviously not serious about hiring her services, and get on with her life.

"I'm in back," Riley said from beyond the chaos.

"I can't get through."

"Right. I'll come to you."

Tracy set her brand-new leather briefcase on the table and tried not to notice the disarray. Office organization was her particular area of expertise and Booker's main reason for hiring her. As much as she hated to admit it, she could do this part of the job.

After a moment, she was startled by the repeat of the door chime behind her. She turned around and noted the jeans and red T-shirt Riley had donned for this meeting. Except for the green bandana he'd wrapped around his head, this version of Riley wasn't vastly different from the teenager she'd known so well.

"Guess you'll have to come this way," he said, turning to head back out the door.

She followed him across the storefronts. He strode past the pet-grooming shop without noticing the patron exiting its door, but the woman's appreciative smile— she'd doubtless noticed Riley's inarguably buff backside—was enough to make Tracy miss a step. Two miniature schnauzers on matching pink leashes tugged the woman along, and Tracy paused to let the trio trot past.

Riley turned at the opening to an alleyway. When he leaned against the redbrick wall of the building to wait for her, she caught a flash of gold underneath the green cloth. An earring?

He'd transformed to pirate. When she reached his side, he furthered the impression by staring boldly at her with his arms crossed in front of his chest. Only an eye patch, a sword and jug of ale would be necessary to complete the picture.

"How long till you open for business?" she asked as she waited for him to stop staring and start walking.

"Two months, max," he answered. "I'd like to be set up and operating by midsummer, but I need to hire a crew."

"Take your time," she advised. "Two months would be barely enough time to shape up your…uh, ship."

"Then you'd better work fast." Riley pushed away from the wall and started down the alley.

He definitely had a stud in one ear. The bandana held his hair back from his face to reveal it. Image coaching might not be Tracy's greatest strength, but Booker had sent her to classes. She could handle that, too.

The sound of a big dog's bark caught her attention, and Tracy glanced back toward the front of the alley. She shivered, aware that she and Riley were alone in the shadowed space.

Her attraction to him was undeniable.

When the alley opened onto a back lot full of trash bins and parked cars, Tracy felt a mixture of regret and relief. She knew she shouldn't relish being alone with him, but the walk had reminded her of the many childhood adventures he'd shared with her. Some days it might be a ring-neck snake they discovered under a rock, other days a fort he'd built in the woods, but she'd often been pulled along behind Riley as he led the way to some new discovery. She'd always felt protected.

Tracy hadn't felt that way for a long, long time. These days, she was the strong one. Devoted mother, thoughtful daughter, hardworking employee and sympathetic friend.

Noting the gleaming motorcycle Riley had parked near a dented purple delivery door, Tracy wasn't surprised when he pulled that door open. He stepped out of the way but kept his arm stretched over the doorway so she'd have to enter beneath his arm.

Was he toying with her? Ignoring the notion, she stepped under his arm into a long room that smelled like sandalwood. This must have been the previous occupant's storeroom.

Riley scooped a pile of folders off a computer chair and tossed them on the floor. "Have a seat," he said.

With her mind on making a professional appearance, Tracy sat down and crossed her legs at the ankles, then slammed both feet flat on the floor when the chair began to roll across the smooth tile. She'd scarcely regained her equilibrium, when she remembered she'd left her briefcase around front, on the light table.

Yesterday she'd given up six months' clothing budget and her entire lunch hour to shop for the case. She'd wanted to appear credible when she turned down the job.

But Booker had dubbed her Ms. Superefficient for a reason. She'd take mental notes. Folding her hands in her lap, Tracy waited while Riley turned a metal trash can on its open end and sat down on top. Even at thirty-one, he was too restless to sit on a normal chair, like a normal person.

She pulled her eyes away from his flexed thighs and peeked through the door at the accumulation of boxes and furniture in the front-office space. "Typically, I would spend this time looking around your office," she announced with a frown. "Then I would write a proposal."

"You can do that after I clear a pathway," he said. "Why don't you start with my image. What would you advise me to do to appear more respectable and professional."

Of course, his image was the bigger challenge.

"Are you sure you want to open a business here?" Tracy asked, studying his ear stud. When she remembered Nellie's comment, she added, "You are Otto's son. People are wondering if you're hiding out. Or running from something."

Riley kept his narrowed eyes adhered to hers. "I haven't seen my father in thirteen years," he said. And shrugged. "I came back because this is home."

Tracy knew he'd read her expression when he added, "I know this town hasn't forgiven my misspent youth, nor my biological tie to Otto. That's why I'm hiring you."

"If I were to take the job, you'd have to listen to my advice," Tracy said with a frown.

He swept a hand down his chest. "Advise away."

She peered at his earlobe. "Lose the earring."

He fingered the stud. "This? It's hardly noticeable."

"*I* noticed it."

Shivering at the look he slipped down her body, Tracy said, "This is the Midwest. At least some of the folks who are affluent enough to require an engineer's services have never caught on to male jewelry."

She noticed Riley's smirk and said, "If you won't listen to my advice, we can forget the whole thing."

When a grin exploded across his face, Tracy realized

she'd sounded shrill. She'd probably reminded him of the young girl who'd once spent an hour trying to convince him that a lemonade stand was a good idea—even though their parents were the only probable customers.

Except this time the tone worked. Riley reached up and removed the stud. "What next?"

That was easy enough, but the removal of his earring hadn't done the job. Maybe the bandana would do the trick. She jerked her thumb over her shoulder. "The bandana."

He swiped it off, and a lock of hair fell across his forehead, only making him seem sexier and more piratelike, if that was possible. Tracy frowned as she watched him fold the cloth. "That's better," she lied. "But you need a haircut."

He shrugged, and lifted a hip to slip the green square into his back pocket. "I was overdue, anyway. What else?"

She almost giggled. The next suggestion was the coup de grâce. "The motorcycle."

His eyes grew serious. "What about it?"

"It doesn't mesh with a professional appearance, and it would remind most folks of your renegade tendencies."

He crossed his arms over his chest. "What else?"

She leaned in and spoke softly. "Watch what you do. Word gets around, even in a town the size of Kirkwood. But you know that."

His eyes bored into hers, and she recognized her friend.

She also recognized the pain of betrayal, but she wasn't sure whose—his or hers.

She hopped off the chair and started pacing. "Attending a few civic events wouldn't be a bad idea," she said. "And start looking for pet charities."

"Sure," he said, causing her to stop walking and study his face. He sounded too agreeable. "Is that all?"

Tracy noted the angled grin. The laughing eyes. The rise and fall of that muscled chest. She sighed. Some things, she wouldn't ask him to change. "For now."

"I can do every single thing you named, except one," he said as he stood and tipped the trash upright.

"What's that?"

"I won't lose the bike."

She shrugged. "Is it worth having affluent members of the community avoid your business because they think you're a member of some biker gang?"

"Absolutely."

She opened her mouth, prepared to argue, but he didn't give her time.

"I could show you why I want to ride it," he said.

She laughed. He'd sounded just like the boy who had been her constant companion through childhood. Until he'd reached puberty and discovered other girls.

And then her sister.

Tracy's smile tightened until her cheeks hurt. "That's not necessary," she said, wincing at her prim tone.

Her place in Riley's adult life was professional, at best. She couldn't allow herself to feel close to him.

And she needed to get out of here.

She barely had the brainpower to further her plan, but she knew it'd be wise to continue her show of acceptance. As if it were base in a childhood game of tag, she backed up to the purple door and put her hand on the knob. "I'll send over a fee schedule," she said as she scanned the room for her car keys. "And give you the weekend to think about it."

Procrastinating again, but it was the only option she had. Since the office visit hadn't provided her with a clue to Riley's motives, she'd have to exhaust a few sources from home. She'd do an Internet search and make a phone call or two, then on Monday morning she could hand Booker a list of all the reasons she couldn't take the job. Maybe he would take pity on her and do the consultation himself.

Or better yet, maybe Riley would have gotten into trouble by then and left.

The keys were nowhere. Tracy remembered that she'd transferred them to her briefcase after she parked. The same case that was now around front on the light table.

So much for Ms. Superefficient.

''You'd need to know what sort of expenses you would incur by using me,'' she said. As Tracy heard the mischosen words fall out of her mouth, she cringed, waiting for the corners of Riley's mouth to lift.

She wasn't disappointed. He had his mischievous smile down to a science. ''I'm sure you're worth any price.''

She didn't return the smile. ''Although it does seem as though you could benefit from help with organization, I'm not sure it would be wise for the two of us to team up.''

At his questioning expression, she explained, ''This is a big job for an inexperienced organizer.''

He shook his head. ''The gold-star girl could have organized this office at fifteen.''

The cornflakes fluttered as Tracy stared out at the clutter of Riley's front office. He was right. That was the sort of turmoil she could handle. Her fingers were practically itching to sort through binders, revamp the filing system and map out the most efficient use of space.

She offered him a brisk smile. ''I'm going back

around front to retrieve my briefcase, but you don't need to walk me out. Will you be here Monday?''

He nodded.

''I'll call you then,'' she promised.

Finally she turned the door handle and stepped outside. Before the door closed between them, she couldn't resist a final look back.

Her heart quickened at the too-long hair and wickedly handsome expression—just as she'd known it would. And when he winked at her, she felt a definite pang of desire.

Which was exactly the sort of turmoil she couldn't handle.

Chapter Four

Tracy stared out at the quiet street in front of the duplex. The midevening surge of vehicles and pedestrians on the through street had died down. Most of the neighborhood residents must have returned from their dinners and soccer games and would now be tucked away inside preparing for work or school tomorrow.

Inside the duplex, things weren't so serene. Oh, Hannah was happy enough. She was in her room listening to music and coloring with a new set of markers. Tracy had brought them out from her secret stash of emergency toys in a ploy to keep Hannah entertained, and it was working beautifully.

Nothing else was. Tracy's computer search had been useless. Every one of her checks had panned out. *R. Collins* had been listed in Berkeley's engineering-course catalog for a two-year stretch; Collins Engineering had been listed as an Oakland Chamber of Commerce member for the past four.

Riley must be on the up-and-up.

And Tracy's list of pros for taking the job was much longer than her list of cons. That side had only one item, really: he was dangerous.

But if her reason for denying the work was only personal, Booker would never understand. Tracy couldn't tell her boss that the potential client was too sexy or that her sister had run off with him thirteen years ago. Booker would tell her to go home and put a cool cloth to her head.

Scooping Claus off the printer stand, Tracy nestled him on her lap and stroked his back. The cat's purr made his pleasure obvious, but Tracy was no less agitated. Unless she came up with a scheme of her own, she was going to spend the next little while working with Riley Collins.

There had to be some other out. If she feigned a sudden and chronic illness, Tracy could call in sick every day until Booker finished the job or hired someone else to do it. But she had only three personal-leave days left. When they ran out, she wouldn't be paid. Bills would pile up, and she and Hannah could wind up on the street.

Claus jumped down with a thud, and Tracy realized she had stopped petting and was clicking a thumbnail between her teeth. She pulled it away and watched the cat jump back up on the printer stand. Before he crawled into his favorite cubbyhole, he bobbed his head curiously at the cell phone Tracy had set next to the printer.

"You're right," Tracy murmured to Claus. "One phone call could provide my excuse. I'll call Karen."

Though Tracy's sister hadn't been Riley's girlfriend for long, she'd been close enough to be able to hazard a guess about his motives. Besides, she must have cared a lot for Riley back then. If this new association provoked a single hurt feeling in her sister, Tracy would turn down the job. If Booker wanted to penalize her for protecting a family member, then so be it. She'd keep plodding along at the job she already had.

Listening intently, Tracy heard Hannah singing along

to her audiotape. The timing was good. After punching in the string of numbers that would ring Karen's posh apartment in San Diego, Tracy listened to the phone ring twice and hoped the time difference would put Alan, her brother-in-law, on his after-work jog.

Karen's voice came on the line, offering a cool hello.

"Hi, Karen. Is this a good time to talk?"

"It's a great time." Her sister's voice warmed.

"Is Alan out running?"

"No, he's working late." Karen chuckled. "I'm lounging on the sofa with a glass of wine and a gossip magazine."

"Sounds relaxing."

"Yes." In one syllable, her sister's voice cooled again. Tracy knew her sister was still nervous about this marriage. Alan provided well for Karen, but he could be controlling. Although Karen seemed willing to comply with his rigid demands for dinner at a specified time, a spotless house and careful upkeep of their clothing, Tracy wondered if her older sister was truly happy. Picturing the handsome but stern man she'd met only once, Tracy asked the question she worried about often: "Are you okay?"

"I'm fine. How's Mom?"

"Better every day." Tracy carried the phone to her night table in the opposite corner of the bedroom. "She has a new neighb—"

"Hang on," her sister interrupted.

Tracy heard the closing of a door, followed by a man's deep voice. Alan must have arrived home. If Tracy guessed correctly, Karen had stuffed her magazine under the sofa cushion and was rushing to the door for a kiss and her husband's approval.

Tracy stretched across her bed to wait. Evening light

slanted across the foot of the bed, illuminating a scattering of stuffed animals Hannah had left there earlier. Alan probably wouldn't allow a child to play in his room, but Tracy enjoyed her daughter's company. She was reminded of the main reason she was a single mom. Finding the right man seemed a formidable task. Too many women settled for good enough and hung on despite a lasting discontent. Others, like her sister, kept starting over.

Tracy had given up her prerogative to make that sort of mistake when she'd adopted a child. Hannah deserved a stable home. Tracy wouldn't upset the precarious balance of their everyday life until she knew the risk was worth taking. And so, men who were clearly wrong were turned down graciously but immediately. These were the men who were too drunk, too dreary, too married or too anything else. The obvious won't-works. Every once in a while, Tracy went through a hopeful cycle. An exceptional man would have entered her life and made her care enough to think future thoughts—until something happened to move him down to won't-work status.

Maybe she was too picky. Maybe Mr. Right didn't exist. If he did, he'd be the one Tracy couldn't bump down. For now, she and Hannah were fine.

Silence interrupted Tracy's thoughts. Briefly, she moved the phone from her ear to listen for Hannah. Within seconds, the music restarted and Hannah's sweet voice joined in. Tracy reclined against the headboard and gathered her courage to ask tough questions.

"I'm back."

Tracy took a deep breath. "I'll be quick."

"Take your time." Karen's tone gave the impression that she was determined to continue the conversation despite whatever opposition she might encounter later.

''Riley moved back to town,'' Tracy said, keeping her voice neutral so she could gauge her sister's true response.

''Really?'' Karen asked. ''That's terrific!''

''You see it as something good?''

''He hated leaving his grandmother,'' Karen said, in a voice so soft Tracy could barely hear it.

''He abandoned you in California,'' Tracy stated bluntly. ''I've never understood why you weren't angry at him.''

''Do we have to talk about this again?'' Karen enunciated each word clearly. ''Riley did not abandon me. Our fling was over before we left town.''

Tracy propped a pillow behind her back. ''Mom and Matthew would have helped both of you if you'd talked to them.''

''Tracy, drop it.''

''It doesn't bother you to know he's living next door to our parents again?''

''Nope.''

Tracy curled her fingers around to stare at her nails. Karen had always avoided discussions about her wild teenage years—and that included her involvement with Riley. Tracy herself was reluctant to admit she'd been devastated by that involvement.

As teenagers, she and Karen had been too different to be friends, even though they were only eighteen months apart. Karen had considered her a Goody Two-shoes, and Tracy certainly hadn't confided in her beautiful but arrogant sister. The relationship had warmed as they'd gotten older, but Tracy rarely brought up the past because Karen had always avoided answering.

Besides, if she pressed the issue, it would broadcast the fact that she still thought about it. Which seemed sort of pathetic, so she usually didn't mention the subject.

"Why would Riley's return be a problem?" Karen asked.

"He wants to hire me to help set up his business," Tracy said. "I'd be promoted to full consultant."

Karen didn't hesitate. "Oh, Tracy, that's great. You're perfect for the job, and you two used to be best buddies."

"With heavy emphasis on the *used to be*."

"Forget what happened between Riley and me," Karen said. "I was a hotshot with a lot to prove. It's ancient history."

Tracy grimaced at the phrase, deciding then and there to remove it from her vocabulary. Unfortunately, she couldn't remove it from anyone else's. Then she bit her lip to keep from mentioning the one thing she absolutely couldn't forget.

An empty pregnancy test carton.

She'd found it in Karen's trash can the morning after they'd left. The box had been rolled in tissue and buried beneath crumpled balls of notebook paper. Karen had obviously been trying to hide it.

In some foolish act of loyalty, Tracy had hidden the container in her gym bag and thrown it in a Dumpster on her way to school the next day. She'd figured it wasn't her news to tell. And no one had ever known she'd found the test. Karen hadn't mentioned the discovery, and no specific outcome had followed—no baby, no quickie marriage or divorce. No real problem.

Except that Karen had struggled to get on her feet after Riley left her out in California, and Tracy's knowledge of the blue cardboard carton had soured the last sweet spot she'd reserved in her heart for Riley. It meant he'd stepped beyond an impetuous bending of rules to real-world risks. It meant he wasn't quite the boy she'd admired.

It meant he preferred her sister.

That was the day Tracy's opinion of men skewed. She knew what they wanted, and it wasn't anything as noble as friendship or loyalty. They wanted long-legged, flirty blondes. Her naive devotion to the boy next door had landed her with a cynical opinion of men at fifteen.

"Tracy? You aren't still holding a grudge, are you?"

"Of course not." Tracy cleared her throat. "I still don't think spending time with Riley is a good idea."

"You don't want the promotion?"

Tracy glanced around her bedroom. She took in the aging computer and used exercise bike. She thought about Hannah's cluttered room and remembered a few of the little girl's recent requests. At Christmas and again on her birthday, Hannah had listed a few simple things. A dollhouse. New skates. A guinea pig. None of the requests were outrageous, and Tracy would love to give her daughter such things. Unfortunately the two-bedroom duplex Tracy rented did not provide ample space.

In truth, she'd love a promotion. She wanted the means to buy a house. She couldn't tell Karen that, though. Her sister seemed to link herself with one wrong man after another, just so she wouldn't have to worry about where or how to live.

Their mother thought it was because Karen remembered when their dad left. He'd quit his job as manager of the pancake house, saying he was too smart to waste his life teaching teenage girls to wait tables. When Gwen had pushed him to find another job, he'd left for Vegas with one of those teenagers, abandoning Gwen with a toddler and infant.

For a while, Gwen couldn't demand child-support payments because he was broke. She couldn't afford diapers and baby food if she paid her rent, so she'd packed up the kids and moved in with a girlfriend. The one-bedroom apartment they'd shared was cramped, but clean and affordable. Her friend's kindness had enabled her to get on her feet.

Karen remembered that six-month time span in the vague, distorted way a toddler remembers a traumatic event. Tracy, of course, had been too young.

But she shivered now, just recalling the family stories. She was fine on her own. She'd live in this cramped duplex forever, rather than spend a day with a man who wasn't right.

"I don't need the promotion," she said. "I'm fine."

"Wait a minute," Karen said. The sound of shuffling in the background indicated that she must be finding a private place to talk. "Okay, I'm out on the balcony."

"Where's Alan?"

"Changing into his sweats."

"Karen, you ought to seek counseling if you have to hide to talk on the phone with your sister."

"Never mind about that," Karen said. "Aren't you buying Mom and Matthew a garden bench for their anniversary?"

Both sisters knew she was. They'd talked about it several times. "Yes."

"Didn't you tell me you wished you had the money to buy one made out of teak?"

"You know I did, but I can use credit."

"So extra money would help?"

Tracy chuckled at her sister's determination. "I can

manage without it, but that does lead to another question.''

"Don't ask," Karen said.

Ever since their mother's illness last winter, Tracy had been trying to talk Karen into coming for a visit. "Have you spoken to Alan about visiting this summer?" she asked.

"No."

Tracy let her silence say what she wouldn't. Karen had never even met Hannah.

After a moment, her sister said, "Airfare from San Diego is too expensive. Besides, I can't upset things around here by asking. Alan can't leave the hotel, and he won't want me to come alone. Mom understands."

"*I* don't understand. Don't you want to see your family?"

"I want to come, but I can't."

A thought intruded upon Tracy's brain. A solution so perfect she didn't know why she hadn't thought of it sooner. Riley had returned and offered her a chance at promotion. Since he was the one who had taken Karen away, it was appropriate that he provide the means to bring her home.

Tracy would take the job. If she worked hard and finished quickly, she might have enough money for a down payment on a house by the end of summer. A house for Hannah. For their future.

It was doable.

"What if I buy your plane ticket?" Tracy asked.

At the other end of the phone line, she heard the opening and closing of a door. Karen must be ensuring the privacy of the phone call, which had taken a dangerous turn. "You can't afford that," Karen whispered.

Tracy smiled into the phone. "Did I tell you I'm due for a promotion at work?"

"Good," Karen said. "Spend some of the money on a new outfit for Mom and Matthew's fifteenth anniversary celebration."

"Promise to come to the celebration."

"I can't."

"Karen, Mom's been thinking a lot about her family."

"I know."

"Her day would only be perfect with you here. I'll send the ticket."

"I can't ask that of my younger sister."

"You didn't ask."

"Tra-ay-cee."

In the past, Karen had used the drawn-out pronunciation of Tracy's name when she'd caught her experimenting with her perfume bottles or wearing her earrings. "It's settled," Tracy said, smiling. "I'll take the job, and send a plane ticket for the second Saturday in June."

"Tra-ay-cee."

"No arguments. I'll buy a round-trip ticket," Tracy said, and then added softly, "But I'll leave the return date open. You can decide for yourself if you want to go back."

THIS ABSURD FASCINATION with the goings-on next door could not be healthy. Tracy pulled her gaze away from the back windows of Riley's house and stepped across her parents' fledgling potato plants. As she knelt next to a row of lettuce, she looked over again and scowled. Riley wasn't even outside, yet she was bothered.

Not that she was looking for him, of course. It was

natural for him to be on her mind because she'd told him she would call his office Monday morning, and it was already Sunday afternoon.

Digging up a thriving mound of lettuce, Tracy shook it off and added it to her basket, then glanced across the fence at the swing set. He'd painted it a glossy aqua, and added new swings and a bright yellow slide. It seemed odd that he would fix up a child's swing set, but maybe he was planning to sell it. Maybe he had a girlfriend with a kid. He could even be married. Tracy had only assumed he wasn't.

It shouldn't matter, anyway. At best, they would have a short-term business relationship. A regular client wouldn't disrupt her personal life, and neither would Riley. Tracy would make sure he didn't by keeping things professional.

Then Riley could disappear into the mysterious details of his everyday life, and she could go house hunting.

Picking up the basket, Tracy stepped out of the garden and scrutinized the yard on her way across it. The teak bench would work well next to the roses. On her parents' anniversary, Tracy had planned to have them come outside to find the bench. She'd hoped to surprise them with a cake and a tiny party. With both daughters here, the day would be more special. Karen could be sitting on the bench alongside Hannah, and the surprise would be bigger. Just that would be worth the trouble.

Feeling perkier, Tracy went inside. The robust smell of her mother's lasagna filled the kitchen, and the mess had already been cleared. If Karen had inherited their mother's looks, Tracy had gotten her efficiency. Although there was a time when she would have traded, she'd learned to be satisfied with herself. Her life was progressing as she wished. Karen seemed to be stuck in an endless search for a decent husband.

Tracy washed and dried the lettuce and tore it into a bowl, putting it in the refrigerator before wandering through the house. Matthew and Hannah were playing cards on the living-room carpet while Tracy's mother read the Sunday paper. Hannah saw her first. "Mama, I beat Poppy Matthew three times so far!"

"What are you playing?"

"Jack-slap." Hannah scrambled the word in a voice so cheery Tracy wouldn't dream of correcting her.

"That's good," she said, smiling at Matthew. He'd always let her win, too.

"The lettuce is ready," Tracy told her mom. "What next?"

"Nothing. Relax." Her mother didn't look up from her paper. "We'll have dinner in an hour."

An hour? Tracy watched the card game for a minute, but she couldn't relax with tomorrow's task looming. Not when she had an hour before dinner.

Riley had probably noticed her in the backyard. He'd probably grinned that goofy grin as he watched her stare at his house and the swing set. He'd probably plotted a hundred different ways to keep her guessing if she accepted the job.

His plot would fail. She'd call all the shots and keep things serious. In fact, she could go over there now to speak to him privately. She could let him know who was boss.

"Mom?"

"Yes, love?"

"Do you mind if I leave Hannah here and run an errand?"

The paper rattled, but her mother still didn't peer over its top. "Always the busy one, aren't you."

"I'd be gone only a few minutes."

"Take as long as you need," her mother said. "Hannah is fine. We'll eat around six if you're here to join us."

"I'll be back long before that."

Tracy stepped on to her parents' front porch and slipped on her shoes, then noticed her car parked behind theirs in the driveway. "Oh! I won't be taking my car," she shouted back inside. "I'm only going next door."

Tracy grinned, knowing without looking that her mother had glanced up from the paper to trade one of those concerned-parent looks with Matthew.

RILEY LUGGED another crate in from the garage and set it in the middle of the living-room floor. His grandmother had told him he needed a few things to set up a proper house, and she'd been kind enough to offer a trunkload. The least he could do was consider what she'd offered.

Pulling a towel off the top, he found more cooking supplies. For a woman who claimed she didn't like to cook, his grandmother sure owned a vast array of kitchen gadgetry. And she'd said these were her duplicates.

He pulled out a flower-shaped waffle iron and set it on the carpet between a set of lace napkins and a cow cookie jar that mooed when its lid was lifted. Scowling at the assortment, which also included a miniature simmer pot and a burnt-orange lava lamp, he felt as if he was the solitary participant in a housewarming shower—except at this party he received things he'd never wanted and would never use.

He would certainly never make flower-shaped waffles.

Any form of from-scratch waffles was labor-intensive. When he thought about it, he realized his grandmother wouldn't make waffles, either. He chuckled. The lady was foisting her unwanted junk off on him. Sly old coot.

The doorbell rang, followed by a knock on the door. One of his first projects had been to rewire the bell. Obviously the person at the door wasn't certain the bell worked. Riley left his odd collection and went to answer the door.

It was Tracy. She stood on the porch with her arms folded around her middle, but rather than looking into his face, she looked behind him, at his living-room floor.

"Come in." Riley worked to curb his astonishment. Of all the people in town, she was the last person he'd have expected to appear on his doorstep on Sunday afternoon. She was also the one he most wanted to see, if with a different expression on her face.

She looked as if she suspected one of the items on his floor was ready to detonate.

"No thank you," she said in a voice too polite to be sincere. "Would you mind stepping out? I won't stay long, but I thought it'd be better if we spoke face-to-face."

He tried not to grin as he joined her. In faded jean shorts and a tank top, she reminded him of the young girl who'd once been his best friend. "Is something wrong?"

"I'm taking the job."

"Good." He offered a smile when her gaze finally met his and held. His initial plan to teach her a lesson was forgotten as he thought about how much fun it would be to spend time with her again.

But her face remained sober, and her eyes bore the same shield of reluctance they had the other day. "I came to talk away from Booker's ears. He doesn't know our history, but you and I know things are complicated.''

Although he respected her honesty and couldn't blame her for the mixed emotions, Riley felt only anticipation. Still, he forced a serious expression. It'd be best to keep things earnest, at least until Tracy relaxed. ''Fair enough.''

She took a deep breath and kept her arms wrapped tight against her middle. ''You have to listen to me.''

He threw both palms up. ''Who's not listening?''

''I mean with this job. You have to listen to my advice, or I'll drop the assignment.''

''Isn't a consulting business based mainly on client preference?'' he asked. ''You can't dictate my needs.''

She put her hands on her hips and glared at him. ''If one of my suggestions won't work for you, by all means let me know. But no game playing. We'll work together as business partners.''

He shrugged. ''Let's agree now to discuss any point of contention.''

''That should work.'' Tracy seemed relieved, but she pulled her eyes away to squint inside his house again.

He hated her avoidance, and it tore him up to know she'd lost her liking for him. He'd love to explore other possibilities with her. If he wasn't making a real go at claiming a life here, he might be tempted to ignore the town gossips and make a real go at claiming Tracy.

She pivoted around to face the street. ''I doubt that you actually need an image consultation,'' she said, standing beside him to converse as if they were two men at a backyard barbecue. ''We'd save time and money if we concentrated on your office.''

Riley bit his cheek to keep from smiling. He knew how to present himself for business, but it'd be fun to have Tracy tutor him. Who knew what he'd learn? Besides, it would also provide more time for the two of them to get reacquainted. For some reason, that was important.

"I'm paying for the works," he insisted.

Her sigh was loud and dramatic. "Are you sure?"

"Absolutely."

"Then let's do the image coaching first and get it out of the way." She was probably on to the very game she'd said she wouldn't join, but she was playing along. It was a cool, professional move. He was impressed.

"Good idea." He turned to grin at her profile. Suddenly it seemed important to chip a hole in her polite veneer.

"Okay," she said, refusing to turn. "I'll get hold of you in the morning. We can set up the appointment with our schedules in front of us."

"Call the home number," he said. "I'll be late getting to the office tomorrow. I have a lot to organize around here now, too."

"What's the number?" Tracy patted her pockets, presumably for something to write on.

"The same as it always was. Do you remember?" It was a loaded question. He probably shouldn't have asked it, but he watched her intently. She'd called his house every day way back when. Would she acknowledge that?

She turned and looked at him with a startled smile that was big enough to drown him in pleasure. Then, abruptly, her face closed off again. "Uh-huh."

He held on to his own smile, unwilling to forget the sweeter memories of childhood. The years of absence couldn't erase the years of closeness.

"We'll spend the bulk of our time getting your office organized, though," she said. "Will that work for you?"

With Tracy making prolonged eye contact, Riley could hardly think about business. He wanted to spend the bulk of his time kissing her face to bring the softness back. He wanted to feel her skin against his, and he wanted to watch her beam another real smile in his direction.

He fought for coolness. "Yes."

"I'll draw up a proposal, with a schedule we can negotiate the next time we meet."

"That's great," he said, his voice deep as he thought of different, more intimate kinds of proposals.

She stretched her frame to a proud height. "You'll take my advice?"

He smiled. "Most of it, probably."

She closed her eyes briefly. "And I should call you Mr. Collins."

He shook his head. "I have a strict rule. Anyone who has shot spit wads at my nose has to use my first name."

She grinned. "You taught me how to shoot those spit wads, and that was the only time I sat in detention with you."

He stared at the gentle upward curve of her mouth, glad to be getting somewhere. It may be the tiniest of smiles, but it was a win, nevertheless.

"You will take me seriously," she said again, as if she didn't believe it was possible.

"If you're working as a consultant, you have to know your advice can be rejected. You'll lose clients if you aren't flexible."

"This is different," she said, shifting her weight. "You tease, but you know my advice will be for your good."

He couldn't help it. He'd been dreaming about this moment since the other day at her office when she'd made the crack about the hairy beast. "Oh, but I beg to differ," he said. "I can already dispute one piece of advice you've listed."

"Which one?"

"The bike."

Her mouth curved into a smile again, but her eyes looked dubious. "I don't care if you ride your motorcycle on weekends," she said. "But not to the office."

"Motor-*cy*-cle," he corrected.

"What?"

"Not sickle, *c*ycle."

She reached down to rub a thumb against her heel, but kept staring at him. "I'm saying that a car gives you the air of respectability you need," she said. "You'll need a car by winter, anyway. Remember? We get snow in Kansas."

He checked to make sure the sedan he'd parked beside his motorcycle was visible. "Something like that?" he asked, nodding toward the garage windows.

She stood up straight and glared into the garage. "Yes! I'm glad you're taking my advice. Get rid of the motorcycle and drive the car."

Riley crossed his arms. His car had been in the shop last week for maintenance work, but now he was tempted to keep it parked. Tracy should know better than to provoke him. "On fair-weather days, I'm taking the bike," he announced.

"You said you'd listen."

The same thing had gotten him into trouble his whole life: a glimmer of an impulse became a goal, and he could never stop his heart from wanting it so badly he'd pay the devil to experience the thrill.

He wanted Tracy to ride his motorcycle with him. He wanted her to admit that the feeling of freedom and power was worth a chink in a man's image. And he wanted her close.

"Let's go for a ride."

She scowled.

"You drove all the way over here to tell me that you're willing to do the consultation," he said. "This is a business decision we're making together."

"I came all the way over here to have dinner with my parents. My little girl is still there. I need to get back."

He ignored her comment. "I've spoken with your parents several times, and they were gracious. They'll forgive us."

She shook her head. "It's not a good idea."

"Yes, it is. Let me take you for a ride."

She peered into his eyes and gasped at his expression. "I won't let you take me for a ride," she said in a quick, staccato rhythm.

Yes! She was biting back. He knew she'd be fun.

"I'm a new client with a special request," he insisted. "Let me convince you the bike is worth working around."

The heartening tinkle of her laughter reached his ears before she could stop it, so he reached back and closed his front door. "After our ride, we can argue as long as you want," he said as he grabbed her hand and led her to the garage. He let go of her hand to pull open the garage door, then hastened across to flip on the light.

There it was, in all its chrome and leather glory. His six-year-old Honda Shadow. He'd bought it the summer after he'd received his master's degree, as a sort of thumbing his nose at the respectability he'd achieved.

He was proud of his bike, and he'd never been

ashamed of the free and easy life it allowed him to return to on occasion.

He looked at Tracy and chuckled. She was glaring at his bike as if *it* were about to detonate. He didn't want to give her time to run away, so he grabbed his extra helmet from a shelf and positioned it on her head. Her hands came up to take over the task, enfolding his as she guided it down. Her surprising acquiescence gained significance as he recognized the importance he was pinning on her reaction to what came next.

This wasn't about a pleasure ride. It was about gauging the way things would be between them. Would she relax enough to get to know him again?

As he pulled the key from his pocket, he noticed her glancing at her watch. "We'll do one loop around the lake," he promised.

She buckled the helmet.

After plugging the key into the ignition, he straddled the seat and kicked the bike off its stand, holding it balanced between his legs as he waited for her to climb on and wrap her arms around his waist. As he waited, he felt stirrings of arousal. Maybe this wasn't such a good idea.

Still, she didn't move. He grabbed his own helmet from the workbench and put it on, then pulled the brake release and looked across at her. Waiting.

Anticipating.

Chapter Five

"I'm finding it hard to believe you bother with a helmet," Tracy said as she got on the motorcycle behind him.

"Why wouldn't I?"

"Too safe."

He buckled the helmet and waited to feel her hands on his waist or chest. "My choices back then were often an effort to goad Otto into showing some concern. One of the best things about growing up is that I can make my own choices. I choose to keep my brains inside my skull."

She chuckled, but her perch was still tentative as she kept inches between them.

He grinned. That wouldn't last long. He brought the bike to life with a powerful roar and made an easy circle around his car. As he turned onto the vacant street, he felt marvelously paired with Tracy. It wasn't long before her arms found their way to his chest, and the series of turns on the road to the lake caused them to pull ever tighter.

As they traveled the one-lane gravel road encircling Willow Lake, Tracy's grip loosened. She must be getting a feel for the shifts in equilibrium. She must be learning to trust him enough to relax.

Sex would be the only thing more satisfying.

Sex with Tracy would be mind-boggling.

Criminy, why would he think such a thing?

And how would he know?

He just *knew*.

He gripped the handlebars, forcing himself to think about the road. Maybe he should head back. Surely by now she'd begun to get a sense of the connection between rider and bike. Surely she'd admit that riding was a worthwhile way for a man to commute.

A lone car entered the road from the other side. The driver seemed to challenge Riley by driving squarely in the middle of the lane. Riley felt a larger threat. He'd ridden most of his adult life. He was willing to accept the risks in exchange for the freedoms, but he didn't want anything to happen to Tracy. He felt a new appreciation for safety that he'd never felt for himself.

He maneuvered the motorcycle to the far right to allow the car to pass, then rounded back toward the house.

If he'd been interested only in feeling Tracy's body plastered against his, he'd have ridden much longer. But there were other things to consider, and too many reasons to keep his distance from Tracy. A temporary surrender to curiosity and passion could hurt one or both of them. He'd known that at seventeen. He needed to remember it now.

Pulling into the garage, Riley held the bike balanced so Tracy could climb off. Both of them were quiet as they removed the matching helmets and replaced them on the shelf. He'd meant to take her for a ride and get her to admit that the feeling was worth the waggling of a few tongues, but she'd taught him something, too.

She made him want to make thoughtful choices.

"Okay," Tracy said, smiling as she crossed her arms. "I can see why you'd want to ride that thing."

He chuckled. Her hair was still perfect, even after being crammed under a helmet. But her face was fresh, as if she'd just been kissed. Or wanted to be.

He wished he could add that to his list of requirements for the job. "Do I hear another condition coming?" he asked.

She nodded, but kept smiling. "I'd leave it home during the week, along with the bandana and ear stud."

His arms ached to pull her close again, but chest to chest so he could kiss a bigger smile onto her face. He crossed his arms, too. "Agreed."

Tracy shifted her weight, rubbing a toe against her opposite heel. "Before I go, I have a question."

"Shoot."

"Why did you ask for me? Booker has years of experience."

Riley shrugged. "Since I don't know Booker, I assume he's unaware of the prejudices I'm facing."

Tracy slipped off the heel of her shoe and bent down to rub her heel with her thumb. "You could tell him."

"I thought you'd agreed to take the job."

"I did," she said, and flopped her heel back down with a clatter that seemed to emphasize her words. "I still don't think it's a good idea."

Riley took her arm, directing her backward a few steps to a chair he'd left by his workbench, urging her into it. "You know me. That makes you my best choice."

"Wouldn't that make me your worst choice?"

"Touché." He feigned nonchalance.

She smiled again. "You'll follow my suggestions?" she asked, returning to her feet.

Her mouth was lovely. But tantalizing when she smiled. "Absolutely."

When her smile grew into the face-lighting wonder he remembered, he knew things would be okay between them. Still, he couldn't resist a tiny tease. "Unless I can convince you that my way is as good or better than yours."

Her smile only faded a touch. "No more rides and no more fooling around," she said. "Image is important." She lifted her chin and stared boldly into his eyes. Then she frowned and bent to adjust her shoe again.

He chuckled. She was likable, as well as gorgeous. If he wasn't so intent on convincing her to trust him, it'd be a blast to tease the primness right out of her. "No fooling around?" he asked, stepping closer. "Is that particular rule set in stone?"

"In granite." She maintained eye contact.

He leaned down and brushed a brief kiss against her mouth. He drew back with a frown, wondering if her lips could have been that soft and pliant. That accepting.

He couldn't resist an extra nip, to test things out. Her mouth opened slightly as she gasped, so he drew closer and let himself fall deeper into it. Much deeper.

He lost track of all intentions and simply enjoyed molding his mouth to hers, letting up occasionally to nibble gratefully as he thrilled at her eager participation.

His hands rested flat against her rib cage, and he forced himself to keep them there. Instinctively, he knew their movement to her more secret curves would force an abrupt halt to this unexpected joyride.

So he satisfied himself with lips. As he kissed, he realized that he'd never wanted any woman more than he wanted Tracy now. That scared the bejeebies out of him.

Still, he didn't stop skidding down the treacherous slope of need until she braced her hands on his chest and shoved.

He gazed at her, waiting for his heart to slow. Before he'd kissed her, he'd started to say something. As he watched her turn her confused face away to leave, he remembered. He'd been ready to make some crack about convincing her that a little fooling around was worth working into the schedule.

He kept his big mouth shut, for once.

TRACY SAT CROSS-LEGGED on the floor of Hannah's room with a red plastic horse in her hand. She sank the miniature hooves into the carpet, dutifully galloping the toy along, but she couldn't pull her mind into the pretend game. Too many other thoughts resided there.

Hannah let out a high-pitched whinny as she moved her animals around a corral made of wooden blocks. She seemed tolerant of the perfunctory companionship her mother was providing, but Tracy wasn't. She wanted to be involved, interested. Not perpetually distracted.

Her initial response to news of Riley's return had been correct, and she'd done nothing but worry since the moment she'd seen him again. The garage kisses hadn't helped. Neither did the knowledge that they'd been partly her fault. The first one had caught her by surprise, but she could've pushed him away much sooner. It was just that she hadn't been kissed that passionately in a while. And she'd been curious about Riley since she was twelve years old. And the ride around the lake had been surprisingly romantic.

And every excuse in the world didn't excuse her behavior.

Those kisses had done more harm than good. They

had roused an ache she'd rarely felt and barely acknowledged, raising her agitation to emergency levels. She had
to fight her way back to normal.

She knew what to do about the kisses. Riley had
promised to discuss controversial issues, and kissing
qualified. She'd simply outlaw them from here on out.

But she also had to get her mind back on business,
and her brain wasn't cooperating. Besides the kisses, a
painted swing set was still looming in her thoughts. So
was the cookie jar she'd seen among Riley's things.

She didn't know if she was hoping he had five kids
who would arrive tomorrow and take him beyond her
won't-work category to bachelor purgatory, or if she was
hoping he didn't.

She only wanted to know.

Fortunately the town's biggest gossip lived one door
away. ''Come on, Bean,'' Tracy said, standing quickly
and smiling down at her daughter. ''Let's go visit Nellie.''

''Why, Mama?''

''We haven't seen her in a while,'' Tracy said.

Hannah brightened as she looked at the toys strewn
around on her bedroom floor. ''Do we hafta pick up?''

''Nope.''

Hannah whooped, and then skipped all the way to the
door.

A quick, information-gathering visit—that was what
Tracy needed. Nellie would have been nosing around for
a while by now. She might have helpful news. Riley
wasn't going to disappear anytime soon, and Tracy
needed armor. Even an ex-lover with a niece or nephew
might help.

A minute later, Tracy squeezed Hannah's hand as she

stared at a wreath of ugly faux fruit surrounding the peephole on Nellie's door. "We'll stay only a minute."

"That's okay," Hannah said. "Nellie has pwetty fish."

Before Tracy could ring the bell, the door whooshed open and Nellie stood in front of them. "Tracy and Hannah, how nice to see you!" She pushed open the screen door.

Tracy waited for Hannah to rush through the door on her way to the tankful of saltwater fish in the corner, then stepped into the duplex that was a mirror image of hers.

As usual, she was struck by the amazing amount of clutter. Nellie was a bit of a recluse, and the fact was reflected in the stacks of magazines and jigsaw puzzles. If Tracy was a craftier saleswoman, she would solicit some work. The woman could use a hand at organizing her life.

"I wasn't expecting a visit this evening," Nellie said with a pleased laugh as she moved some newspapers from the sofa so Tracy could sit down.

Tracy waited patiently while Nellie bustled into the kitchen on an urgent mission. When she returned with a tray crowded with plates, Tracy stifled a groan. This snooping visit could cost her an entire evening.

But Nellie didn't get a lot of visitors, and it would be cruel for Tracy to satisfy her curiosity and leave. She accepted an exquisite red glass plate piled high with coconut macaroon cookies, and watched as Nellie offered Hannah a similar treat.

So much for an uneventful bedtime routine tonight. Hannah would be full of sugar-induced energy. "Be careful with crumbs," Tracy said when Hannah plopped down in front of the fish tank and crunched into a cookie.

Nellie situated herself on the threadbare rocker across from Tracy. "I've thought for a long time that we should get together in the evenings," she said. "Since neither one of us is dating, we're both home an awful lot."

Tracy picked up a cookie and smiled.

Nellie lifted an eyebrow. "I've wondered if you were lonely since you broke up with your redheaded track coach. What was his name?"

Tracy frowned. Counting boyfriends was Nellie's favorite game. She seemed to live her romantic life vicariously through Tracy, and the questions were repeated nearly every time they saw one another.

"Samuel," she answered, taking a big bite of cookie in hopes of avoiding Nellie's next question.

"Whatever happened to you two?"

Tracy chewed slowly, willing Nellie to start chattering about something else. When her neighbor leaned to the very edge of her chair and maintained a rapt expression, Tracy offered the shortest version of the story. "We split up."

Nellie wasn't deterred. "Why?"

He told me I'd have been the perfect girl for him if I hadn't adopted Hannah. He wants redheaded kids.

"I realized he wasn't the guy for me."

Nellie didn't bat a lash at the elusive answer, probably because she was planning her next question. "Anywho, he wasn't as good-looking as the dentist before him. Mike? With the bike shorts and long fingers?"

And long tales of his escapades with his previous girl-friend. Tales that proved to be prophetic, in the end.

Tracy nibbled her cookie. "Mike was handsome."

"Whatever happened to him?"

Tracy rested her half-eaten cookie on the plate. "Last time I heard, he was living in Denver with a wife and new baby."

Finally Nellie took a cookie off her own plate and waved it around in front of her face. "We're unlucky in love, aren't we, Tracy?"

Tracy shrugged. "We're focusing on our careers."

When Nellie paused to shove the entire cookie into her mouth, Tracy decided it was time to ask her own question. "Speaking of careers, have you heard any more buzz about Riley Collins?"

Nellie chewed frantically and leaned so far forward that her knees banged against the coffee table.

Tracy leaned closer, too.

"No changing the subject," Nellie said. "It's odd that you don't date much." She looked across at Hannah, then lowered her voice. "In high school, I'd have bet dollars to doughnuts you'd be the first in your class to marry."

"Would you?"

"We have bad luck with men, but it isn't our fault," Nellie insisted as she devoured another cookie.

"I thought you were going to try Internet dating."

"My friend Ruth said I should."

"I think you should, too," Tracy said gently, realizing her chances of gleaning information from Nellie were fading.

One more try. Tracy would attempt to bring the topic back around to Riley one more time before she left. After waiting until Nellie was between cookies, Tracy asked, "Has your friend said anything about Riley's present-day life?"

"Why? What are you wondering about?"

A wife, a lover, an ex-wife, stray children. Any reason

for a man to own a swing set and a cookie jar. Any reason for his kisses to be meaningless. "Anything."

Nellie tilted her head. "I've heard he's starting a business and using your services to get set up," she said. "Isn't that true?"

"Yes, it is."

"Then why are you asking me about him?"

Tracy shrugged. "Research."

"I do know he was putting up a basketball hoop at his grandma's retirement village the other night. The manager wasn't happy, but she let him put it up because Lydia always pays her bills on time."

"Where was Lydia?"

"Hanging around, bouncing a ball." Nellie said this as if it were a news flash. Then her voice lowered to a whisper. "That woman is an odd one."

Tracy had heard it said that Lydia was eccentric, but she'd always been charmed by the lady's pluck. "How so?"

"She has no idea she's getting old," Nellie said.

"And what's wrong with that?"

Nellie looked perplexed. "I don't know. It seems to me that old women shouldn't trot around with basketballs."

"If I can heave a ball into a hoop when I'm Lydia's age, I hope I'm bold enough to do it." Tracy watched Nellie press her fingers into the crumbs on her plate, collecting them all on the ends and shoving them into her mouth. She sent a silent plea to the heavens that her idiosyncrasies were more like Lydia's than Nellie's.

"Did you know she's going to college?" Nellie asked.

Tracy nodded, her heart sinking as slowly and grandly as the *Titanic*. Tonight, Nellie's gossip seemed to include everything Tracy admired about the grandmother, and nothing at all about the grandson. Another mission had failed.

LYDIA TOSSED a white lace square into the giveaway box and shook her head. ''I'm not surprised about the napkins,'' she said, ''but I think every bachelor needs a waffle iron to feed their lady friends breakfast in bed.''

Riley grinned. ''Be nice, Gran. That's only bachelors who cook and have current lady friends.''

Lydia chuckled and followed him to the back bedroom, where boxes of her castoffs were stacked. ''M'dear, under certain circumstances even Friday night's hot date would go for a daisy-shaped waffle.''

''I seem to recall asking a sassy chick out to dinner last Friday night,'' Riley said as he put the box with the others. ''She said she'd rather shoot hoops and eat hot dogs.''

''What time are you expecting Friday morning's hot date?''

Riley looked at his watch. ''You mean Tracy?'' He didn't wait for an answer to his admittedly stupid question. ''Now.''

''Then I'll get out of here before she notices you're two-timing her.'' Lydia cackled as she made her way out Riley's front door, directly into the rain. She paced steadily to her car, seemingly unconcerned about getting wet. Before she climbed inside, she turned and called out, ''My best grandmotherly advice is to score the first kiss before you lose your nerve!''

Riley chuckled, but even after Lydia drove away, he remained at the door, watching the clouds squeeze the last bit of blue from the western sky. Gran didn't know it, but he'd already gotten that first kiss knocked out.

Since then, he was discovering nerves he'd never known he had.

He'd intended to teach Tracy a lesson in the perils of misjudging a person. He'd wanted to rock her boat a little. Get her to think.

He seemed to be the one doing the thinking.

Abruptly, he left the doorway and crossed the house to his bedroom. Besides a little paint, he hadn't done much to the room. He'd brought in a cheap dresser, added a good mattress and box spring and called it finished. A few of Gran's contributions had added a homier feel, but the red-glowing lava lamp she'd set up on his dresser this morning didn't add anything dignified to the room. The slow-moving shapes seemed languid and sexy, like something a couple would watch from bed. Clicking off the lamp, Riley swiveled around to scrutinize the room further. He wasn't as sloppy as Otto, but he wouldn't want Tracy to see dirty socks or a pair of boxers on the floor.

When the doorbell rang, Riley knew exactly who it was and why she was here. He walked slowly and purposefully, pausing to pull in a deep breath before opening the door.

Tracy made a stunning picture as she stood under an oversize black umbrella in a well-fitting red blazer and skirt. She looked quite composed as she turned to look down the street. "I just missed your grandmother, didn't I?"

"She's been helping me get moved in," Riley said, noticing that Tracy had colored her lips the same bright shade as her suit. She had the best lips. When she was a kid, their fullness had made teaching her to whistle easier. Now they made him want to teach her other things.

Tracy closed the umbrella and shook it before picking up her briefcase and stepping into the house. After she'd leaned the umbrella next to the door, she moved into the living room and glanced around.

Businesslike. That was how she looked. And that was how he should act. He'd concentrate on what she was saying instead of the lips forming the words.

She wouldn't learn to trust him if he kept staring at her mouth. Or if he kissed her again.

She didn't give him time to think about it. She glanced at the new bamboo shade covering the picture window and frowned. "Let's make an agreement," she said.

"What about?"

She crossed to the window, where she grabbed the string at the bottom of the shade and yanked, sending it flapping toward the ceiling. Then, looking across at him in the muted light of a gray day, she simply said, "Kissing."

Chapter Six

"Kissing?"

"Yes, kissing," Tracy said. "It's off limits."

Ah! Another dare. Riley crossed his arms. "All kissing? Everywhere? Forever?"

She looked confused. "Well, no. Only between us. It's unprofessional and we're working together now."

"Let me get this straight," he said, trying not to grin. "We're agreeing not to kiss when we're working together?"

She seemed even more confused, but she said, "Right."

She'd made it too easy. He let go of a smile. "Agreed."

Her gaze moved around his living room again. "The old house is looking good." Her eyes lit up, her mouth turned up—and his heart started skipping every other beat.

Criminy.

When she set her briefcase near a couple of boards he'd shoved next to the wall, he realized she might trip over something if she didn't watch where she was going. He picked up the boards and crossed the room to lean them against the wall near the kitchen. "Sorry, I'm not quite moved in yet."

She raised her eyebrows but didn't comment.

"My clothes are back here." Riley led Tracy toward his bedroom, and acknowledged to himself that he was getting revved up at the thought of having her there.

It was odd. Whenever Tracy was away, he summoned ample resolve to make a mature impression. Whenever she was within kissing distance, his hormones took over. At present, his desire for her was so great he couldn't think about anything but kissing Tracy, whether it was sanctioned or not. Suddenly it seemed as if it would be wise to get the kissing out of the way first, so he could think.

Gran's comments hadn't helped. Neither had Tracy's dare. But those red lips should be outlawed.

As Riley turned into the hallway, he noticed Tracy frowning into the back bedroom. She was probably wondering about the boxes. "I'm trying to get organized," he said. "Gran gave me a few hand-me-downs and I haven't kept up."

"Oh?"

"She thinks my bachelor lifestyle is too bohemian," he said. "That's sort of funny, if you think about it."

Tracy frowned. "You're a bachelor?"

Of course, he thought. Why would she think otherwise? He followed her gaze out the window to the swing set. Oh, that. He'd painted it soon after Tracy had left on the Saturday after his return. It was probably foolish, but he'd had hopes of meeting Tracy's little girl.

It was a little trouble to go to on the off chance that the child would be using the swing set, but refurbishing it had cost only pocket change and an afternoon's time. Nothing major.

"Yes, I'm a bachelor," he said. "And I don't have kids, if that point is in question, too."

Her eyes rested on his. "Why did you paint the swing set?"

He sensed she'd stepped closer. A business relationship would preclude kisses, all right. It would also disallow any talk beyond polite discussions of weather or lunch plans. This was curiosity, and it was personal.

"I thought your little girl might like to swing over here when she visits your parents."

There was Tracy's beaming smile. "How thoughtful," she said, and left the smile in place.

Riley was no fool. Her smile was well worth the time and paint. He watched for a minute, wondering if he should break a rule and kiss her now, or take her to his bedroom.

Both ideas seemed dangerous.

Both appealed.

Tracy raised an eyebrow. "Are we going to do this consultation in your hallway?"

He took a giant step, three feet to the left. "In here."

As soon as Tracy followed him in, her smile reverted to a frown. He knew why. His mattress and box spring seemed to dominate the room. Even the plain, coffee-colored comforter Lydia had brought seemed to suggest decadence. Sure enough, Tracy's gaze lingered there.

Back when they were school chums, Tracy would have flopped across his bed without a single thought. She'd have chattered happily about school and weekend plans. Her demeanor would have been animated and innocent.

The chances of her flopping across his bed now were slim to none. That opportunity had ceased to exist at about the same time she'd started developing curves.

This was the first time she'd been in his bedroom since she was twelve. He'd missed her.

But times had changed. The sight of Tracy standing in his bedroom now was so enticing he thought he'd leave it this way. Suddenly, just a mattress and box spring seemed the perfect bachelor decor. Maybe he'd add a few candles over on the dresser, but that was it. Well, perhaps a bedful of rose petals the same color as her lips… *Stop.*

''Here's the closet,'' he said. Why was he pointing out the obvious? He must really be losing it.

When Tracy brushed by to peer into his closet, he caught the scent of her perfume. He listened to her soft puffs of breath as she started to rummage through his clothes. She was so near. He'd only have to lean forward a little bit to make physical contact… He stepped back and watched her derriere wiggle as her arms moved clothes from side to side.

Then the squeak of metal hangers sliding against the rod ceased, and she glanced back at him. ''How many suits do you have?'' she asked.

''About ten, I guess. On the left.''

Tracy stepped deeper into the closet, and the scrape of metal against wood grew louder before she turned around and emerged from the closet with an armful of suits.

She held them against her chest and looked at the mattress again. ''There's only a mattress and box spring in here,'' she said in a breathy monotone, and looked at him questioningly.

''I'm not quite moved in yet,'' he repeated.

Her eyes narrowed suspiciously. ''Is it okay if we use it?'' she asked.

You bet we can use it, gold-star girl.

He shrugged. "I don't see why not."

She laid the suits at the end of the mattress and returned to the closet to peek inside again. "Do you have any casual business clothes?"

"Casual business?"

"You know—nice pants and shirts that don't necessarily go together?" she prompted, and clicked her fingers. "Like what you wore to my office."

"Oh. Sure. Those are somewhere under all the boxes in the back bedroom."

Tracy put her hands on her hips and surveyed the bed. "Then let's just look at your suits."

Frowning as she looked around the room again, Tracy rubbed a toe against her opposite heel. She always seemed uncomfortable in her shoes, he noted, puzzled. He swept his hand over the mattress. "Have a seat."

Her eyes narrowed, but she sank down at the end of the mattress and picked up the top suit. Smoothing the lapel, she gave the suit her full attention. "This is nice."

It'd be so easy to slide down on top of her and all those suits. If he unbuttoned her blazer, would he discover lacy lingerie in seductive black or simple white? He didn't know how he knew it would be lacy, but he did. Either color would be fine.

She looked up, and the lilt of her voice changed. She must have asked a question.

"I think so," he answered, frowning.

The bridge of her nose wrinkled when she laughed. He'd always been fascinated by that wrinkle. "Surely you know whether or not you've worn this lately."

He glanced at the gray-stripe suit she was studying. "I wore it all last winter."

She chuckled again. "Then it should fit."

Why was she obsessed with the suit? "It fits."

Tracy frowned up at him. "You're not listening," she announced. "Maybe if you sit down, you can concentrate."

His eyes moved from her curves to the pillows, about a body length up.

So easy.

He sat down opposite the stack of clothes and tried harder to focus. Although he believed dressing well was important for business, talking about clothes was anything but stimulating. Using the strategy he always used when he wanted to put mind over matter, he started solving equations in his head.

But Tracy was too close. The numbers in his head became fingers curling around her waist to coax her down. The symbols became himself, leaning on top of her—

"This one's out of date," she said, picking up an old suit of Otto's that his mother had left. "The others are fine, but you might want to invest in one more light-weight suit—maybe an olive tweed. And get a few new ties."

"Uh-huh."

"Don't forget what we talked about the other day," she said, looking at his head. "Get a good haircut and nix the bandana."

Criminy. He'd forgotten to take off the bandana after he touched up the kitchen cabinets this morning. Riley tugged at the material and tossed it on the bed.

"Riley, it looks great!" Tracy exclaimed. She got up and walked around the corner of the bed. She lifted her hand, as if she was going to touch his hair. But instead, she brought her thumbnail to her lips, letting her gaze drift down to his.

Oops! She didn't say it out loud, but they both heard it.

Riley frowned. He had a lovely view of full breasts on a slender frame, and the scent Tracy wore today was potent. He wished she would touch him. He could imagine how her fingers would feel against his scalp. Against his face and chest. Beyond.

All he'd have to do is reach out a few inches to tug her down on top of him. He sucked air through his teeth and said, "What do you think?"

"It looks great," she repeated. The darkness of her eyes seemed to indicate that she wouldn't resist a simple tug.

Then she backed up so quickly she stepped out of a shoe. Her toenails matched the suit and lipstick. Suddenly he knew the exact color of her lingerie. "Red today, is it?" he asked, imagining the color against a full and satisfying cleavage.

Tracy peered down at her toes before scrambling forward to slip her foot into the shoe. "Orange."

He pulled his eyes away from her top button. "What?"

She backed all the way to the wall. "This is a deep orange—the label on the bottle says Punchy Paprika.

"Okay."

Tracy stood against the wall and slipped her heel up and down in her shoe.

"Why don't you leave it off?" he suggested.

"I beg your pardon?"

"The shoe," he said, watching her cross her foot behind the opposite leg. "It seems to bother you."

Tracy smiled nervously. "Booker would kill me."

Unable to resist, Riley rose from the mattress and walked across the room. He knelt in front of Tracy, pulled her shoe off and tossed it behind him. "Is that better?" he asked as he massaged a chafed spot on her heel.

"This is so-o-o unprofessional," Tracy said in a worried tone, but she discounted her own words by leaning against the wall so he could keep working.

"As long as we don't break the kissing rule, what's a little relaxation between friends?" he asked, looking up as he kept smoothing his thumb over the sore spot. "We are still friends, aren't we, Tracy?"

"Why wouldn't we be?" she squeaked.

"You tell me." He couldn't help it. Speaking of the past wasn't what he'd planned, but it bothered him that she'd believed the worst of him. Maybe it was time for the truth.

Tracy didn't give it a chance. She pulled her foot away and strode across the room to pick up her shoe. Without bothering to slip it on, she hobbled out of the room. "Our appointment is over," she said as she continued to the living room. "Your wardrobe is fine. Just wear a suit when you're working and devote some time to maintaining a refined appearance."

As she paused at the door and looked backward, he sent her bare foot a pointed glance. "I'll keep a refined appearance in mind at all times."

He followed her out into a day that had turned sunny, and waited near her car as she tossed her shoe in the passenger seat, then got in and poised her bare foot over the gas pedal. "Wednesday. Your office," she said.

Riley nodded. He thought he detected a blush, even against the Punchy Paprika background.

THE FAMILIAR STRANGER in the nice Italian suit was a sight to behold—that was the first thing Tracy thought as Riley walked through the maze of furniture in his office space. Gone was the pirate, replaced by the distinguished gentleman. He looked rich and powerful, and as sexy as any man she'd ever seen. Tracy looked at the jeans and sweatshirt she'd pulled on earlier, and wondered which of them was dressed inappropriately. "Weren't we sorting through files this morning?"

"Absolutely," he said with a grin. "But I wanted to follow your instructions, and you said to suit up for work."

He had to be toying with her again, but since she was determined to keep things businesslike, she'd have to assume he was serious. She sighed. "You've gone overboard for a morning when we'll be sorting through dusty papers and shoving furniture around. I meant to dress for customers."

"Work is work," he said with a shrug. "I'm comfortable."

"Fine," Tracy said with an exasperated smile. "It's my fault, anyway. I brought notes to your house last week, outlining which type of suit you should wear to which function. Obviously I forgot to give them to you."

So far, she'd been anything but professional around Riley. Any other client would think her an amateur.

"Give them to me now."

"They're in my briefcase, which I've misplaced," she said feebly, knowing there was no way to make that confession and still sound proficient.

He grinned, stepping a few feet over to unlock a file cabinet. The charcoal suit fit him well, reminding Tracy that at least some portion of this gig was a ruse. As soon as he opened the cabinet, he pulled out her briefcase and umbrella and walked across to hand them to her. "You left them at my house."

Of course she had. She'd left there in a hurry, after his bedroom had started seeming a mite too dangerous. Tracy remembered the hour she'd wasted early this morning, scouring her house in search of the briefcase. She'd even questioned Hannah about it. The little girl had told her that "pack-packs" belonged next to the front door. And when Tracy had called Booker at the office to have him look around her desk, he'd politely suggested that she pull herself together if she wanted to work as an organizer.

She was keeping things serious today, all right. Her status as Ms. Superefficient was falling into the same question as her nomination for mother of the year.

Tracy set her case on the nearest table to open it. "Here's a list of suggested attire for events you might wish to attend," she said. "Wear a nice suit for presentations, and tone it down a little for everyday business. The suit you have on today is overkill for anything but a major public event."

"Uh-huh," he said, grinning at her mouth. He wasn't listening again.

"Since we'll be hiding away inside today, jeans or sweats would have been fine."

"Do you want me to strip down to my skivvies?"

"No," she said, smiling. "Quit teasing."

He took off his jacket and draped it over the back of a swivel stool. "This will have to do."

It did fine, and he was still gorgeous. "I've allotted three hours for this appointment," Tracy said, deciding she didn't have to look at him. After learning of his bachelor status, she was feeling dangerously close to Riley again. She needed to back up.

For three hours, she could keep them both busy. They wouldn't have time for anything as frivolous as a motorcycle ride. She looked around the office space. She had noticed immediately that she could get through the front door. A lot of the file cabinets and tables had been shoved aside to clear a pathway. Even so, there was plenty to do.

"Do you want to devote our morning to anything in particular?" she asked.

Riley looked dead on her mouth and didn't answer.

When she put a hand over it to fake a cough, he said, "Office setup, filing. Let's just tackle things as we come to them."

Tracy started along the path, counting furniture and file cabinets and asking questions. Riley followed. Though he answered every question fully, she had the impression that his mind wasn't on the task. It seemed as if he knew how he wanted to organize things and could handle the task alone.

She'd had that impression from the start. Still, a job was a job, and she wanted this promotion. It was just that Riley followed too close behind her, brushing against her and keeping her very aware of him. Several times, he seemed to stare at her mouth as if he wanted to kiss her again.

He didn't, thanks to luck and Tracy's own foresight.

After they divided up tasks, he became a productive and companionable workmate. The morning passed quickly.

A few hours later, Tracy felt more like her old self as she created new file folders. They'd accomplished quite a bit. Most of the filing system was updated, and the space was more organized.

Riley appeared from the back room. "The computer system's up and ready," he said as he pulled up a chair and sat down beside her. "How are you doing?"

"I need to file these, and then I have a few marketing reports to go over with you."

He picked up some folders. "If I help you file, can we do the reports over lunch? I'm famished."

"Lunch?" Tracy checked her watch. Sure enough, it was well past lunchtime. And she'd logged enough restaurant receipts in Booker's ledger to know that she should offer her client a meal. It was expected business protocol.

As if it was glad to have finally caught her notice, her stomach started to ache. Tracy couldn't tell if the vague pain stemmed from hunger or an attack of nerves.

She'd intended to go home during the break between her morning at Riley's office and her afternoon at Vanderveer's. She wanted to change into office clothes, start a load of laundry and sort her mail. Leave it to Riley to dump her plans upside down again. He seemed determined to keep her guessing.

Well, Tracy was just as determined to do a good job. If that included treating her client to lunch, then so be it. They'd had a productive morning. If she needed to keep Riley at arm's length while they were away from the work setting, she could always summon an image of her sister.

Tracy watched Riley file a couple of folders, then smiled when he glanced up at her. "What sounds good?" she asked.

Riley snapped the cabinet drawer shut and let his gaze travel from her mouth to her sweatshirt to her sneakers. "Fast food would be fine," he said with a shrug.

Tracy had forgotten their mismatched attire, but apparently he hadn't. She frowned. "Booker would drop me back to flunky status if I fed a client fast food."

"Booker won't be joining us, will he?"

Tracy shook her head. "Vanderveer's has an account at Tiers, near the lake," she said. "It's a fantastic restaurant, but neither of us is dressed for it. You're too dressy and I'm too casual."

"Maybe we'd start a trend," he said amicably as he took the last file from her hand and filled it with receipts.

"I could go home to change and meet you there."

"Or we could forget Booker's view of proper entertaining, and I could show up at your place with food. We'd have enough privacy to talk about the market reports, and you wouldn't have to rush around."

And just like that, their problem would be solved. "You'd do that?" she asked, smiling.

"What could it hurt?" He was staring at her mouth again.

She closed her mouth and tried to remember. Friendly. Arm's length. No kissing.

The solution made sense. After all, Riley was the same guy who'd kept a protective eye on her in her tender years. Things hadn't changed all that much.

She drew her pinkie finger up, tasted the foul anti-nail-biting cream and let it drift down. "Okay, but we won't tell Booker."

"That's fine with me," Riley said, and lowered his voice. "You were always good at keeping secrets."

Tracy squinted at Riley, reminded of the secret that had formed a bond between him and Karen. She wondered if either one of them would ever confess. Or if Tracy would ever figure out whether Riley was friend or foe. She changed her mind by the minute.

She handed him enough bills to cover a simple lunch for a half-dozen people, then wrote her address on the back of a discarded invoice.

"What's this?" he asked.

She frowned. "You were bringing food to my place, right?"

He copied her frown, but stuck the money and note in his jacket pocket before slipping the coat on. "What sounds good?"

"Surprise me."

Ten minutes later, Tracy rushed into her duplex and went straight to her bedroom, tossing her umbrella and briefcase on the bed with a bounce that shot Claus beneath it. She returned to the living room and grabbed a carpeted cat pole, shoving it under her arm so she could toss a pile of Hannah's coloring books into a drawer. Finally she rushed back to her bedroom to hide the pole behind the door.

And stared into her own closet. This morning, Riley had looked extremely handsome in his snazzy suit. He must have worn it partly for her reaction. She wanted to upgrade her own outfit before he arrived, just to see his.

But the navy jacket she'd planned to wear to Vander-veer's this afternoon didn't seem right. She left it on the rack and dug deeper. She was in the mood for something more feminine. Her black georgette made her feel confident. She'd bought it for last New Year's Eve when Booker had let her attend Kirkwood's Grand Charity Ball on behalf of Vanderveer's. But it was too dressy for a business lunch. Especially a lunch that was being eaten in Tracy's own kitchen.

But nothing else appealed, and Riley was actually dressed in a suit that would match. Tracy chuckled as she pulled out the dress to look at it. She was tempted to wear it as a silent acknowledgment of Riley's little game. It sounded fun and as soon as Riley left she could change into her blue suit for the office. No one else would know.

She laughed again when she imagined Riley's reaction, and the decision was made. Dressing quickly, Tracy remembered the plunging neckline only after she'd zipped herself in. But one glimpse into the mirror showed a flattering cut, and she admitted to herself that she was wearing this particular dress for more than just a joke. She wanted him to really notice her.

After she'd brushed her hair and dabbed on lipstick, Tracy closed the bedroom door behind her and walked through the house, picking up a stray toy here and there and tossing each into the nearest cubbyhole. For some reason, she wanted to give an illusion of sophistication.

She wasn't Tracy Gilbert, a nice woman who spent her days playing with her daughter, typing reports for her boss and picking up after a plump tomcat.

She was a bewitching woman with an abundant life, a brilliant child and a feline familiar. She was a princess with a charming way of being kind to those around her. An enchantress who lived an enchanted life. A socialite who thought nothing of wearing a cocktail dress at home.

And one who'd forgotten the shoes to match her dress.

She reentered her room and found the shoes she'd bought for the ball. They were spiky and sexy—very fitting for the classy lady who resided here. Tracy slipped them on, half expecting magical sparkles to float up around her head.

Then she sat down on the sofa to frown at her nails.

Enchantresses didn't chomp on their nails.

When Riley rang the bell a few minutes after Tracy's panic attack started, she was tempted to follow Claus under the bed.

Chapter Seven

The woman in the doorway was a vision of creamy cleavage and lustrous hair. Apparently, while Riley had been inching toward their lunch at a favorite local drive-thru, Tracy had been changing clothes. Her grin was subdued, but broad enough to let him know she was enjoying his reaction.

He grinned back, conceding her victory in their scuffle over proper business attire. Without saying a word, she'd let him know that she'd recognized his game and was playing along.

Once again, he was impressed. And not only by her joke. Tracy's chestnut hair stole the light from the doorway, and her green eyes glittered. He'd always suspected Tracy would grow up pretty, but this woman had an inner glow that no amount of fuss could have produced.

He stepped inside and stared at her for what seemed like an eternity before he felt something brush against his calves. A big white cat curled through his legs and left patches of fur clinging to the bottom of his pants.

"Claus, you're mussing the man's suit," Tracy said with a husky laugh.

Frowning, Riley bent down to pick up the cat. When he saw the unusual blue eyes, he asked, "Is this the scrawny kitten I found out in Otto's shed the Christmas before I left?''

Tracy scratched Claus behind the ears. "This is the same cat," she said. "I'd forgotten that you gave him to me.''

When Tracy's eyes met his, he knew she'd fibbed. She remembered exactly who had given her the cat. The poor kitten had been cold and half-starved when Riley discovered it behind a stack of Otto's junk. Riley had offered it to Tracy, telling her he couldn't think of anyone who would do a better job nursing it back to health.

A few weeks later, he'd started up with Karen. His relationship with Tracy had grown more distant, and his life had seemed to veer off-course for quite a little while.

It was all a long time ago, but Claus linked past to present in a very real way.

"He must be ancient." Riley watched Tracy stroke the cat to a loud, rumbling purr.

Tracy chuckled. "Thirteen might be old for a house cat, but it's not ancient. He's led a charmed life.''

Riley smiled at her laughter and kept holding the cat until Tracy moved away from the door. "Come on in,'' she said. "If my neighbor sees you, I'll never hear the end of it.''

He bent down to drop Claus, and they both watched as the big cat floated his hooked tail somewhere beyond Tracy's cozy but tidy living room.

Tracy started to close the door, but Riley caught it and stepped back out on the porch. "We're forgetting something,'' he said as he picked up their lunch bags. "I hope you still like chili dogs and limeades.''

Judging from Tracy's smile, she was delighted. She took the drink bag and headed toward the back of the duplex, chatting all the way. "Actually, that sounds good. I don't indulge often anymore, so it'll be a treat."

As Riley followed her into a small kitchen, she set the drinks on the table and motioned for him to sit. Then she took the trouble to move a couple of bowls from the dish drainer to a cabinet, hide the drainer under the sink, and pull plates and silverware from the pantry.

When she turned around and picked up the lunch bag to slip the plates beneath, he caught on. They were being casual—but not too casual.

Smoothing her dress under her thighs, Tracy sat down across from him. He was struck again by her elegant appearance. It seemed funny that the two of them, who used to wear cutoffs and eat chili dogs straight out of the foil wrappers, would now be sitting in a suit and fancy dress eating the same thing off stoneware. He liked the idea.

With a decorum to fit the occasion, he transferred food from the bag to the plates, then smiled across at Tracy as he unfolded his napkin and began to eat.

After a few bites of her chili dog, Tracy said, "Were you surprised when Lydia started taking college classes?"

"I've learned not to be surprised by anything Gran does," he said, watching Tracy press her lips around her straw. He should look at his food. Her mouth was too sexy.

"Will she continue them this summer?"

Another question about Grandma Lydia. He recognized what Tracy was doing—she was making casual conversation. One that any two friends would have, or even business acquaintances who were thrown together over the lunch hour.

If it kept him from licking the chili sauce off the corner of her mouth, it was another good idea. He licked his own lips and started factoring equations.

"Riley? Did you hear me?"

"Yep. She said she was planning to sleep half the day and eat pizza every night, in keeping with expectations for college students."

"That's great," Tracy said with a laugh, watching him bite into a French fry.

He chewed slowly, more aware of her attention on his mouth than the taste of the food. If any other woman had been sitting across the table watching him so avidly, he would have crossed the space to take what her eyes dared.

But it was Tracy.

He didn't want to mislead her or scare her away. And if he wanted her to think well of him again, he had to control his impulses.

Somehow, he managed to finish lunch with behavior that suited his style of dress, rather than his thoughts. When Tracy finished, she tossed her napkin beside her plate and scooted her chair back. "Excuse me while I go grab those marketing reports," she said, and padded out of the kitchen.

Riley smiled and peeked under the table, where Tracy's heels were tipped on their sides. Her concession to comfort was heartening. When she returned with a handful of papers, they pushed their empty plates aside to discuss business.

Afterward, Riley dug in his pocket and laid the bundle of bills she'd given him on the table between them. "Lunch was my treat," he said, pushing the money toward her.

"Why?"

"To return a favor. I know you didn't want to take me on as a client."

"Actually, your request came at a good time," she said in a show of the fairness he'd always associated with her. "I've been working toward a promotion, and you accelerated the process for me."

"Great, but let me know if things don't work out. I could use a gold-star office manager."

Tracy rolled her eyes, then got up to carry the plates to the sink to be rinsed. He knew it would be best to leave now. Lunch was finished, the reports had been discussed, and Tracy was off limits.

But he didn't want to leave. Since Riley had always been inclined to rush headlong toward want, he followed her.

As she turned to face him next to the sink, she didn't seem to mind him being close. She seemed to welcome it.

Testing both of them, he touched his finger to a spot beside her mouth to remove a smudge of chili. Then he sucked his finger clean and returned it to her lips, skimming slowly across them.

Her breath came out in a warm rush, bringing him back to reality. He stepped back and tried to think of something to say. An excuse. An off-the-wall comment. Anything to allow him to pause long enough to think.

They were alone in her house for a business lunch. A stolen kiss seemed too clandestine for a good girl. He'd hooked up with women during lunch before, but this woman was built for rings and promises. Riley couldn't fathom such things for himself.

Returning to the table, he began to push wrappers into the lunch sack. When he thought about it, Tracy's single status was curious. And he'd wondered about the little black-haired girl he'd seen only from a distance, getting in and out of Tracy's car at her parents'. What had happened to the girl's father?

"Why aren't you married?" he asked, crumpling the bag into a ball and looking around the kitchen for her trash can.

Tracy finished loading the dishes into the dishwasher and turned to tilt her eyes up to his. "Why do people always ask me that?"

Her eyes seemed to summon rather than retreat. "Because you've got all the bases covered," he said.

She wrinkled her nose. "Bases?"

"Sexy, savvy and sensible," he said, tossing the ball of trash from one hand to the other with each point. "I'd think you'd hit a home run with someone."

"Don't you have to get past third base to score?"

"Third base?" He smiled, trying to keep his attention up in the vicinity of her face. She couldn't be a virgin.

"I meant you listed only three things," she explained with a blush. "A point would be scored on the fourth."

He frowned at her. "Genuine—that would be your fourth winning quality. And so you see, you've got it all."

She opened a cabinet under the sink to point out the trash can. "Thanks," she said as he tossed the trash inside. "But even before Hannah came into my life, I didn't exactly lead a whirlwind social life."

She frowned as she kicked the cabinet shut. Her admission seemed to embarrass her. She was the same charming blend of sophistication and naiveté she'd been at fifteen.

He thought again about the little girl. "You must have had somewhat of one," he said.

"Sure." Again, she seemed embarrassed. Hannah's

dad must have been a jerk. Maybe he'd been Tracy's first lover.

Riley didn't like thinking about Tracy with some other man. His old protective instinct must be kicking in. He reminded himself that he'd hired Tracy to help him start a business. Beyond that, she was none of *his* business.

Now that he and Tracy were spending time together, his thoughts were turning dangerous. He could damage both of their reputations by getting involved with her. When it ended, he'd feel compelled to move on, just as he always did. "Maybe your right guy hasn't found you yet," he said belatedly.

She nodded. "What about you?"

"I've never been anyone's right guy."

She picked up her limeade and sipped, so Riley did, too. The kitchen seemed even tinier with the two of them standing in its middle talking about things they shouldn't.

"But you have been someone's okay-for-right-now guy." She tugged on his lapel, indicating silently that he should follow her.

"I've had my share of girlfriends," he said, following wherever she led. "But nothing deadly serious."

"Interesting choice of words, Riley." She led him into the laundry room and immediately started pulling clothes from a basket and loading her washing machine. She seemed to be perpetually busy, and he knew he was probably in the way.

Since she hadn't pointed him toward the door, he grabbed an armful of clothes from her basket and tossed them into the washer.

Tracy paused just long enough to glance at him. "I see. You're a 'love 'em and leave 'em' kind of guy."

He shook his head. "I've had four long-term girlfriends, but I haven't been engaged. The relationships never developed to that last step. I guess I could never picture any of those women as my wife.''

''What's long-term for you?''

''My longest was three years. Brianna's married with a kid or two now, back in Oakland. I'm happy for her. She wasn't right for me, which means I wasn't right for her.''

Tracy nodded.

''The single man's greatest fear has to be making a bad choice in partners,'' he said.

She frowned at the washer, removed a miniature pair of red jeans, then added detergent. ''Quite a few single women share that fear.''

He smiled. Touché again.

She closed the washer lid, clicked the control knob around to start the machine running and returned her attention to him. ''Okay, I'm just going to ask,'' she said, raising her voice to sound over the running water. ''Thirteen years ago, you carted my sister all the way across the country just to break up with her. Why?''

''That's not the way it happened,'' Riley said, and hoped Tracy would drop the subject. He'd rarely handled inquiries into his motives with grace, and he didn't want to yell this conversation to Tracy while she did her laundry.

She didn't budge. She leaned on the washer and kept her eyes on his. Then she turned around and punched the control, silencing the noise. ''What were you thinking?''

''I wasn't,'' he said, thankful at least for quiet. ''I had just turned eighteen and I wasn't thinking about anything but getting away from Otto. Karen asked for a ride out to California.''

Tracy frowned. "Really?"

"You know she was making crazy choices in those days."

"She was wild," Tracy admitted. "I thought you two had run away together."

"Didn't Karen talk to you?"

Tracy laughed. "Not back then. I was the pesky little sister. She never confided in me. And later, she didn't want to talk about the past." She paused. Then asked, "Why did you break up?"

"A more apt question might be to ask why we got together," he said with a small smile. Karen had been a mistake from the start. He'd probably been trying to cool his interest in Tracy by dallying with her sister.

Karen had wrapped sophistication around herself like a cloak; it was the most evident part of her. He'd thought he could have the best of both worlds—someone like Tracy, but with a tough exterior he couldn't damage.

The first simply hadn't been true—Karen and Tracy were very different. And he didn't know about the second. He'd felt some affection for Karen, but in the end she'd only been another excuse for Otto to yell at him.

Tracy was still watching him. She seemed to be waiting for an answer. "We both needed too much attention," he finally answered. "That's the truth."

Tracy turned to restart the washer.

"And I had a thing for her little sister," he said.

He'd meant to say this in a teasing tone, adding a chuckle to take the seriousness out of it. But the declaration had come from deep inside, and that was how it sounded.

Tracy didn't turn around, but her shoulders hitched up protectively. "No, you didn't."

Riley wasn't surprised by her reaction. "It's true," he said. "In any case, Karen and I weren't right together."

Tracy turned and shook her head, meeting his look squarely. "It didn't seem that way to me, either."

She was still fully engaged. If he was going to kiss her, it was time. She was close, and they were both admitting feelings that had never been in the open.

Just then, a violent screech sounded, and was followed by a rhythmic pounding that shot Riley's nerves into the stratosphere.

TRACY LET OUT a breath as she turned to open the washer lid. Something strange was in the laundry again, and the interruption could not have come at a better time.

Riley had been about to kiss her, she was certain.

And she'd been about to kiss him back.

After waiting for the washer barrel to stop turning, she reached inside to pull out one of Hannah's clogs. It must have been stuck inside a pant leg.

Which meant the other one was probably still immersed. If there was any hope of saving it, Tracy needed to get it out now. She thrust an arm back into the frigid water, swirling her hand through clothes and suds in her search.

But she didn't hurry. The air still felt too charged.

"What about you?" Riley asked from behind her.

She shivered, and not because her arm was cold. More because the situation seemed so unreal. Riley was back and she was not only working with him, she was feeling close to him. Less than a minute ago, his face had been only inches away from hers, and he'd seemed ready to kiss her.

And now he was asking some obscure question while

her back was turned. She swung around halfway. "What?"

"Any long-term, grown-up relationships?"

She felt the shoe, but it slipped out of reach. "Nothing deadly serious," she said, leaning in and deliberately furrowing her forehead. She hoped he would notice she was busy and let up.

"Why not?"

She scowled into the gray wash water. She'd have tossed her own shoes in if it would've halted this conversation. "I guess I haven't grown up enough to allow a man to intrude on my life with Hannah," she said.

"You've been grown up forever, Tracy."

There it was. Tracy pulled out the second clog, placed it beside the first on the dryer, and restarted the wash cycle. Then she turned to grin at Riley. "And you've been a troublemaker for just as long." She hoped the teasing would defuse the air a little.

"I'm trying to make better choices."

Seriousness wasn't a quality the young Riley had adopted often. The mature Riley seemed stuck there right now. Another surprise in an altogether surprising day.

A productive morning had extended into an enjoyable lunch break, and she'd even managed to cross a chore off her list. And all had been enhanced by the company of Riley.

"You had obstacles to overcome," she said. "But you've become a respectable man."

She felt seriously in like with him again. Not in love. In love she wouldn't allow. Not now, not with Riley. He was a won't-work man.

But Lord, he looked good. It was probably some psychological phenomenon, but Riley always reminded her of lazy summer afternoons under a cottonwood tree.

She let her eyes slide down his chest, past his narrow hips and back up.

And felt seriously in trouble.

He took a step toward her. "Tracy?"

She remembered that she had things to do and that keeping busy would keep her safe. She reached back to drop the washer lid, hoping to break the spell.

Praying not to.

"We aren't working now, are we?" he asked.

She shook her head.

As Riley's mouth moved toward hers, she felt herself quaking with the potential of a simple kiss. She knew he'd stop if she whispered a word of protest. But she didn't.

A strong hand spread across her back, tugging her closer. She opened her wet hand against his chest, loving the solid warmth of him as she slid it to his stomach. She felt his muscles there tighten, and knew she was affecting him. He hadn't even kissed her yet, but she knew.

Suddenly fear made her step back, yanking her hand away. Tracy looked down at her handprint, smudged down the front of Riley's crisp dress shirt. Dear Lord, she'd come so close!

"We can't do this," she said. She looked up into Riley's eyes and recognized the same raw fear she was feeling.

"You're right," he said, stepping back, too. "The timing's off."

"My job is to *improve* your image."

"I couldn't look your mother in the eye."

"I think Booker has a rule against this sort of thing."

"Booker has a thing for you."

Tracy blushed. "What makes you say that?"

"A hunch."

"Booker's married," she said, again staring at the handprint. She wondered how she could be relieved and disappointed at the same time. "And speaking of Booker, I need to get back to work," she added.

"Me, too. Friends?"

She smiled. "Friends."

Riley stepped forward to brush a kiss across her lips.

Tracy knew it was meant to be short and sweet, a simple gesture of affection from friend to friend. But once his lips touched hers, she couldn't resist softening hers, pulling closer, taking more than he offered.

Allowing herself one more taste of chili and limes and forbidden fruit before he left.

Knowing she'd always crave more.

TRACY TOSSED the last report into her done basket and reclined against her chair back, satisfied with another end to another productive week.

"Stop in before you leave, Tracy," Booker said from his office. She smiled. She and Booker often chatted late on Friday afternoons, and they usually divided the weekend tasks. She'd never leave without checking with him. Slipping her feet into her shoes, she headed back. "If you want me to go over the books, I can take them home," she said on her way in.

"Nope. Have a seat."

This was odd. Booker was sitting with his hands folded across a desk that had been cleared of everything except a wine bottle and two glasses. Paperwork wasn't stacked in the middle awaiting last-minute explanation, and Booker seemed prepared to celebrate.

Tracy sat in one of the client chairs and stared at the wine bottle.

Booker grinned. "You didn't see this coming, did you."

"See what coming?"

Booker opened his desk drawer and took out an envelope, barely glancing at the front before sliding it across his desk. "Your first commission check."

Tracy fingered it lightly, feeling as if it couldn't truly be hers. "But this is premature," she said. "My follow-up visit with Ri— with Mr. Collins isn't until next week."

"The follow-up is a formality," Booker said. "The job is essentially finished, right?"

It was. Tracy had spent a lot of time at Riley's office over the past couple of weeks, and his business was ready for start-up. "I guess."

Booker pulled the wineglasses in front of him. "I've been organizing long enough to know exactly what's been going on across town at Collins Engineering."

Tracy straightened in her chair, *remembering* exactly what had been going on across town. Four organizing sessions had passed by in a blink. Twelve hours of teasing chatter had floated between file cabinets and computer workstations, making the work seem effortless. After the first session, Tracy and Riley had fallen into the routine of sharing lunch. Except for that first day, they'd always eaten in public. Twice, they'd shared meals across linen tablecloths, and once across a sun-dappled park bench. Kisses hadn't been expected or offered, but whatever force had drawn them together as children was still at work. Tracy had never had so much fun with a grown man.

A crackle drew her attention as Booker peeled the foil

off the wine bottle. "I'd say it's time to celebrate your new position, wouldn't you?"

"Sure." As Tracy watched Booker pour the wine, she thought how nice it was of him to mark the occasion in a special way. Many bosses wouldn't.

She accepted a glass and didn't even listen to Booker's toast before she clinked her glass to his and sipped. Was this a beginning? Or an ending?

The promotion was wonderful, but it would end her scheduled appointments with Riley. She didn't know what would happen after the follow-up visit. She and Riley wouldn't be working together, but they would see one another on occasion. After all, he lived next door to her parents. She had no reason to feel bereft.

Booker chuckled, and Tracy realized she'd finished a full glass of wine before he'd finished a third of his.

"More?" he asked, pointing to her glass.

"No thanks," she said. "I need to pick up Hannah from day care in a half hour."

"Well, congratulations," Booker said. "I'll channel some new accounts to you. When we're both too busy to manage the office, we'll hire a secretary."

"Fine."

"In fact, remember the call you took last week from the sorority woman who wanted us to organize an Independence Day fund-raiser? Are you willing to take that on?"

Tracy ran a finger around the rim of the glass. "Sure."

"Tracy?"

She looked up. "Yes."

He laughed. "We're done. Finish up and get out of here."

"'Kay."

Twenty minutes later, Hannah chattered about her day as Tracy drove away from the day-care center. Without thinking, Tracy turned down the street toward Riley's office. This route took her two miles out of her way, but she'd taken it every evening this week. His entry door had been cleaned off today, and his inside lights were on. Apparently he was working long days.

Tracy knew if she didn't have a tired four-year-old in the back seat, she might feel compelled to stop by and check things out. She might even become a nuisance.

As she had a million times in the past two years, she said a silent prayer of thanks for Hannah. She'd never let herself grow dependent on a man. She wouldn't start now.

It was time to disconnect.

Driving past Riley's office, Tracy turned at the next corner. Maybe she and Hannah should have their own celebration. She didn't want to spend the evening thinking about him, and keeping busy would pass the time. "What do you want to do tonight, Bean?" she asked.

"Stay up late an' eat popcorn!" Hannah shrieked, obviously excited at being given a choice.

"That sounds fun," Tracy agreed. Hannah couldn't tell time yet. If she fell asleep on the sofa at nine o'clock, she'd consider it a treat.

"Before that, we can go out to dinner," Tracy suggested. "Then we can drive around looking at houses for sale."

"Why, Mama?"

Tracy smiled at Hannah in the rearview mirror. "Because I got a better job today."

Hannah was quiet.

"I'll bring home more money," Tracy explained. "Soon we'll be able to move into a nicer house."

"I like our 'partment with Claus and all my toys."

"Claus and your toys will move with us. We'll find a bigger house with a nice yard."

"Could I get a gwinny pig?"

"A guinea pig? We'll see."

Hannah's shriek was jarring within the confines of the car, but it reminded Tracy of one very important fact— acquiring the means to provide well for her child had been reason enough to risk getting to know Riley again, despite the resurrected trauma of seeing him leave.

Chapter Eight

A young man in khaki pants and a white dress shirt looked up from the set of plans on his drafting table. "Morning, ma'am," he said with a grin. "May I help you?"

Tracy paused midstride, wondering if she'd entered the wrong door. She was accustomed to seeing only Riley when she visited his office. She glanced back, but the inverted lettering on the glass door clearly identified this office as Collins Engineering. A scan of the space revealed a roomful of familiar things. The only thing throwing her off was the smiling stranger.

"I'm Tracy Gilbert. I have a nine o'clock appointment with Mr. Collins?" She lifted her briefcase briefly, as if this man was a guard who would need proof.

Already, her plan to rush Riley through a flawlessly professional follow-up appointment seemed upended. Before the man could speak, Riley strode in from the back. "I'm here," he said on the way toward her. "I see you've met Duncan, my new draftsman."

After a round of introductions, Riley cupped a hand under Tracy's elbow and asked, "This follow-up visit is scheduled for an hour?"

"Up to an hour."

"Great," Riley said, tugging her toward the back. "Don't we have some paperwork to complete?"

This was a switch. Riley seemed to be in a bigger hurry than she was. Tracy removed a clipped assortment of papers from her briefcase. "Right here," she said quietly, wishing Riley wasn't quite so handsome in his well-cut olive sports jacket and dark brown dress pants. He even smelled good. She didn't remember him wearing a scent before, but the crisp cologne he'd chosen suited him.

He paused to take the papers and skimmed the top page. "'File cabinets updated and ready for daily use,' he read out loud. "Absolutely. Where do I sign?"

She pointed to a spot at the bottom of the document. "Only initials until the last page," she said, mystified as he marked the page and continued his trek toward the back.

She followed, but felt nervous about this curious reversal of roles. She'd expected Riley to joke and tease, not pull her along behind him. She'd planned to make a supreme effort to keep things sober. Still, as long as the meeting was quick and productive, it shouldn't matter who shoved whom through it.

When they arrived at the taped-off area that would eventually become Riley's office, he sat down in a swivel chair and rolled a second around to his side. "Have a seat," he said. "Since you wore dress shoes, we don't have to do a walk-through assessment."

She sat down and crossed her legs, glancing down at her tan mules. "I'm fine walking in these."

"Sure you are," he said, grinning. "In any case, I don't need to see what we did to know we did it."

Tracy didn't answer. His grin had felt as cozy as a flannel nightgown, and she was trying to figure out why it pleased her so much. After all, Riley smiled all the time.

He started leafing through pages, muttering phrases from each before signing. "Computer system update, check...office set to maximum efficiency, check..."

Somewhere in the middle of his mumbles, Tracy realized that his grin had been her first glimpse this morning of the Riley she knew. This take-charge businessman was foreign, and the change seemed abrupt. She shook her head. Obviously she'd gotten too attached.

He scrawled his signature across the last page. "It all looks great to me. How 'bout you?"

Tracy whistled when she checked her watch. She'd hoped to condense this follow-up visit into a half hour, but they were finished within eight minutes. "It looks fine," she said, standing up to offer her hand.

Riley stood, too, but rather than taking her hand, he shoved the paperwork into her grasp. "Put these away."

She sniffed, but did as he asked. "Do you have any questions?" she asked as she buckled her briefcase.

"No. Do you?"

"No."

"Great." He finally extended his hand.

She took it, but instead of the expected handshake, she felt herself being pulled toward the delivery door. "We're leaving," Riley shouted toward the front.

"Catch you later," came Duncan's faint reply.

"What are you doing?" Tracy squealed.

"We have almost an hour left, don't we?"

"Yes, but..."

As Riley shoved a shoulder against the heavy purple door, he turned halfway around to grin at her. "I have something to show you."

"In the back lot?" She couldn't resist smiling at this swift return to out-and-out Riley.

"Not exactly." He stepped outside to where his motorcycle was parked near the door. Both helmets were balanced on the seat.

"No, Riley."

"I don't see why not."

"We're finished, that's why not."

He frowned into her eyes and jiggled their linked hands. "We don't feel finished."

Tracy sighed. She didn't think so, either. She looked up at the gray sky, smelled the earthiness of the air and recognized that it could start raining any minute. She could use that as an excuse to make a clean break now, or she could risk the weather and delay the end by fifty minutes.

Minutes that had already been accounted for, anyway. "A quick ride," she said. "But I need to be back at work by ten-fifteen at the latest."

"Absolutely." Riley grinned as he put on his helmet and handed her the second. Swinging a leg over the motorcycle, he pulled it upright. As Tracy climbed on, she wasted no time being tentative. She wrapped her arms around Riley and held tight, starting the thrill before the first rev of the engine.

Riley headed north, and soon they were passing into the limestone hills and flowered grasses along the western edge of Willow Lake. An occasional patch of fog and the scarcity of other vehicles combined to make Tracy feel as if she and Riley were very much alone.

This time, instead of circling the lake and returning home, he turned into a narrow gravel driveway that sloped sharply upward. Tracy was surprised when it opened out onto a secluded plateau with a wide, stunning view of the water.

Riley parked the motorcycle and waited for her to get off. "Thirty-nine minutes," he announced as they walked toward an old wooden bench with grass growing up through the broken middle slat.

Tracy checked her watch, then noted the patch of rain already slanting across the western sky. "Thirty-nine minutes if it doesn't pour," she corrected.

Riley glanced at the clouds, then walked closer to the overlook. He picked up a stone and tossed it down to the silvery water below.

"Hannah loves to skip rocks," Tracy said, plucking the grass from between the bench slats before she sat down. "I brought her to the lake once this spring, and we wound up spending the entire day searching for good rock piles."

He threw another stone. "I haven't met Hannah."

Tracy knew that, of course. With her last boyfriend— there'd been very few—she'd waited months before introducing Hannah to him. But Riley wasn't a boyfriend. He was a *friend,* and he could never be more than that.

She'd avoided the introduction for altogether different reasons—mostly self-protection. Keeping from caring by separating the two worlds.

"What's she like?"

"She's tiny and energetic and the light of my life," Tracy said. "I knew I wanted a child, but I didn't realize how much I would love motherhood."

Riley sat down beside her and started sifting through a handful of colorful pebbles. "I feel that way about my work," he said. "I got the degree to thumb my nose at Otto, but once I started working, I took a lot of pride in the process of designing a plan and watching it become reality.''

She looked at him. "I'm not surprised.''

He looked at her, too. "You always had more faith in me than I had in myself.''

Abruptly, Tracy faced forward. She stared out at a boat with rainbow-colored sails as she let Riley's comment reverberate in her mind. He was right. Even after he'd had a decade of Otto's harsh punishments, scores of school detentions and a few scrapes with the local law, she'd trusted Riley's goodness. She'd always believed he was unjustly accused of whatever trouble he was in. Until Karen.

Now, even that mistake seemed appropriate for the reckless teenager he'd been. The man beside her seemed different—he was the same person, and yet he wasn't. Tracy admired this man as much as she'd admired the boy, but she couldn't allow her feelings to go further. It would be too risky.

Drizzle started falling seconds later. The wetness cooled Tracy's face, easing the intensity of her discomfort. Rather than acknowledging the rain and looking for cover, Tracy and Riley continued to sit side by side on the neglected old bench. "Twenty-seven minutes,'' she said softly. "Do you ever talk to Otto?''

"I call him every year on Father's Day,'' Riley said. "But he doesn't seem interested. He wasn't meant to be a dad.''

Tracy nodded. She'd thought the same thing often enough, and she was glad Riley seemed to have come to terms with it. "I wonder what made him so ornery.''

"Otto had a tough childhood,'' Riley explained. "His dad was a mean drunk, and his mom neglected him.''

The story sounded familiar. "And the war of pain and

retaliation continued with you and Otto,'' Tracy said softly.

''It happens.''

''But it doesn't have to continue,'' she said. ''You're not like your parents.''

''Ah, but I had you and Grandma Lydia to give me balance. Besides, I'm not trying to be a dad.'' He took her hand and turned it palm up. ''For Hannah,'' he said, dropping a small stone there.

Tracy smiled as she examined the irregular shape. ''It looks like a horse's head.''

''Turn it over.''

''And now a chick.'' She rubbed her thumb over the stone's surface, which still held the warmth from Riley's hands. ''Thanks. She'll love it.''

''You ready to go?'' He stood abruptly, allowing the remaining pebbles to clatter down to his feet.

Tracy looked at her watch again. They still had time, but maybe he'd grown tired of the rain and gloomy talk. She dropped the stone into her jacket pocket and answered by returning to the motorcycle to put on her helmet.

On the way back, Riley seemed to take the curves more recklessly. Tracy wondered if he realized he was hurrying them back to the real world, where separation was their only reasonable choice.

The scattered drizzle had left the road dry in spots, and traffic was sparse. When the hum of a car began at some distance behind them and grew increasingly louder, Tracy was bothered. She knew why when Riley slowed and pulled to the shoulder, allowing the car to pass around the next bend. The return to privacy was welcome. It seemed this road, this rain and these remaining few moments should belong only to the two of them.

And then they were back at his office. Riley was quiet as he got off the motorcycle and removed his helmet. His hair was damp, and it curled appealingly around his face. She stared for a moment, allowing her mind an image of the two of them, slick and naked and anywhere together. She removed her helmet with trembling hands.

"Wait here," he said, frowning as he took both helmets inside the dented back door.

In seconds, he returned with her briefcase. "I'll walk you out the back way."

Tracy didn't question his directive. At this moment, a walk down the alley with Riley seemed good and right. It was tomorrow without him that frightened her.

As they approached the alley's entry, Tracy checked her watch one last time. Twelve minutes left. She knew Riley had noticed her movements when he nodded, as if silently acknowledging the length of time remaining.

Halfway down the alley, he pulled her around to face him and she wasn't surprised. He guided her backward until she was sandwiched between the equally unyielding pressures of brick and his body, and she felt no need to shove him away. They were still on fantasy time.

She moved forward, meeting his boldness with her own. This kiss didn't begin with teasing nips or nibbles. It started at passionate and spread like wildfire toward erotic. His tongue thrust into her mouth, and his hands roamed her body possessively.

She dropped her briefcase and shoved her own hands up into his hair, pulling him closer. He slid both arms inside her suit jacket, and she was glad. Glad to feel his hands peel her blouse away to reach the skin beneath.

Glad to feel his fingers undo and slide her bra out of the way. Glad when his mouth replaced fabric.

When he began to suckle her nipple, she gasped, but tangled her fingers in his hair to keep him there. When he moved across to attend to the other side, her need for him grew so intense she felt herself droop in his arms.

Tracy had never felt such an acute ache of desire. She would never before have considered indulging in some back-alley tryst, but something about this felt right. His exploring hands grew firm against her hips, pulling her so close that there was no question about the intensity of his hunger.

And then, abruptly, he stopped. He pulled her blouse closed over her naked chest. "I'm sorry," he said. "Grappling in a hidden alleyway isn't your style. Are you okay?"

"I'm fine." Tracy stepped away to fasten her clothes, leaving Riley to collect himself. She'd always known she wasn't the kind of woman who inspired more than momentary abandon. She was a good girl. Hot-blooded men didn't fall for good girls, and passion was fleeting, anyway. Her sister and a preponderance of divorce statistics had proved that.

Tracy reminded herself that she expected to choose her man late, and choose wisely. She planned to spend her middle years enjoying his companionship. She needed someone warm enough for the good times, and comforting enough for the bad ones. She deserved no less.

And Riley deserved some wild, exotic woman he wouldn't be able to stop kissing.

WITH NIMBLE MOVEMENTS, Riley dribbled the basketball toward the goal. He ignored Lydia's expectant stance as she waited under the net, and pretended instead she was a fierce opponent as he dodged her to shoot a layup. The ball bounced off the backboard and circled the rim, adding drama to a game he normally toned down for his grandmother. When it fell through, Riley caught the ball before it bounced off her silvery hair. He handed it to Gran, finally relinquishing one of the turns he'd stolen.

As he waited for her to make her shot, he chastised himself for showing up at the retirement village. Their regular Friday-afternoon jabber-and-shoot session wasn't satisfying. The net was too low, the play was too mild, and he was in no mood for talk.

But Gran didn't complain. She planted her fancy white athletic shoes square on the court and bounced the ball twice, making a clean shot. Riley caught it immediately and jumped to slam it through again. He didn't mean to be rude, but he needed to work hard enough to sweat. He needed to work out a few kinks and forget a few kisses. He needed to keep his thoughts breezy.

"Something bugging you, doll?" Lydia asked as he skipped another of her turns and dribbled toward the back court.

"Nothing I can't figure out." He turned to make the shot, and watched the ball ricochet off the rim and bounce toward a group of parked cars.

He chased it down and walked casually toward his grandmother. He held out the ball to her, but she shook her head. "You're as nervous as a cat in a roomful of rockers," she said. "I'll sit out and let you work off energy if you'll entertain me."

"How?"

"You miss a basket, you answer a question," she said. "You make one, I do."

He tossed the ball through and caught it on the rebound. "I already tell you too much."

"You haven't told me what's been bugging you for the past week, and you've used up all your fake excuses."

He should have known Gran would call him on his surly behavior, and he would have been smart to stay home. But Lydia had done him a million favors, and she was the most nonjudgmental person he knew. He'd survive her inquisition.

"I'll do it if we switch it around," he said. "If I make a basket, I keep shooting with no chitchat. If I miss, you get an answer."

"Deal, with one condition."

"What's that?"

"You have to answer in more than one syllable."

He grinned. "Deal."

Gran sat in one of the lawn chairs Riley had set up in the grass, pulled out two bottles of a caramel-colored beverage and waited for his first miss. After a short turn of vigorous play, a hook shot fell on the wrong side of the net. Lydia's first question was shrewd and direct. "Does your bad mood have something to do with Tracy Gilbert?"

He scowled. "Probably." At his grandmother's cocked eyebrow, he added, "But I can handle it."

Gran sipped her drink and nodded toward the basket. This time, he shot a longer series to give his heart and lungs a workout. When he missed, he was tired enough for a break, and anticipating her next question. He dropped the ball and accepted the bottle Lydia handed him. After a single swig, he considered spitting the liquid out on the grass. It was atrocious. He swallowed hard, then swiped his T-shirt sleeve across his mouth. "What is this?"

"Instant tea and grape drink." Lydia took another sip and puckered her mouth slightly, as if assessing the taste. "I was out of orange, but this is just as good."

He handed her the bottle and didn't comment. Everything about Lydia was unconventional, including her taste buds.

"How are you going to handle this problem with Tracy?"

"That's easy," he said with a shrug. "I'll stay away from her. I've been swamped at work, anyway. It seems that there are quite a few rebels in town who don't care about my genetic background, or my past."

Lydia squinted at him. "Speaking of which, are you the same guy who once stole Bluemont High's mascot and left it to graze in your backyard?"

He grinned. Otto had been livid about the damage the goat had done to their fence posts, as well as the two-week expulsion Riley had taken in punishment. "The goat looked thin," Riley said. "Besides, their football team sacked our quarterback twice the night before."

"Where's your sense of adventure?" Lydia asked.

Riley dropped into the second chair. "My interest in Tracy is too intense, so I'm backing off."

Lydia sat forward and frowned. "How can a man's interest in a woman be too intense?"

"That's too many questions," he said, and got up to play.

When he returned, Lydia was waiting with a smile. "You already know the question," she said.

He sat down and stared at the basketball for a moment before resting it in the grass beside him. "I've always backed away from girlfriends before things got complicated,'' he finally said. ''With Tracy, things start at difficult and get worse.''

''In what way?''

''For one thing, she's marriage material and I'm not.''

''How do you know?''

Riley shook his head. ''I never took you for the type to nag for grandkids, if that's what this is about.'' He picked up the basketball and flipped it from hand to hand.

''Does Tracy want you to back off?''

He frowned, remembering the exquisite sweetness of Tracy's response to him. He'd relived that morning several times, but even if he never forgot it, he'd know the mature choice was to put distance between them. ''I don't know.''

A mud-splattered sedan pulled into the parking lot and drove over their basketball court. Riley watched as it stopped in front of the retirement-village office. A middle-aged couple climbed out and, hands joined, walked into the building. ''I have a question for *you* now,'' Riley said, setting the ball down.

''Shoot.''

''When you met Grandpa, did you know the good in the relationship would last thirty-five years?''

''It would have been fifty years next August,'' Lydia said, smiling. ''But no, I didn't. His mother predicted that we would be together two weeks or less.''

Riley took his grandmother's hand and squeezed it. ''She didn't understand your independence.''

''No, she thought I was too conventional,'' Lydia said with a chuckle. ''But it didn't matter if it lasted two weeks or fifty years. I needed to try and so did your grandfather.''

Riley leaned back in the chair and frowned. ''That's

nice, Gran, but some people aren't so lucky. My parents weren't.''

''Yes, their marriage *was* a disappointment, wasn't it.''

Turning to face his grandmother, Riley took a deep breath. ''I'm afraid I'll become an Otto.''

Lydia's jaw dropped. She seemed truly stunned. When the light went back on in her eyes, she laughed. ''There's very little Otto in you, m'dear.''

Criminy, he hoped so. But who knew what could happen?

''I knew Otto was wrong for Vanessa from the beginning,'' Lydia announced. ''Their first date was on an evening much like this one—the sky was perfectly blue and the breeze was picking up enough to gentle the heat of the sun. Otto showed up with a six-pack of warm beer and a withered rose he'd picked from our neighbor's bush.''

Riley had never heard this story before. ''Was the six-pack for Grandpa?''

''It was for Vanessa, and she was thrilled. She was crazy about your father in those days. Your grandpa and I didn't think there was any point in interfering.''

Riley had known his parents as two people who were disillusioned by life and each other. He must have assumed they'd started out that way. He laughed now, amazed at this new perspective. ''So even my parents had their two weeks.''

Lydia shrugged. ''I'm sure they did.''

Riley got up and folded his chair, suddenly feeling as if he had somewhere important to go. He glanced at the armpits of his T-shirt, checking for sweat stains, then shrugged. ''You think it's worth the risk?''

''The fun is in finding out for yourself,'' his grandmother said. ''But not if you keep running the wrong way.''

Chapter Nine

Hannah bounced through the kitchen doorway and climbed on to the stool next to the counter. She peered wistfully inside the bowl Tracy was holding.

"Would you like to taste it?" Tracy asked.

"Yeah!"

Tracy scooped a tiny morsel of the cookie dough onto a teaspoon, then handed it to Hannah. "Did Nellie have an egg?"

Hannah's mouth was occupied with the spoon and dough, so she shrugged and hummed three notes Tracy recognized as an *I don't know.*

"Are you sure you pushed the doorbell?" Tracy asked, still working the wooden spoon though the mix. "She's usually home on Friday night."

"But Mom—"

"Hannah, just ask if she can spare an egg," Tracy said gently. "You can do it." The little girl was naturally bold, but she'd never rung a doorbell alone.

"Mo-om."

Hannah's tone made her sound more like an embarrassed teenager than the independent little girl who'd begged to fetch the egg alone five minutes before.

"What, Hannah?"

Hannah's eyes sparkled. "There's a big man out there."

"A big man?"

Tracy stepped around the kitchen doorway with the bowl, and was astonished to see Riley standing just inside the front door. Hannah must have let him in.

"Riley? Is something wrong?"

Even though he was tall enough to fill the doorway, he managed to look sheepish. "Not at all," he said.

Tracy set the bowl of cookie dough on a side table and turned to see that Hannah had followed her. "You're not supposed to open the door to strangers," she told her.

"But that big Wiley asked if he was at Twacy's door."

Tracy directed a quick smile to that big Riley, who seemed even more uncomfortable. "Were you coming to see us?"

"Yes. I was startled when Hannah met me on the porch."

Tracy noticed his eyes on Hannah's glossy black hair and Asian features, and realization struck. He must have expected her child to be one of birth rather than adoption. Hannah was so much her little girl she seldom remembered to mention it.

Picking up the bowl, Tracy handed it to Hannah. "Go put this in the fridge, Bean. We'll bake cookies later."

"But I want cookies for my snack," Hannah said in a childish whine.

"I know, but we need an egg," Tracy explained. "If we're too late to finish the cookies tonight, we'll go to Kerry's Dairy and get ice cream for your snack."

"Ice cweam, yummy!" Hannah made a slurping sound. She loved cookies, but ice cream was her favorite. She'd tried nearly every flavor offered by the neighborhood shop. Grinning at Riley, Hannah stretched out her arms around the bowl and hurried with it back to the kitchen.

After Tracy had heard the refrigerator door open and close without a catastrophe, she explained, "I adopted Hannah from an orphanage in central Asia two years ago."

"She's great," he said. "I suppose I expected a miniature version of you."

He wasn't the only one who was surprised. His presence here on her doorstep, dressed and groomed as if for a date, astonished Tracy, and she stepped back. "You didn't come here on Friday evening to meet my daughter, did you?"

Riley didn't get a chance to answer before Hannah reappeared to take his hand and lead him to the living-room sofa. "Sit down," she said in the bossy tone only a very young girl could use with charm. "Mama gets comp'ny a dwink."

"I'm not company," Riley said as he sat down. "I'm an old friend of your mom's, and I dropped by to say hello. I'll only stay a minute so you can bake your cookies."

Hannah managed a rather dramatic wilt. Tracy smiled, prepared to tell Hannah the ice-cream promise would hold, when Riley interrupted. "We could all go to Kerry's Dairy together," he said. "I love ice cream."

His smile started with Hannah, but rested on Tracy. He seemed awfully pleased with himself.

"You do?" Hannah stepped close enough to lean against Riley's legs and stare up at him. She seemed completely smitten. Kids were too gullible. "I like candy cane best."

Tracy watched in horror as Riley and Hannah grinned at each other and started discussing ice-cream flavors. The past week had been hard enough to get through. Tracy had tried to numb her feelings with a frenzied schedule of work and activities. By nine o'clock this morning, she'd finished the office chores. She and Booker would have their first free weekend in months. She'd also researched ideas for the college fund-raiser, and she'd planned her parents' anniversary celebration down to the tiniest detail.

In the evenings, she'd taken Hannah to two movies, four restaurants and five different parks. She'd talked on the phone to Karen twice, and she'd run numerous pre-party errands. She'd even managed to drive straight home from work on three days out of five.

She'd still thought about Riley constantly.

And not only about Riley, but about sleeping with him.

And not only once, but a lot of times—all lined up side by side and night by night in a relationship that would be anything but orderly.

The dreams would fade eventually, but not if Riley began to make a habit of showing up at her door. He might be able to indulge in casual and sundry relationships, but she could not.

Especially not with him.

She studied Riley's and Hannah's mutually charmed faces, and knew she had to stop a bad idea at its beginning. "Riley, we can't go," she said firmly. "Hannah and I have a big day planned for tomorrow."

"I don't see why not," Riley said. "You told your daughter she could have ice cream. I'll just come along."

Hannah put her hands on her hips and scowled. "I ate

sixteen peas at dinner," she reminded her. "You said eat ten if I want a snack."

"I know, Hannah."

"I 'membered to put my cwayons back in the box." Tracy half expected Hannah to tap her foot in impatience.

When she did just that, Tracy frowned. Despite her attempts to keep things fun, Hannah had suffered from the week's pace. "I know."

"You took Apwil Max to the movie. Why can't you take your big Wiley to get ice cweam?"

Riley raised an eyebrow. "Yeah. If April Max got to go to a movie, why can't I get ice cream?"

Tracy scowled at him. "Because you're a grown man with your own transportation. Get your own ice cream."

"Mama, that's mean!"

Riley smiled.

Tracy brought a thumbnail to her mouth. If she allowed this outing with Riley, maybe she could find a quiet moment to question him about why he'd shown up on her doorstep. Maybe she could warn him against future visits.

Hannah squealed and started hopping around the room, apparently reading a lot into her mother's momentary hesitation.

And with that, Tracy was committed. She drew her hand back down and rubbed her thumb against her hip. "Let me get my shoes," she said. "We can all go for ice cream, but let's take separate cars."

Fifteen minutes later, Riley had finished reading off the extensive selection of flavors to Hannah. The little girl decided against candy cane and chose bubble gum swirl, then took her cone and skipped off happily to find a booth.

Tracy felt Riley's arm slide across her shoulders. His breath was warm against her ear when he asked, "And what about you, gold-star girl? Cappuccino crunch or toasted marshmallow?"

She smiled, trying to ignore the heat of his arm before she shrugged it off. "Are you kidding? They have the classics. For me, that means butter pecan."

Riley stayed close as she ordered and waited. She felt his eyes on her as she walked to the booth to join her daughter.

Seconds later, Riley arrived at the table with a banana split. He grinned at Hannah as he plunked the heaping bowl in front of him. "My teeny-tiny bedtime snack."

"Wow, you do like ice cweam." Hannah shoved the tip of her blue-and-pink swirled ice cream in her mouth, adding to the sticky mess surrounding it.

Tracy started to taste her cone and noticed Riley watching her. His gaze was focused on her mouth. Clamping her lips together, she pointed. "Pay attention to your teeny-tiny snack or it'll melt and make a great big mess."

Riley grinned and picked up his spoon, but he kept his eyes on her mouth with an interest that seemed almost predatory. Tracy discovered that it was impossible to eat her ice-cream cone without opening her mouth and using her tongue. When Riley finally turned his eyes to Hannah, Tracy took the opportunity to sample her ice cream.

"Mo-om!" Hannah said loudly, in her exasperated tone. "I *said* can I taste *yours?*"

Tracy looked back at Riley with a start. How long had Hannah been trying to get her attention? She gave her daughter a taste and wiped the little girl's drippy chin with a napkin.

This wasn't going well. The ice cream was going to melt down Tracy's hand unless she tossed it in the trash or took charge of the situation. And the butter pecan was too delicious to throw away.

Tracy narrowed her eyes at Riley, then opened her mouth and took a long, slow lick. She sucked in her cheeks, savoring the creamy sweetness, then ran the tip of her tongue from one side of her lips to the other.

Riley's eyes turned dark and his smile vanished, but he kept watching.

She smiled. "Are you going to tell me why you showed up on my porch?"

He cleared his throat and gave her the satisfaction of looking uneasy. "Later," he said, his eyes darting briefly toward Hannah. Whatever it was, he didn't want to talk about it in front of a child.

Tracy took another lick and kept watching him.

He finally picked up his spoon and started eating, turning his attention to Hannah. "Your mom told me you're already in school," he said. "What are you learning?"

"The alphabet," Hannah said proudly. "I can sing the whole song. Wanna hear?"

"Absolutely." Riley proceeded to listen carefully, then he carried on a conversation with Hannah that flowed from a graphic analysis of how to catch bugs without smashing them, to a vehement agreement that naps were for babies.

Hannah was infatuated already. Of course, she would be. Riley's playful nature would appeal to most any child. Most any mother would feel less flustered if Riley wasn't quite so attractive.

Tracy managed to get most of her ice cream eaten

under the cover of Hannah's chatter, but Riley looked again just in time to see her crunch into the cone.

This time she was stunned by the open desire in his expression. It sent sparks of fear and joy shooting around like a Fourth of July sparkler.

She looked away, watching Hannah eat. If the reason for Riley's visit had been to confuse her, it had worked. She felt intrigued, frustrated, elated and nervous. She knew she couldn't ask him questions about this impromptu visit unless she was ready for his answers. It'd be best to let the subject drop.

When she had regained some portion of her composure, she finally focused on Hannah. The rainbow of colors had spread from ear to ear. Tracy knew her daughter would swipe her bare arm across the mess, if left to her own devices.

"I need to take Hannah to the rest room to clean up," she said to Riley.

Then she spoke to Hannah. "I don't think I've seen anyone enjoy ice cream more than you do, Bean."

Riley's eyes dropped to Tracy's mouth, and his cockeyed smile told his contrary opinion.

Tracy shook her head, silently acknowledging his point, then took Hannah's hand and headed for the rest room.

A few minutes later, Tracy was leading Hannah back to the booth, when she saw Nellie enter the ice-cream shop. Quickly, she pulled her daughter back to the hallway. The last thing Tracy needed was for Nellie to see her here with Riley. The questions would be hard to answer, and rumors would fly.

"Mama, what you doin'?" Hannah asked. "Your big Wiley's out here."

"We're playing a game," Tracy whispered, scrambling to think of a plan. "Let's see if we can get Riley's attention without going back to the table. Just stand here by my side and wave toward him."

Hannah bounced on her toes. "Yay!" she hollered. "What's our game called?"

Tracy put a finger to her lips and said softly, "Secret spies. We need to be really quiet, okay?"

SOMETHING WAS ODD, Riley thought. Tracy and Hannah were standing in the rest room hallway waving at him. Tracy's frown looked worried, but Hannah was trying to stifle a giggle behind her hands.

Of course, he got up to check on them. As soon as he rounded the corner, Tracy backed farther into the hallway and said, "My next-door neighbor just came in."

"We're playing secwet spies," Hannah said, snickering as she hopped from one green floor tile to the next. Tracy wasn't amused. She pulled a stick of gum from her purse and handed it to her daughter, then slanted an annoyed look at Riley. "You remember Nellie. She was two years ahead of you in school? Talks about everyone but fills in her own details? She's the one who started the rumor about the principal and the Channel Three weather anchor."

"Oh. *That* Nellie." He laughed. "I guess she has to be someone's next door neighbor. Aren't you lucky."

"Yes, aren't I."

Riley looped an arm over Tracy's shoulder and tugged her close. "The thing to do is to go out and say hello."

Tracy pulled away. "You paid me to improve your reputation. Are you willing to risk a rumor about the two of us being involved?"

He'd be willing to drill a hole in Tracy's bedroom wall and give Nellie a peep show so wild it couldn't possibly be embellished. He grinned. "It wouldn't bother me."

Tracy moved confused-looking eyes over his face. He should quit teasing her. He hadn't told her the reason for his visit, and he had the feeling he'd scare Tracy off if he admitted the truth.

That he still had a thing for her.

That he suspected it might very well last forever.

And that he was inclined to stick around and find out.

Despite the twenty-plus years he'd known Tracy, it seemed too soon for that confession.

He stared at her for a minute, and then shrugged. "We could leave separately. Pretend we weren't together."

"I thought we were gonna play a *game,*" Hannah said, gazing up at her mother. Her bulging bottom lip told Riley the little girl had expected more excitement.

He thought for a moment, wishing to appease them both. "Okay, here's our plan," he said, jerking his thumb toward the kitchen door. "We'll take the back way out."

Tracy peered around his shoulder. "That entrance is for staff. I'm sure they don't want customers using it."

Riley grinned at Hannah. "But we're customers pretending to be spies. I'm sure a place that sells bubble gum swirl would make an allowance for fun."

Tracy scowled. Hannah jumped around and cheered until her mother clamped a hand over the girl's mouth.

He bent down to speak to Hannah. "We'll pretend the bad guy is there in front, and we have to make a sneak getaway. Can you be very, very quiet?"

Hannah nodded, then darted her eyes from side to side. She'd entered easily into the game of pretend.

Tracy's frown of reluctance indicated that she'd

grown up a tad too much. She needed encouragement just to play.

"Let's go," he said conspiratorially. He took Tracy's hand and led them through the service door to the kitchen. They crouched for a moment behind a shake machine, waiting for Nellie to leave the front.

When the attendant noticed them, Riley put his finger to his lips as if he was actually on some undercover mission.

The attendant glared at him, Hannah giggled at the attendant and Tracy shushed her daughter.

Then laughed along with her.

Riley smiled. If Tracy's gossipy neighbor noticed them, it wouldn't be his fault. But the woman got her ice cream and then her back was turned to them, so he grabbed Tracy's hand and led them all out the back door.

Hannah stopped just outside to clap both hands against her knees and laugh. "That was fun!" she said when she calmed down. "Can we do it again?"

Tracy grinned, but she said, "No. It's time for us to say good-night to Riley. We need to get ready for our big day tomorrow, and he needs to go home."

Hannah seemed disappointed, but she looked up at him with an impish smile. "Guess what?"

"What?"

"You're my second-favorite big man after Poppy Matthew!"

Riley chuckled. His efforts hadn't been completely wasted. In an evening's time, he'd met Hannah and won her over. He glanced at Tracy one more time, noted her frown and knew he still had work to do. He waved good-bye on his way to his car.

Things had seemed so clear after talking to Gran. He'd gone home to shower and change, then he'd sped across town to find Tracy. He'd wanted to lure her out beneath the vast and perfect Kansas nighttime sky. He'd wanted to woo her with reckless confessions and nonstop kisses.

Until he'd been stopped at the porch step by a pre-school child. Hannah was wonderful—cute, personable and bright.

In fact, she was very much like Tracy in those aspects. But the face-to-face reality of her existence gave him pause. And it wasn't because of her appearance. It was because of her adoption.

Tracy had made responsible choices in her life, long-term, life-changing choices that had everything to do with deliberation, and nothing to do with impulse. Riley may be the type to jump off rooftops on a dare, but Tracy wasn't. She'd need more than warm beer and dead roses. She'd need thoughtful wooing. That wasn't Riley's usual style, but he was willing to give it a shot.

Chapter Ten

Kirkwood's tiny, two-runway airport was quiet, even for a Saturday evening. Only a few tired passengers had emerged from the jetway before Hannah pointed to a platinum blonde in a stunning white suit. "I like her bear."

When Tracy saw the woman with a humongous purple teddy bear tucked under her arm, she tugged Hannah forward. "Come on!" she said with a smile. "That's your aunt Karen."

Karen spotted them, too, and rushed forward for a round of hugs. She gave the bear to Hannah, and within seconds the three of them started toward the luggage trolley. On the way, they chatted about tomorrow's party, Karen's day of travel and Hannah's plans to introduce her new teddy bear—which she'd named Violet Plumtree—to the rest of her stuffed menagerie.

Tracy kept up her part of the conversation, but she noticed the same thing she always noticed when she ventured into public with her sister: people stared. Especially male people. From the teenage boy in baggy khakis and headphones who craned his neck around to watch her sister pass, to the older man in a wheelchair who offered a wry, unnoticed smile, they puffed out their chests and looked hopeful, as if one peek from the sexy blonde would brighten their day.

As Tracy drove them toward the duplex for an evening of rest and catching up, all she could think was that she hadn't grown up at all. She was still a five-year-old girl in a red felt ladybug costume, standing under a porch light waiting for her lollipop while the person at the door gushed over the blond princess in pink taffeta and silver sequins.

Tracy had wanted to be a princess that Halloween, too. She'd asked if she could wear the same costume in blue or purple, but Karen had pitched a fit and her mother had said it didn't matter, anyway—the store didn't have a princess costume in Tracy's size.

But Karen seemed different now. Eyes that had once been coated with makeup were more natural, and the soul behind them seemed less hungry. For the first time, she showed interest in Tracy's life with Hannah. She even played Candyland with Hannah on the sunny back-porch step while Tracy grilled shrimp kebabs on the lawn.

After dinner, Tracy shooed Karen and Hannah to the living room so she could clean up the kitchen. She claimed that she could never let another person scour her grill pans, but she really just wanted the time alone.

Time to deal with a simmering pot of feelings that threatened to boil over with each added ingredient. She closed the dishwasher door and leaned against the counter, listening as Hannah tried to teach her aunt a clapping rhyme. Every time one of them missed, they both burst into giggles. It was a happy sound, and Tracy knew she should get out there to enjoy the evening with her sister. This problem shouldn't be a problem at all.

It was just that her gorgeous sister was going to be

there tomorrow at her parents' party. And her parents' equally gorgeous neighbor could drop by to say hello.

Tracy knew she was being petty. She also knew that she'd be holding her breath, waiting for Riley's eyes to show the tiniest spark as they focused on the wrong sister.

The older one. The princess. The one he'd run off with all those years ago.

It didn't matter that Karen was married and wearing a too-big-to-miss diamond and sapphire set on her left hand. It didn't matter if nothing happened beyond a smile. Tracy would be watching for anything until Karen left, and that meant she cared more than she wanted to.

She could kick herself for that.

Tracy should call Riley and invite him to the party. She should get the reunion over with, pretend indifference to whatever happened and get on with her life.

While her sensible side fought to do just that, her inner Jezebel wanted to stand up in front of everyone and proclaim Riley her man, starting now and continuing for as long as it lasted. But there was a third choice—and it was the safest. It would be best to avoid him. If he was home during the party, he was home. Tracy didn't have to call him over. She didn't have to torture herself.

"I can't wait to surprise Mom and Matthew," Karen said after they had tucked Hannah into bed and settled on each end of the sofa to talk. "But I'm glad we have tonight. I've missed you, sis."

"Me, too." Tracy added a dollop of guilt to the pot. "I hope this trip doesn't get you in trouble with Alan."

Karen rested her head against the sofa back and massaged her temples, but she smiled. "We'll survive," she said. "The break will be good for our relationship."

"Well, I'm glad you're here," Tracy said.

And she was. That was part of the problem, too. This weekend was about family, and she wanted to devote herself to it. Tonight, she wanted to enjoy her time with Karen. What had happened was so long ago it could hardly matter now, and Tracy was old enough to admit that. She didn't have to let thoughts of Riley intrude. If she didn't mention his name, maybe Karen wouldn't, either. They could have their first slumber party as sisters, and maybe Tracy could get through an entire evening without thinking about him.

Both sisters watched as Claus poked his head around the doorway, then shot through the living room on his way to the back bedrooms. "I don't remember your cat being afraid of me before," Karen said.

"I never know how he's going to react," Tracy said. "Cats are peculiar. Don't worry about it."

"Anyway, thanks," Karen said. "I'm paying you back for the plane fare as soon as I can."

"There's no need." Tracy got up and crossed the room to pull a small satchel from an end-table drawer. "Thanks to Riley, I got my promotion. I'm earning a percentage on top of my regular salary now."

Lord. Riley's name had slipped out of her mouth in record time, hadn't it? Tracy returned to her end of the sofa and put the satchel between them. Then held her breath.

"How *is* Riley?"

You expected this. Play it cool. "Fine. In some ways, he's just like the boy we both knew. In other ways, he's different."

"I knew he'd grow into someone special," Karen said, causing Tracy's heart to twist. "Maybe he'll be home when we're at Mom and Matthew's tomorrow."

"Maybe." Keeping a neutral face, Tracy shrugged and opened the satchel. "Want to do nails?"

It was one of the few things they'd done together as girls. She'd paint Karen's nails; Karen would paint hers and chastise her, every time, for biting them.

Karen chose a coppery taupe, and Tracy began to apply it to nicely shaped fingernails, which were attached to a flawless hand, which was attached to a perfect body.

Tracy felt a little rough around the edges. "Are you happy with Alan?" she asked.

Karen pulled her hand away slightly, and when Tracy looked into her sister's face she was struck by the gentle expression. "I'm as happy as I've ever been," Karen said. "I've never been good at relationships."

Tracy laughed. "*You've* never been good at relationships? But you've had at least one male orbiting your path from the day you hit puberty. Sometimes it was two or three at once."

"That doesn't mean I know what I'm doing when it comes to making things work with one man," Karen said. "Alan's the longest I've been with anyone."

Tracy lifted her sister's finished hand to the sofa arm. She'd always thought the rapid succession of men had been Karen's choice. She remembered the blue carton that contained the pregnancy test, and wondered how much her sister had gone through and never confided. "Things haven't been easy for you, have they."

"Not really." Karen offered her left hand.

Tracy studied her sister's ring before starting on her thumbnail. "You seem calmer. Do you think Alan's the one that will last?"

"I hope so. I'm too old to keep starting over. I'd like to provide Hannah with a cousin or two someday."

Tracy had never thought of her sister as mom material,

but she seemed to have grown up quite a bit. Digging through the satchel for the bottle of Luscious Lime polish that would match tomorrow's outfit, Tracy pulled it out and balanced it on the sofa cushion. "Why do you think your other relationships ended?"

Karen frowned and touched her pinkie nail, then blew on her fingers. After a moment, she waved her hands in the air and said, "My therapist says it's because I blame myself for our father's departure. I choose men who won't stick around so I don't have to blame myself when they go."

Her sister's tone was light, but Tracy recognized the hint of pain behind her words. The erroneous guilt had affected them both, in different ways. "But he left three months to the day after I was born," Tracy said. "I thought it was *my* fault."

"But how could a rosy-cheeked baby cause a grown man to leave his family?" Karen asked.

"The same way a rosy-cheeked toddler could."

They looked at each other and laughed. "I'm glad we're talking now," Karen said. "I know I wasn't very nice to you when we were kids, but I've wished that we'd been closer."

"I have, too," Tracy said.

Karen grabbed the green polish and pulled Tracy's hand across to her knee. "Our father left under his own steam, and it was his loss," she said. "Have you seen him?"

"Not since my college graduation."

Karen tsked as she started applying polish to Tracy's stubby nails. "I can hardly believe Mom and Matthew have been married for fifteen years," she said.

"I can believe it. Dad's a great guy."

"You've always called Matthew Dad, haven't you?" Karen asked, smiling. "Maybe I'll try it tomorrow."

"He'd be touched." Tracy replaced her finished hand with the opposite one, and the conversation turned to tomorrow's party. As they polished toenails and put on nightgowns, it turned again, several times.

Despite Karen's fatigue, she seemed eager to stay awake and whisper in bed, mostly about Alan. How he drove her crazy but kept her grounded. She said she'd left him once last year and stayed in a motel for a week. She'd considered returning to Kirkwood, but missed sleeping beside him. She went back, and they were both changed by the experience. They'd softened their approaches to each other, determined to give it another try.

As Tracy listened, she realized Karen still had something she wanted—someone to miss, someone to welcome her home and accept her flaws. Maybe what Karen had was as good as it got. Maybe a won't-work man worked—if you loved him.

At six minutes before midnight, Karen neglected to answer a whispered question. Tracy peered across to the opposite pillow and realized her sister was asleep.

She must have fallen asleep missing Alan. Tracy could imagine how that would feel. She could imagine getting used to a pair of smoke-gray eyes and a cocky sweet smile turned toward her in the darkness.

She'd get too used to it, though. She'd fall too hard and make a fool of herself. Riley was too hot. Too uncertain. She needed the warm, safe man of her dreams. Which was exactly why she couldn't keep falling asleep missing Riley.

Maybe tomorrow night, she'd do better.

RILEY ROLLED the shade up partway, watching as a big white van groaned to a stop at the curb between his house and the Gilberts'. The gravel road they shared was so remote that he noticed any traffic, whether it was bound for his house or not. Handsome black lettering clued Riley in on the van's probable contents. The renowned local builder of fine wood furniture would have plenty he could use, but he hadn't ordered anything from them. And even Grandma Lydia wouldn't go that far to fill his house.

An angular old man and a portly young one jumped out and went to the back of the van. Without bothering to ring the bell at either house, they unloaded some sort of bench and carried it toward the gate between the houses.

A little more than an hour ago, Riley had hollered a greeting across the lawn to Tracy's parents as they'd loaded his-and-hers golf clubs in their trunk and left. He doubted they'd be home anytime soon.

Riley stepped over the Sunday paper he'd spread out on the floor to read. He wasn't inclined toward spying, but it seemed foolish to deliver a nice piece of furniture to an absent recipient. He peeked out the back bedroom window to note that the men had stopped in the middle of the Gilberts' backyard, but were holding the bench midair between them. The older guy was looking droopy, but didn't seem to realize that he could just put the bench down.

Deciding he should go out to see whether Laurel and Hardy needed directions or help, Riley had just turned to head for the back door, when a movement caught his eye. He returned to the window to watch Tracy jog into the yard and speak to the men. She pointed toward a rose trellis, and the men lugged the bench farther across the yard. She gestured again, and they turned it around to face the hills. Finally, they put it down. The little guy rotated his shoulders a few times while Tracy sat on the bench and looked around.

As the deliverymen were leaving, Hannah skipped into the yard with a bundle of white balloons. A blonde with a yellow laundry tub followed. Tracy summoned them toward the bench, then separated a couple of the balloons and fastened each to one of the bench's scrolled arms.

Something was definitely up next door, but apparently the delivery was sanctioned. Riley could quit watching.

Less than a minute later, Riley waited for one of the trio to notice him as he walked out toward the fence.

"Big Wiley!" Hannah charged over. "We're having a 'versry party for Gwamma and Poppy Matthew! Wanna come?"

"Ah! A party." He started to respond, but paused when he observed the blonde rocketing toward him almost as fast as Hannah had. As she neared the fence, he recognized Tracy's sister, Karen. She advanced so quickly he was tempted to dive for cover. She opened her arms wide, gave him an across-the-fence hug, then backed away. "I see the boy next door has grown more handsome than ever," she said.

"Nah, I'm the same," he said. "But I didn't recognize you at first."

"Holy maltballs!"

Riley smiled down at Hannah as she planted her hands on her hips and scrunched her face into an expression of extreme bother. Then he chuckled. He'd seen Tracy assume a similar stance of exasperation at least dozens of times. Hannah looked a lot like her mother, after all.

Karen bent down to Hannah. "What's wrong, sweetheart?"

''Big people talk a lot, and I don't get to eat cake 'til the party. I'm gonna go help Mama.''

Hannah started toward Tracy, but when she spotted a butterfly near the garden, she veered off after it, instead.

Riley turned back to Karen. ''I never figured we'd run into each other back here in Middle America. How are you?''

''Good. I've only been in town a day, but Tracy and I have had a nice visit.''

He directed his eyes across the lawn. Tracy was scowling as she stapled a tablecloth onto a long folding table. ''Hannah says there's a party in the works,'' he said.

''Yes, Mom and Matthew's anniversary is today, and Tracy planned a surprise for them.''

''A big social event like the ones I remember?''

''Nope. Just family this time,'' Karen said. ''I suppose I'm the big surprise for the day.''

He frowned. ''I saw your parents leave to play golf a while ago. I hope this thing isn't supposed to start soon.''

''Tracy set that up, too. They're playing an easy nine holes and having a late brunch at the country club. They think it's their anniversary present.''

''I should have known she'd cover everything,'' he said, watching as Tracy worked her way around the table. She finally came to the side facing him, but she still didn't look up. She seemed to be avoiding his gaze.

''I should go help,'' Karen said.

Riley pulled his gaze back to Karen briefly, then looked at Tracy, willing her to come over. It'd only been two days since the ice-cream date, but he'd missed her. As much as he wanted to prove his sincerity with a slow and steady wooing, it had been hard to stay away. He'd driven past her duplex four times yesterday. When he'd finally decided to stop, she hadn't been home. Good thing.

Tracy finished the table and hunkered down to speak to Hannah, then got up and looked inside the tub. She wasn't going to acknowledge him at all. "Hey! Gold-star girl!" he hollered, causing her to shoot a frown across the fence. "Nice day for a party!"

The comment was lame, but at least she looked at him. She offered an equally lame smile and lifted a hand.

Great. Progress. He kept staring intently, never allowing his eyes to waver until she tossed a red streamer into the tub and came across. "We're having a party," she said, her voice heavy with reluctance. "Join us. One o'clock."

She turned around and walked away. Her rear view was sexy in the hip-hugging denim skirt she was wearing, but he couldn't truly appreciate it because she seemed angry. At him, probably. Riley frowned. He'd love to spend time with Tracy and her family, but her invitation had seemed forced. Karen came near with the dwindling bouquet of balloons, so he summoned her in a whisper.

She left a white balloon suspended above the lawn and returned with raised eyebrows.

"Did something set your sister off?"

"Not until you came out." Karen frowned at him. "You aren't messing with my little sister, are you?"

He wished. "I'm crazy about your little sister, but crazy isn't working for her. Any ideas?"

Karen's mouth dropped open. Then she squealed and reached her free arm across the fence to hug him again. "I'm not surprised." She turned around to smile at Tracy.

Who looked as if she wanted to throttle both of them.

"Wow, she looks mad."

"Criminy."

They'd both spoken at once, but Karen was the first to move. She slid her arm off his shoulder, stepped away and gaped at her sister.

But Tracy was back to glaring into her yellow plastic tub and seemed unaware of any change.

He joined Karen in staring, but Tracy ignored them both.

Finally he backed up a few paces and made a running hurdle over the fence he'd installed a few weeks ago. He cleared it easily, sending Karen shuffling backward with the balloons. "Keep Hannah busy," he said as he passed.

He wished Tracy would at least blink to show that she'd noticed his impressive jump. He jogged a steady path toward her until he was too close to be ignored.

She edged to the side with a pile of paper plates. "I have a lot to do, Riley. I think Mom and Dad will be gone a while, but I can't be sure."

He moved closer, and didn't bother trying to keep the warmth from his voice. "I came by the duplex yesterday," he said, and took her plates from her hand. "I wanted to take you and Hannah out to dinner. Maybe take her to the park."

She stopped moving and looked up, but she still seemed edgy. "You came by?"

Ah. A flicker of interest. He nodded. "At five. After I rang the doorbell a few times, your neighbor came out and told me you'd left. She asked if we were dating."

Tracy's eyes widened. "What did you tell her?"

"I told her I was hungry for an enchilada and knew

Hannah liked the ones at Taco City. Then I said that I was too hungry to wait around, and I left.''

Tracy nodded and stepped back about a foot. ''Good save.''

He closed the gap again. ''It was all true, but it wasn't the whole story.''

''Oh?''

''I wanted to see you. Talk to you.''

Kiss you and see whether you'd kiss me back.

Tracy looked around. When she located Hannah near the fence chasing after another butterfly, she said, ''Listen, I heard Hannah invite you to the party. Karen wants you here, too. You should come.''

''What about you?''

She shrugged. ''You attended a lot of Gilbert parties when you were a kid. It seems right to have you here.''

He tossed the plates into the tub and took both of her hands. ''Good, because I want…''

She was staring at their hands. He hoped she felt the kick-in-the-gut attraction that made it hard to keep a clear head. She tugged her hands away and bounced back a few feet. Her face was flushed, but her eyes were shuttered. She was teetering near the edge, but she could fall either way.

Slow and steady.

''…to wish your parents well. One o'clock, you said?''

She nodded, so he smiled and walked around to leave through the gate, satisfied with the knowledge that Tracy was watching *his* rear view this time.

Chapter Eleven

Riley's whistle meant that it was time. Tracy's parents were arriving for the party. Her stomach flipped as she heard their car's approach, around front. Tracy slammed the lid to the drink cooler closed, then turned to holler at Hannah, "Come to the fence, Bean! They're here." Hannah shrieked and jumped out of the swing in Riley's backyard. Tracy ran across to pull her daughter over the fence and sail her back across to the bench.

After plopping Hannah down beside Karen, Tracy stood beside them and surveyed her parents' backyard. Pearl balloons and crimson streamers fluttered in a gentle breeze; a two-tiered bakery cake and leaf-shaped mints glistened under their net covering; and the three instigators of the surprise waited in bright summer colors. It was one-twenty.

Riley had been here on time, but her parents hadn't. After a five-minute discussion, they'd all decided Riley should go out front and pretend to work on his motorcycle, then whistle to warn them of the car's approach.

Tracy didn't know if her excitement was because she knew Riley would be here with them, or if it was because of the party in general.

No. That was wrong. She *did* know.

It was him.

Something shifted in her mind as she realized he wasn't flirting with her because she was around and available. He'd practically catapulted past the princess on his way to the ladybug. His interest seemed as focused as a blowtorch, and its blast of fire was directed right at her.

Her joints loosened.

She grasped the arm of the bench and let out a nervous breath, then heard tires crunch against the gravel of the driveway. Hannah tittered. Tracy felt like chuckling herself, but held back in fear that hers would carry the mad sound of a lunatic.

Karen leaned down to Hannah. "Zip your lips, sweetie," she said. "We want to surprise them."

Ever the pleaser, Hannah pinched her thumb and index finger next to her mouth and made a zipping motion, then pursed her lips. But when the car engine stopped, a round of giggles erupted from both Hannah and Karen. Their eyes barely contained their excitement as two car doors slammed closed and the buzz of the couple's voices took over.

"Shh!" Tracy touched a finger to her lips.

Once again, all was quiet. Tracy imagined her parents walking into the house to notice the balloon she'd left in the middle of their living room, its string weighted by a tiny crimson bottle of bubble-making solution. If the lure worked, they would follow the trail of balloons through the kitchen and out the door.

Karen smirked at Tracy, then let a chuckle escape. By the time the back door opened, Karen and Hannah were shaking with laughter. The jig was up.

Tracy let go of the bench. "One, two, three. Go!"

Everyone jumped forward and yelled "Surprise!" in

varying degrees of hilarity. Despite the unplanned final moment, it worked. Her mother cried out, then scooted across the lawn to hug Karen. Her dad followed quickly to pick up Hannah and swing her around.

When he stopped, he looked over Tracy's shoulder and gave the sort of nod one man gives another in greeting. Without looking, Tracy knew that Riley was joining them.

"Tracy invited me," he said. "I hope you don't mind."

"You were always a part of our family gatherings," her mother said, and the circle broke as they made space for one more.

"Tracy convinced me to come, too," Karen said. "In fact, this whole idea was hers."

After kissing Karen on the cheek, their mother turned to cup her palms around Tracy's face. "You've given us a precious gift, love. Thank you."

Everyone was quiet as Tracy accepted her mother's praise. Even after they'd hugged and kissed and broken apart, the rest of the group watched. Tracy shifted her weight and smiled painfully. She'd always felt strange in the limelight, no matter how fleeting.

When everyone started talking at once, Tracy relaxed. She looked from face to face and felt grateful. This was what she'd wanted. Her whole family, talking and smiling, together and home.

Her mother's voice was cheerful as she spoke across the group to Matthew about how well they'd been duped. Karen's tone was sweetly patient as she answered Hannah's questions about when they would cut the cake.

Riley was the only one who was quiet. The warmth of his gaze trapped Tracy's attention, and she tilted her head at him. He sent her a grin, the sort of grin that confirmed his interest.

She squinted past him.

Today wouldn't be easy with Riley around, but if she could stop noticing him and think about what she was doing, she'd be fine. Keep her distance, keep smiling, keep her mind on the details of the party. She'd hold an umbrella of calm against the onslaught of feelings he provoked, and she'd survive.

Karen had cleared her throat twice. When Tracy finally looked at her sister, she caught an odd tilt of a nicely shaped eyebrow and recognized that she was being prompted.

"Oh!" She turned and swept her arm toward the new garden bench. "Mom and Dad, did you see your gift?"

Her mother gasped. Scurrying across the lawn, she sat down on it and exclaimed, "This is wonderful!"

Matthew didn't get a chance to speak before Hannah bounced in his arms and said, sweet and clear, "The big man at the store said your bench is made of tea!"

Everyone laughed, and Tracy smiled at Hannah. "Teak. It's made of teak, which is a good wood for outdoor furniture because it lasts through rain and snow."

Riley stepped forward to take Hannah from Matthew's arms and said, "Go sit with your bride, Matt."

Tracy's attention was divided between her parents, who sat on the bench looking out at the hills, and her daughter, who seemed awfully comfortable with her arms looped around Riley's neck.

The little girl hollered over his shoulder. "Mama! Can I do bubbles?"

Good idea, a way to untangle them before the bond

grew too strong. Tracy reached out to sway a balloon her way and removed the bottle to hand to her daughter.

Riley put Hannah down, and soon the little girl was ripping around the yard sending trails of bubbles over their heads. Karen crossed the yard to talk to their parents a minute, then walked toward the house saying she wanted to call Alan.

Leaving Tracy to talk to Riley.

"You have a minute?" he asked.

She had an afternoon full of them, all set aside for her family and this party. And he'd be here as long as he wanted, to keep her in need of that flimsy umbrella.

"I have something for your parents, but I want you to look at it first."

He'd brought them a gift?

Tracy's gaze flicked across a copper crew neck that fit Riley's torso snugly, then to hands that looked strong but empty, and finally down to dark pants that emphasized long, muscular legs.

He had a garage-door opener clipped over his belt, but he couldn't be hiding much. When she looked back up to his eyes, she saw awareness. He knew he'd been noticed and appreciated. He was noticing and appreciating back.

She played dumb. "Where is it?"

He caught her hand and started tugging. "In my garage," he answered. "It was too big to wrap."

She started after him, speculating on the sorts of things a bachelor would buy for an anniversary couple. Bottled wine, baseball tickets and geometric picture frames seemed likely choices, but they were all wrappable.

Hannah was still flying her bubbles, so Tracy hollered

across. "Stay here with Grandma and Poppy, Bean. I'll be back in a minute."

When they rounded the corner, he clicked his garage door open. She saw the gift and let go of his hand to rush forward. Riley must have gone out to the furniture store after they'd spoken this morning. The teak armchair was the perfect match to her parents' bench.

She felt his warmth and knew he'd come to stand beside her. "This was too expensive," she said.

"Not at all," he said, his breath caressing her cheek. "Your parents have always been good to me."

Most everyone's garage would be hot in mid-June Kansas, but the melting sensation in Tracy's heart could only be her imagination. She should get back to Hannah and all those party details.

Before she did, Tracy reached out to grab the balloon that was tied to the chair. She followed its string down the back spindles, located the bottle of bubbles and pulled it free. "I'm amazed that you found crimson bottles here in Kirkwood. Karen bought ours in San Diego."

He chuckled. "Okay, so I nabbed a balloon when you weren't looking. You went to a lot of trouble with decorating, and I wanted my gift to match."

She rolled her eyes. "I've heard this before. You take what isn't yours with the best of intentions."

He moved closer. "Uh-huh."

She saw a kiss coming and wanted to step into it but didn't. "I need to get back to Hannah."

He shook his head slightly, but kept his mouth within two inches of hers. "She'll be fine for another thirty seconds."

The soft, hungry kiss probably cleared his professed time limit, but it was long enough to slide most of her resistance to the floor. When that kiss ended, Riley spoke against her mouth. "Make that a minute."

The add-on kiss was different—firmer and sexier. It was more dedicated, as if he was proving a point. And it sent Tracy into a massive puddle of want. If it weren't for her family next door, she'd probably be leading him into his house to see what would happen next.

When he finally backed away, he had the balloon string in his hand. He rewrapped it around the chair back and picked up the whole thing. "Let's go."

Somewhere on the way back, Tracy managed to speak, but only to make a banal comment about how much her parents would love his gift.

Of course, they did. And of course, Tracy survived the next little while even though she felt as if she was holding a tiny cocktail umbrella against a tidal wave of feelings.

Almost an hour later, her parents had admired the new chair, exclaimed over a watercolor painting from Hannah and commented on the cut of the crystal-decanter-and-goblet set from Karen and Alan. They'd eaten cake and chatted, and several of the adults had even joined in Hannah's bubble chase for a while.

Riley had stayed close. He'd delivered discarded gift wrap to the trash, passed out drinks and rattled off enough rambling jokes to keep everyone laughing and Tracy hot and loose-limbed.

She finally escaped when she and Karen carried empty plates and food containers into the kitchen. Tracy intended to take a minute to collect herself, but Karen kept the turmoil rolling. "I'm glad to see you and Riley finally worked out your problems," she said as she slid a finger across an edge of icing left on the cardboard circle.

Tracy started rinsing forks and didn't comment.

Karen collapsed the plastic cake covering and stuffed it into the trash container. "I can't believe you held a grudge that long."

Tracy turned around with a drippy fork in her hand. "I wasn't holding a grudge."

"Well, your feelings were hurt, though."

Tracy frowned. Of course she'd been hurt. She'd been too young to truly understand adult relationships, but she'd been horrified by that blue carton.

Her sister frowned back. "You and Riley haven't talked about it at all, have you?"

Tracy shrugged. "You've got it wrong, Karen. What happened was your personal business. If you'd wanted anyone else involved, you wouldn't have hidden the truth."

Karen snickered as she started transferring leftover mints to a small plastic bag. "What truth? The handsome guy out there has always had eyes for only you. Nothing personal happened."

With careful movements, Tracy put the fork in the dishwasher rack and walked across to touch her sister's hand and still her movements. After glancing toward the door, she said quietly, "I know about the test."

Karen looked truly confused. "What test?"

"The day after you left with Riley, I found the pregnancy test carton in your trash can. He took you away to take care of things, didn't he?"

Karen shook her head. "What things?"

"A baby, or the possibility of one."

Her sister stared out the glass panes of the door. "I'd forgotten about that."

The insanely sexy guy outside had once made Karen worry about a pregnancy, and she'd forgotten? Tracy thought. How? That didn't make sense. Tracy pulled out a stool and sat next to the counter. The air in the kitchen seemed too warm, so she kicked off her shoes. ''You weren't pregnant?''

''No, thank God.''

Tracy sniffed, relieved at least for that.

Karen plopped onto the stool next to her. ''It wouldn't have been Riley's.''

''What?''

''I never slept with Riley,'' Karen said quite clearly.

Tracy realized her mouth was open. She snapped it closed, then opened it again immediately. ''But I saw you two kissing down by the train trestle.''

Her sister seemed embarrassed.

Tracy continued, ''I ran away when I recognized you, but I saw enough.''

''Everyone saw us because I staged it that way,'' Karen said. ''But we never did more than kiss.''

Tracy shook her head. ''No other boy was hanging around you then, and you were sneaking out every night,'' she said softly. ''Besides, I found the evidence.''

When Karen pushed a hand through her hair, it fell into a disarray that was somehow more human than Karen's usual style. ''Okay, here's the truth,'' she said.

Tracy held her breath.

''I was seeing a married man,'' Karen said, and lowered her voice to a whisper. ''A teacher.''

Tracy put her hand over Karen's. ''At the same time you were seeing Riley?''

Karen closed her eyes. ''Yes. My…er, *friend* said it would be smart to pretend to be Riley's girlfriend so no one would catch on to what *we* were doing.''

Tracy shook her head again, unable to believe her

sister would get into that kind of trouble at seventeen. Or that she would have used Riley so callously.

Karen slid off the stool and paced in front of it. "I did everything my friend asked," she said. "But when I told him I thought I might be pregnant, he ended our relationship."

"But why would you want to be with a married man?"

"He convinced me that I was too mature for boys my age," Karen said with a rueful smile. "I believed him."

All of a sudden, the sugary tastes of cake and mint that lingered in Tracy's mouth seemed disgustingly sweet. Her mouth felt parched. "Mr. Mars?" she whispered.

"Yes."

The story must be true, then. The man had been fired several years ago, when one of his female students had accused him of a similar incident. Tracy padded across to the sink to fill a glass with water. She drank in big, slow gulps before stacking the glass in the dishwasher. Then she looked at her sister and shook her head. "You let everyone believe Riley had hurt you. You let me believe it."

"I figured it couldn't harm Riley's reputation to be known as my boyfriend, and I didn't think beyond that," Karen said.

Tracy averted her eyes, too shaken to continue the conversation. Glimpsing a movement outside, she stared out at the yard. How many summer days had she spent with Riley? How many days just like today, filled with sunshine and laughter and friendship?

She wished she could turn back time to any one of those days. Much of her confusion and pain would be erased, and there would be no need for the deep regret she felt now.

Lord. Her entire life might be different.

Tracy's throat felt tight and she still had a funny taste in her mouth. She pulled a new glass from the cabinet and filled it at the tap, then drank with her eyes closed so she wouldn't have to look at Karen. The only sound in the kitchen was the hum of the refrigerator, and Tracy liked it that way. She wanted her sister to go away. Outside, back to the duplex, even back to sunny California.

They could try to forge a closer relationship in another thirteen years or so.

"I see now that I was wrong, and I'm sorry."

Karen's soft voice was meant to soothe, but it didn't. Tracy wasn't ready to be comforted. She wanted a few moments to herself. Carrying her water, she returned to the stool and sat. "I know. I'll get over it. Would you mind checking on Hannah?"

Karen headed for the door, but on her way out she said, "If it helps, kissing Riley was like kissing a brother."

Tracy snorted. Riley's kisses had never been anywhere close to brotherly. And Karen's confession didn't fully explain his role in the pretense.

Just before Karen slid the door open, Tracy asked, "Did Riley know about any of this?"

"Ask him." Karen slipped outside and left the door open behind her.

Immediately, Riley's frame filled the doorway.

Tracy wasn't sure she was ready to see him.

He seemed so big. So gorgeous. So different.

And he wasn't off limits anymore.

Despite her quaking nerves, Tracy couldn't break eye

contact with Riley. He strolled into the house, pulled out the shiny red stool next to hers and sat.

"What's Hannah doing?" Tracy asked.

His eyes were grave and steady, as if she'd asked him to resolve world hunger and he was prepared to give a viable solution. "Gran showed up at my place, and she and Hannah started tossing a Frisbee back and forth over the fence."

"Good."

He shifted on the seat. "You seem upset. What were you and Karen talking about in here?"

Tracy felt exposed, as if even the cocktail umbrella was gone. "Oh, I just found out that you didn't get her pregnant thirteen years ago," she said, her voice too melodious for the weight of the words.

Riley frowned. "That wouldn't have been possible. As I told you before, things didn't work out with your sister."

"I know. Now."

He took her hand. "You could have asked."

Tracy looked at their linked hands resting on the countertop between them. "I was mad at you for a long time, but my anger didn't feel right since I had no claim on you." She smiled. "Then again, you were gone."

"I guess I was," he said, smiling back. "Your anger at my connection with Karen was justified. I didn't feel right about what I was doing, even if it didn't go far."

She squeezed his hand. "You and I weren't close then, though. We'd grown apart."

"I know."

Tracy had always wondered who had started avoiding whom first. It was as if in one day her friend had transformed into a stranger. She'd lost confidence in herself. "Why was that, do you think?"

"Confusion. Hormones. I was noticing you too much."

She looked at their fingers, fitted together like zipper teeth, and was astonished to note that she wasn't at all tempted to tug hers free to bite her nails.

"Otto told me he'd have me arrested for child molestation if I touched you."

She frowned. "But you didn't turn eighteen until two days before you left. You were as much a child as I was."

His eyes were pensive. "I know that now." He slid off the stool and slipped between her bare and dangling feet, offering the sort of embrace the seventeen-year-old Riley would have given the fifteen-year-old Tracy.

"I forgot about you for a while," he said against her ear. He backed up and looked at her. "Until I came back and felt the bond again."

She knew what he meant. Although she didn't move, she felt a last little nudge toward him, felt it like a physical push.

From the day she'd confronted Riley in his own backyard a couple of months ago, fate had pointed them toward the time when they'd find out what it was like to be together.

Almost without thought, she put a hand on his chest and slid it down to his thigh, watching his eyes gleam like silver. She felt the heat mingling between them, and was grateful for the divine anticipation.

Then she put all the passion of the day, the past two months and the previous thirteen years behind her movements. Her lips were the first to taste and her fingers were the first to slide beneath clothing and caress bare skin.

Moving her knees past his hips, Tracy slid forward,

wanting to get closer to this male who'd always fascinated her. When she felt his hot, proud body pressing into her lower abdomen, she nestled herself against it.

Their fit was perfect, their movements sensual.

Fated.

A thud against the house made them both jump.

Riley seemed undaunted as he lifted her from the stool and held her braced against him. He walked them to a secluded spot between the refrigerator and pantry, wedged them into the narrow space and offered a quick smile. "Are you okay?" he whispered.

She'd heard that question before, in a similar situation and from the same person. This time, instead of risking his departure by answering, she wrapped her limbs tighter around him and offered another kiss.

Riley's chuckle vanished with the touch of her mouth, but he took control within seconds. His lips and hands made obvious his desire to continue. And the husky words of encouragement he breathed against her skin laid rest to any lingering doubt.

When he released her legs, her feet slid to the floor and her body almost slumped down with them. The cramped pressure of their narrow hideaway had numbed her legs, and their lack of sensation seemed in sharp contrast to the vital need at their juncture.

As she caught her balance, she thought she heard a door open and close. She kept kissing Riley, but she realized that she still had no choice. Not now. Whether Riley was available to her or not, she couldn't go on because the party was now. Her entire family was on the other side of a door that wasn't hers to lock.

Tracy sighed against Riley's mouth. She'd planned her parents' anniversary party for months, and had even paid her sister's way to attend. At this moment, she wished every one of them would find somewhere else to go so she could keep making out with Riley.

She wasn't a love-struck teenager, and neither was he. They were adults, and they had come to the point where they needed to finish or stop.

And she had no real choice.

Tracy shoved a hand between their mouths, almost forgetting her resolve when she felt his breath against the palm of her hand. She could imagine that soft heat tickling against her ear, moving down her neck…she could imagine it *everywhere*. But she shouldn't.

"My sister's staying with me tonight," she said. Her words seemed to echo through the quiet kitchen, and seemed so out of place among the heated nibbles, they sounded bizarre even to her own ears.

Riley backed out of the tiny space, looking dazed.

Tracy grinned. "Karen's sleeping in my bed. We're having a grown-up slumber party." She hoped he'd understand that this afternoon's fervor had no chance for a satisfying end.

He groaned. Then chuckled. Then groaned again, probably when he understood what her statement implied. He shot a glance toward the hall to the bedrooms.

Tracy giggled. "They'll miss us if we disappear for any length of time. They'll hunt for us."

He looked pained. "Are you sure?"

She nodded.

"Why didn't you invite the usual crowd?"

"I was going for something warm and intimate."

His eyes teased, and she wondered what he would have said if Hannah's voice hadn't interrupted. "Mama and big Wiley? Are you playing hide-and-seek now?"

Chapter Twelve

Riley inched back until he bumped into the counter on the opposite side of the Gilberts' kitchen. He made an effort to pull himself together, but Tracy was wriggling around in the cramped space. Apparently, she was stuck. Her eyes were still bright with the passion of a moment before, but her cheeks were growing pinker. She seemed embarrassed and annoyed in such an adorable way that Riley chuckled.

Tracy didn't seem to think the situation was funny at all. She glared at him while Hannah twirled around the kitchen, apparently waiting for an answer to her question.

Riley stepped forward to grasp Tracy's hand and tug her out, then wound up chuckling again as she bent down to explain the situation to Hannah.

Tracy's tale changed as it progressed, beginning with a fib about searching for extra mints and ending with a confession that she and her friend Riley were just playing a game, as Hannah had suspected.

Hannah must have been satisfied with the answer, because she skipped on into the house.

Riley was pleased that Tracy had referred to him as a friend, but he hadn't been playing any game. He'd never been more serious. Hannah's interruption was a good thing. So was Tracy's obligation to entertain her sister. He thought.

Hannah galloped back through the kitchen on a hobbyhorse, and Tracy followed her daughter outside. Riley followed, too. It might be okay for him to crash a Gilbert party, but he couldn't skulk around their house alone.

As he stepped out onto the patio, his eyes hurt from the rapid adjustment to the bright sunlight. He was making adjustments, too, on every level. His body, his emotions, even his pores felt needful. He hoped it wasn't noticeable.

He blinked a few times, and when his eyes adapted, he realized his grandmother had made her way to this side of the fence. Lydia noticed everything, and usually commented on it. Loudly and explicitly. In front of whomever.

Riley glared at his grandmother, prepared to send a silent warning, but she was speaking to Hannah as the child stuck the hobbyhorse handle under a bush to slide the Frisbee out from beneath it. Once again, the little girl had saved him. He'd have to take her out for her own banana split real soon.

Hannah shrieked. She'd dislodged some pill bugs with the handle, and was dropping them into the upturned circle of the Frisbee. When she plopped down on the patio to nudge them around with her finger, Gran's attention was free.

Riley whipped a glance across at Tracy, who was standing beside him and blinking. With her pink cheeks and pouty lips, she looked as if she'd just been kissed rather soundly. If Gran made some off-color comment, Tracy would be more embarrassed and upset. She might even retreat again.

Riley decided to put distance between himself and Tracy. "See you, ladies," he said. "I'm going to mingle." He strode across the lawn and stopped near Tracy's parents, who were sitting on their bench chatting with Karen. Riley couldn't have said what they were discussing, though, because his eyes and ears were on the two women on the patio.

Tracy's smile for his grandmother was generous. "How are you, Lydia?" she said, and opened her arms for a hug.

Gran stepped forward, looking as awkward as Riley felt. Riley knew that few people in town welcomed her so warmly. Tracy had an open mind and a kind heart.

"I came by to rope my grandson into entertaining me this afternoon, but I guess he jumped the fence again."

"He most certainly did that," Tracy said with a chuckle.

Riley smiled. She *had* noticed.

"You were always a pair, weren't you?" Gran said. "And he's such a stud now. You two should hook up."

Tracy's mouth dropped open. Even from this distance, Riley could tell she'd lost her pink.

Gran's heart was in the right place, but she was going to ruin Riley's efforts to execute a slow and thoughtful wooing. She might thwart his ability to woo at all.

He couldn't let that happen. "Nice chatting with you," he said to the startled Gilberts, and hurtled himself back across the lawn to try to salvage the situation.

But Hannah had already done so. She'd caught both ladies' notice by flopping belly down across the brick patio, propping her chin between both hands and chanting a nursery rhyme to her round of crustaceans.

Gran was smiling, but Tracy wasn't. She frowned and

shifted her weight, then slipped the tip of her finger into her mouth.

"Pleasant weather for a party," Lydia said.

"Mmm," Tracy said distractedly.

"It's too damn hot," Riley interjected as he walked up.

Both ladies ignored him.

"And how is work, m'dear?" Gran looked directly at Tracy.

"Busy." Tracy frowned off toward the hills. "It *is* getting pretty hot. I think I'll head for home."

Riley rocked back on his heels and told himself that he was satisfied. He didn't want to see Tracy go, but if she left now, his grandmother wouldn't be able to meddle.

He could do his own romancing, at his own pace. Maybe he'd even go by tonight and ask Tracy and Hannah out for ice cream again. "I think I'll go, too," he said. "Thanks for the invite."

"Why go so soon?" Gran asked Tracy.

"I have an early alarm tomorrow," Tracy said. "I'm organizing a fund-raiser for a group of college kids, and we're meeting for coffee."

Before his grandmother could form an argument, Tracy called out across the space. "Hannah, put the bugs back where you found them and go inside to wash your hands."

"Can I take my woly-polies home?" Hannah asked her mother. "I named them Dopey, Doc and Sleepy."

Tracy smiled. "Clever names, but let's leave them here. Maybe you can find seven next time we visit."

Hannah got up and tipped the Frisbee next to the grill, nudging each bug until it fell to the ground. "I'll be back," she said. "Don't get squashed."

"May I borrow Hannah this evening?" Gran asked abruptly.

Tracy, who had started toward her parents, stopped at the edge of the patio and turned around. "I beg your pardon?"

"I'm attending a production of *Beauty and the Beast* at the arts center this evening," Gran said. "Your daughter would make a fine companion."

Riley laughed out loud. His grandmother wasn't the theater type. Maybe she was bored. "Don't worry, Gran," he said. "I'll come by and shoot hoops with you later."

"Hoops, shnoops," she said, frowning across at him. "I'm asking Tracy if I might spend time with her daughter."

Riley caught the gleam in his grandmother's eyes and knew she wasn't motivated by boredom. She must be trying to occupy the child so the mother's time would be free for kisses. Or for *hooking up*.

That thought was enough to heat him up and send him a step back at the same time, making him an observer in a conversation that was beyond his control, anyway.

"Tracy?" Gran said. "Hannah is charming and I'd like to get to know her better. Would you mind?"

"I appreciate the offer," Tracy said. "But Hannah has day care early tomorrow, and she'll need a good dinner and a bath tonight. Besides, she missed her nap. She's cranky."

"But, Mama, I love that movie." Hannah tossed the empty Frisbee into the yard and bounced around the patio in a decidedly uncranky manner.

"This isn't a movie, Hannah-bean."

The little girl stopped jumping and turned her sloe eyes toward Lydia. "It's the weal *Beast?*"

Gran smiled. "No, it's a marionette show—with puppets on strings. I read somewhere that a local second-grader is supposed to be doing the voice of Teacup."

The battle was lost. Hannah tugged at the hem of her mother's skirt. "Poppy Matthew calls you Teacup!"

"I know, Bean."

The child yanked again. "I let the woly-polies go, and I don't need to eat gween stuff for dinner cuz I had seventeen mints."

Tracy looked horrified. "Seventeen?"

"Not counting the bwoken ones." Hannah turned her bright eyes toward Gran and tried to wink.

Lydia was clearly captivated.

Tracy leveled a gaze at Gran. "Are you sure about this?"

"I'd love company, and fairy tales aren't Riley's bag."

Riley had grown used to being ignored, so he only grunted. He liked the happy endings well enough, but he'd never end the whole shebang with just a kiss.

"What time would you need to leave?" Tracy asked.

"Now would work," Gran said with a shrug. "We could have hot dogs at my place and head out to the show a bit later."

Tracy sighed and bent down to her daughter. "Would you be very good?"

Hannah nodded, and seemed to make a humongous effort to stand still while her mother tugged at her socks, dusted grass off her knees and examined her clothes.

Riley took advantage of the moment to whisper to his grandmother, "Whaddaya think yer doin'?"

"Taking a little girl to a play," she whispered back.

"Why?"

"To help."

"Don't need it."

"You're moving as slow as a snail over molasses," Gran murmured a notch too loudly. "I'll die before you get to second base."

He'd already been there and done that, but he'd never tell his grandmother. He grunted again.

Tracy stood up and looked at both of them, and her expression made it clear that she'd heard every word. "I can't send her out in public like this," she announced, pointing to a large dirt stain on the hem of Hannah's pants.

"Allow me." Gran stepped forward. In a flash, she bent down on one knee and rolled the hem of Hannah's pants up twice, turning them into neatly cuffed pedal pushers. Then she stood back. "They look better this way, don't they?" she said, her tone precluding an answer.

When Tracy started ticking off detailed child-care instructions, Lydia cackled and shot him a victory glance.

Riley shrugged, silently conceding her victory until Karen approached the group.

"We'll be alone tonight," Tracy said to Karen as she finger-combed her daughter's hair. "Hannah's going to a puppet show with Riley's grandmother."

Gran scowled.

Riley grinned. He'd forgotten that Karen was staying with Tracy. The sisters started listing possibilities for their evening together, and Hannah skipped across the patio toward the house. Nodding complaisantly when her mother yelled a last-minute command to use soap, she went inside.

"Would you like to come along?" Lydia asked loudly.

Both Tracy and her sister stopped talking and looked at her. Gran kept her eyes pointed directly at Karen.

"You want me to go to a puppet show with you and Hannah?" Karen asked, seeming startled.

"I know you're here to visit your family," Lydia said, "but I believe that an old classmate of yours might have a part in the production."

"Really? Who?"

"His name escapes me, but he's a brawny guy with a dark scruff of hair and soulful eyes."

Karen gasped. "That could be Pete—a senior I dated in my sophomore year!"

Riley was probably the only one who suspected that his grandmother had just given a description of the *Beast* marionette.

"I suppose it could be Pete," Gran said.

Karen glanced at her sister. "We might wrangle an invitation to the after-party," Lydia added. Riley was probably the only one who could have seen Gran's fingers, crossed behind her back. Sly old fox.

Karen tilted her head. Tracy scowled.

"We would stay a few minutes," Gran said, obviously trying to squelch Tracy's motherly concerns before they got out of hand. "I'd have Hannah home by nine o'clock."

Then she turned to Karen. "And if you wanted to stay at the party, I could return to pick you up later."

"Would you mind?" Karen asked Tracy.

Tracy didn't answer because Hannah had slammed the back door and was galloping toward them. "I used soap to my owbows!" she hollered in a voice so piercing it caught everyone's attention and lured them toward the patio.

Tracy scooped her daughter up and held her perched on a hip. When the rest of the gang had gathered around, she asked, "Should we all wash to our elbows and go to a show together this evening?"

"Count us out," Gwen said, smiling at her husband as she spoke for both of them. "We've had a big day already." She shrugged apologetically and left the circle to carry a set of crystal glasses inside. Matthew followed her with the matching decanter.

As soon as the sliding door closed again, Riley grinned charismatically. "I'm game," he announced. A group date would be more conducive to slow and thoughtful wooing.

Gran glared at him. "It's a *puppet* show."

He frowned back at her. "I know."

"My car seats four comfortably," she said. "But since Hannah needs the built-in booster seat, it will fit only three today." She scowled harder.

When Tracy opened her mouth, presumably to offer a seating solution, Lydia gave her a foul look. Tracy's mouth snapped closed.

Gran put a hand on Tracy's shoulder and shot a look of challenge toward Riley. "My persnickety grandson prefers even green food to my hot dogs."

Riley stared at Lydia. He was a grown man with a grown man's self-control. He could spend an evening alone with Tracy and still go slow.

Very, very slow. Then faster and... "That's right," he said abruptly, and attempted a nonchalant shrug. "I'd rather eat brussels sprouts."

Lydia smiled at Tracy. "And if you came along, who would be responsible for cleanup?" She pointed at the yard. Three balloons and some tattered streamers were the only items that hadn't already been cleared away, but they were enough to disturb a true perfectionist.

"Right." Tracy lowered her daughter to the ground. "I suppose I should stay and finish things here."

Hannah skipped across the circle to take Gran's hand. "It's okay," she consoled. "I'll go to the *Beast* with you."

"Of course you will, and so will your aunt Karen."

Within minutes, Gran was driving down the street with Karen at her side and Hannah in back in the booster seat—both headed out for an evening away from Tracy.

Riley had spent the afternoon being ignored, tempted and challenged by his two favorite women. He felt like a puppet himself. So when Tracy smiled brightly at him and asked him to help her clean up, he did exactly that.

Ten minutes later, he tied the last three balloon strings to a handle of Tracy's laundry basket and watched her disappear inside to grab her shoes and tell her parents she was leaving. As he picked up the basket to wait, he wondered how to approach the subject of their free evening.

He wanted to spend the time with her, doing whatever. He also wanted her to know that his intentions were honorable. If that meant he needed to ask her for a date, then that's what he'd do—with his heart pounding until the moment she said yes. If she said yes.

The basket slipped. He put it down to wipe his palms against his trousers and tried to remember the last time he'd been so nervous. He couldn't even remember the last time he'd formally asked a woman for a date.

Criminy. A date sounded mild when compared to the wicked thoughts he'd been battling for the past few hours, but thanks to Gran, an evening alone together was an option.

As tempting as it sounded, skipping the date and heading straight for the bedroom would be worse than Otto's six-pack and dead-flower offerings.

Riley didn't want to dishonor Tracy. He'd romance her with wine and candles, if that was what she wanted. They could paint the town red, or go to a movie. Anything. He cared only about having her company.

Or at least that was what he kept telling himself.

Tracy slid the door open, stepped out and summoned him with one of her beaming smiles. With balloons sailing past his head, he followed her to the front yard and stopped when he noted the empty curb. "Where did you park?" he asked, realizing she would have hidden her car to ensure her parents' surprise.

Tracy was halfway across his yard. "On the other side of the farm field," she said over her shoulder. "Near the wooded area where you used to build your forts. Hannah and Karen and I walked past the spot earlier, but I didn't tell them about that."

Tracy was the only person who'd known about his forts. He was glad she'd kept it secret. He bopped a balloon away from his face and rushed to catch up.

"Do you mind if I cut through your yard, instead of going around?" Tracy asked as she rounded the cedar bush.

"Of course not. I'll come with you." And on the way, he would ask her out on a date.

She opened his gate and walked through, but paused in the yard to admire the storm door he'd installed a few days ago. "You've done a great job fixing up the house."

"Thanks." He nudged a bothersome balloon away

from his line of vision again and waited for her to continue.

She didn't.

The wicked thoughts returned with a vengeance. She turned around to face him, and he was glad the balloons were floating out between them. Her full lips and brilliant eyes suggested passion. He didn't need to look below her chin to know what the rest suggested.

But he did.

Truly wicked thoughts.

And asking her in would be asking for trouble. Did any woman take bedroom romance seriously? He shuffled the laundry basket to one side to rub a palm against his pant leg. "I've done more inside since you've been here," he said, switching hands to repeat the motion. "Want to see?"

She nodded.

In a valiant attempt to maintain some degree of decorum, Riley left the basket near the back door and led Tracy upstairs to show her a freshly painted bedroom, then back down to admire a new kitchen sink and faucet.

She seemed impressed. And they returned promptly to the back door. Tracy stood near the laundry basket as if she was really going to pick it up and leave, and Riley pulled his extra house key off the nail as if he was really going to walk her out to her car.

"I'm not leaving," Tracy said softly.

"God, I hope not."

His mouth got to her first, but everything else followed as if attached to his lips by a tightly coiled spring. He kissed her, and at the same time moved the two of them back inside the house and through the kitchen.

They paused in the middle of the living room for a while. Tidy Tracy, gold-star girl and indisputable perfectionist, was also an accomplished kisser. She did things with her lips and tongue that made him forget to move his feet. Things that tempted him to forget a thoughtful wooing and take advantage of the wide expanse of carpet in his sparsely furnished room.

But soon, she grabbed his collar and tugged him forward, setting his feet back into motion. There was no question about where they were headed. Or why.

With supreme efficiency, Tracy stepped out of her shoes, then unzipped the denim skirt he'd admired all afternoon. She wriggled out of the garment and kicked it out of the way before they both tripped over it.

His pants were next. The funny thing was, Tracy helped him remove them and let her hands show an appreciation of what was underneath. All while kissing him. All while leading him toward his bed.

Tidy Tracy was hot enough to melt steel.

By the time they made it to the bedroom doorway, she was peeling off her ruffled green top and revealing a sexy piece of lingerie that stopped at her midriff and accented a topaz belly-button ring.

His chest hurt. Would he ever learn not to be surprised by Tracy? He picked her up and made a mad dash for the mattress. But as he laid her across it, he reminded himself that romance and passion could work together if he kept control. This was an area where he prided himself in his own expertise. He wanted to satisfy Tracy, all right. He also wanted to leave her yearning for more. He pulled off his shirt and lay down beside her, then propped up on one elbow, facing her.

He smiled, pretending his body wasn't anywhere near explosion level. "What do you call this?" he asked, running an index finger across the silky fabric covering her chest.

"A bustier. Do you like it?"

Grinning his answer, he moved his lips to her neck, kissing the tender skin there while he explored her body with a curious hand. But instead of invading her most private places, he only flirted with them.

Remained a gentleman. Bided his time.

When he bumped into an earring, he noticed that it matched the stud in her navel. "Did I tell you you have sexy ears?" he asked, moving his lips against her earlobe. "I've admired them since we were teenagers."

"Your jaw drove me crazy," she confessed huskily. "I've wanted to feel your face against my skin."

He backed up and looked in her eyes. "Really? You had those kinds of thoughts as a teenager?"

"I had those kinds of thoughts this afternoon."

He laughed and touched her navel ring. "As soon as I saw this, I wanted to put my face down there."

Her breath caught. "Okay."

He nibbled his way down and touched his tongue against the jewelry, then kissed all the way around it. Her skin felt as warm as summer sun; its vanilla scent was both exotic and comforting.

Her hips bucked up when he slid his fingers across her hipbone and across the band of her panties. He knew she wanted him to remove them. He wanted to remove them.

But he could wait.

Returning to her side, he propped back up on his elbow and smiled as if he had all the time in the world. Tracy raised an eyebrow, then reached back and unfastened her bustier. Slowly, she peeled it off, smiling boldly as she bared her breasts to him.

He'd seen them before, so he shouldn't have been so

astonished by them. "And there are two other things I've admired," he confessed.

"This afternoon?"

"Yes. And at least a thousand other times since the first day of swim season in 1990. You wore a brown polka-dot bikini that made my knees shake."

She closed her eyes, waiting with an expectancy that was hard to resist. But he touched her gently, rubbing his palm in lazy circles against each nipple.

They responded so beautifully his fingers trembled.

She laughed shortly. Taking his hand, she moved it to the small of her back while shoving her chest forward. "Stop teasing!"

He accepted what she offered, swirling his tongue around her pink, delicate nipples until they glistened. He loved the feel of her inside his mouth. As he inhaled her scent again, he knew he recognized it as clearly as he did the color of her eyes. He wanted to memorize her taste, too.

Her whispers and sensual movements let him know she was affected. She wanted this as much as he did.

In a moment of clarity he recognized that she was moving her limbs methodically, working away at some task while he took pleasure from her breasts.

He knew what she'd done when she shoved him onto his back and straddled his body. She moved against him, sliding her naked flesh against his arousal. He shuddered, wishing the thin cotton cloth of his boxers wasn't separating them. Her heat seemed to welcome his. Her soul seemed to shout that it was time.

He agreed.

He slid his underwear off and rolled on top of Tracy, letting their bodies settle together, anticipating for the briefest of moments what would come next. He opened his mouth to hers and let his tongue explore erotically. Let his body sink deeper into her sensuality.

And finally, pushed inside her.

She felt so good. Hot and right. She sucked in her breath and turned her face to one side, then closed her eyes tightly, as if she was savoring his feel.

He closed his eyes, too, concentrating on self-restraint. He wanted to avoid movement long enough to let their minds and bodies adjust to the intense connection.

Finally he let himself move, slowly and deeply, as if this first time with Tracy might also be the last. He wanted the experience to haunt both of them.

Tracy seemed to follow his thoughts. She matched his patient rhythms for a long time. Sweetness teased and lingered as they drifted on a plane of shared and secret joy. Until he was straining with effort and her movements were growing frantic.

And still, he curbed his passion. Kept thinking about restraint. Kept thinking about pace.

"Riley?" She shoved her hips forward, then pressed her fingertips into his back. "Let go! *Please.*"

She was right—it was time.

He opened his eyes and kissed her beyond comprehension, then abandoned rational thought. They rose up so fast and hard she screamed.

A minute later, Riley eased down beside her on the bed. He wasn't sure what would happen next. This was the moment he usually parted ways with his lady friends. Whoever was in the wrong house got up and went home.

It was different with Tracy. For one thing, he didn't want her to leave. He also felt compelled to tell her how much she meant to him. He held back, though. Would any woman believe words of caring only a minute after a climax?

Instead, he tried to adjust to a new situation by making light of it. He flattened a palm against her belly and said, ''That was a first for me.''

Tracy turned over, so that her back rested against his front, but she didn't ask what he meant.

He answered, anyway. ''It was my first time with a woman who knows my spit-wad technique.''

''Don't talk,'' she whispered. ''Relax.''

Maybe she was right. The experience had been deeply intimate. Maybe he shouldn't try to force conversation now. He nestled closer to Tracy. Her need for quiet seemed to indicate that she was sorting out some powerful feelings. He'd give her time to do so.

Chapter Thirteen

Tracy stared down at Riley's hand as he draped it around her waist. His tanned flesh looked startlingly dark against the pale skin of her belly—almost as startling as her response to him a moment before. She couldn't believe she'd screamed. She couldn't believe much about this entire evening. She'd been so reckless. Sex had never been this shattering before. It had never evoked such a profound response.

A fold of dark fabric bulged out of the second drawer of Riley's dresser and pulled Tracy's attention across his bedroom. His walls were bare, and the shade covering his window was a basic white. Except for the keys and coins cluttering the top of his dresser, there was little evidence of Riley's personality in this room. The changes he'd made to the house were all structural.

He didn't seem to be settling in.

That bit of knowledge lodged in Tracy's brain like a splinter. At the same time, she felt as if she was a reluctant intruder, digging through closets and cubbyholes to search for returned feelings.

Fearing the very thing she was seeking.

Her emotions were too intense. This afternoon she'd learned a piece of truth about Riley's past. Then she'd slept with him. Now, her "hopeless romantic" switch seemed to have been flipped on. She craved bent-knee promises and vows of undying devotion, but knew it was foolish to start planning the wedding. She wasn't even sure she wanted one. Not with Riley. He was reckless, dangerous. Not at all the kind of man she pictured herself marrying.

It was really just sex. Although it had been cataclysmic for her, it could have been just another pleasurable evening for him. He'd told her that he involved himself in a relationship only until the woman he was dating wanted more.

A part of her wanted more now.

The silence felt awkward. Maybe Riley had been right to make such a lighthearted comment. Tracy frowned, trying to think of something funny to say in return.

She must have made a slight movement, because he flattened his palm on her belly and pulled her closer. "You okay?" he asked.

She attempted a grin over her shoulder. "Yes. I was just admiring your elaborate decorating scheme."

"The dime-store dresser or the minimalist bed?"

"I like your lava lamp."

"Oh, that. It's one of Gran's hand-me-downs." He rolled off the bed and crossed the room to switch it on. The sight of his bare backside moving across the room was enough to make Tracy shiver. Then he turned around. She was amazed that she could feel a need for him again so soon.

She flopped onto her back, pulled the sheet higher on her chest and said the first nonsexy thing that came to mind. "You don't have a lot of furniture in here, do you?"

He slid back between the sheets. "Not yet. Maybe I've got Gypsy ancestors. I don't mind simple living."

She'd noticed. But the topic wasn't exactly blithe. She'd have to try again. Bumping her elbow against his side, she said, "You're a Gypsy and a fraud."

"A fraud?"

"The motorcycle you ride isn't a Harley, is it. Don't think I haven't noticed. And since you own more than one helmet and buy ice cream for little girls, it's safe to assume you aren't a bad boy at all."

"Watch it, lady." He turned onto his side, facing her, and moved a hand across the sheet until he felt her belly button stud through it. "I noticed that you've been hiding something here. Maybe you're a closet rebel."

"Maybe you're losing your edge."

Riley eased on top of her again, grabbing her hands to pull them over their heads. "I'll show you my edge."

Tracy's self-consciousness was lost in laughter and renewed desire. Despite the worry she felt when she was out of his arms, she felt daring within them. She did a few more things she'd never done before. Riley met each of her moves with two of his own. Their lovemaking felt wild and exotic and…forbidden. The word kept coming to mind.

Afterward, Tracy lay beside him and felt the same awkwardness. Instead of a person she'd known all her life, Riley seemed like some stranger she'd met in a bar two hours ago. She felt very aware of herself. Of him.

She had no idea how to get up and leave. Should she just hop out of bed, stark naked, and start dressing while they exchanged quips?

She'd been brazen enough to strip, but without intense passion fueling her actions, she couldn't quite muster the courage to reverse the process. And her earlier attempt at joking was impossible to resume.

She made a huge show of checking her watch, then grabbed her underthings and sprang out of bed.

"What are you doing?"

She turned her back to him while she slipped into her panties. "Leaving."

"Already?

"Your grandmother will be taking Hannah and Karen home."

"Don't worry. If you're not there, Gran will find some way to entertain them. Or she'll bring them here."

As Tracy fumbled with the hooks to her bustier, she glanced over her shoulder at Riley. "Think she knows?"

His gaze moved down her back, and he grinned that wicked, lopsided grin. "I think she set us up."

That was what she'd thought, too. Tracy felt her entire body blush, but she resisted the urge to cover all that hot, bare skin. "I want to beat them home."

"I'll walk you to your car." He grabbed his boxer shorts and climbed out of bed again.

He seemed quite unconcerned about his nudity, stunning as it was. She averted her gaze. "No, just relax. I'm in a hurry. I'm sure I'll see you soon."

Tracy headed for the hallway, hoping Riley wouldn't follow her. She wanted time to compose herself before returning home to Hannah and Karen. The walk across the farm field would provide the opportunity.

When she located her blouse on the floor, she pulled it on over her head. Scrambling toward her skirt, she zipped into it and managed to scoot into her shoes on her dash out the back door. Then she stumbled over the laundry basket. She righted her footing and picked it up. With a careful glance next door to make sure her parents weren't outside, she strode across Riley's yard with a trio of balloons flying out behind her head.

THE NEXT AFTERNOON, Tracy left work early to spend time with her family. Karen was finishing her visit at their parents' house, and Tracy and Hannah had been invited to join them all for dinner. When they arrived, Matthew and Karen were outside talking near the grill. Hannah saw them through the glass door, and her face lit up. "Can I look for woly-polies?"

"Just look, but don't pick them up," Tracy said, smiling at her mother. "It smells like dinner's ready."

Hannah flew out to the patio while Tracy helped her mother put finishing touches on the table. She started laying out silverware and realized there was one too many place settings. "Mom, did you realize you set the table for six?"

"Oh! Didn't I tell you?" Her mother's look was sly. "We saw Riley this morning and thought it would be nice to have him over, too. When you finish there, would you walk over and tell him dinner's ready?"

Tracy finished setting the table, but her appetite had vanished. Suddenly the smell of Matthew's famous tequila-lime chicken made her feel nauseated.

She'd missed Riley today. She'd gone to her coffee meeting to plan a celebration for the college girls, then she'd gone into the office and found the flowers.

Riley had sent a bouquet of wildflowers tied up in a red grosgrain bow. He'd signed the card with just his name. She'd called him at work to thank him, but that was the only conversation. She'd hung up quickly.

Their bedroom antics loomed in her thoughts constantly. She alternated between delight and confusion. As excited as she was to be seeing him tonight, she was reluctant to spend an evening with him and her entire family.

When she rang his bell, he opened the door immediately and summoned her inside, but he was talking on the phone. "Five minutes," he mouthed, extending five fingers. "Make yourself comfortable."

Tracy watched him disappear into his bedroom. He was speaking to someone about barricades and construction crews—must be a client. She stood in the living room for a moment, waiting. The room smelled of paint and looked clean and bare. He'd upended a box to use as a telephone stand, but that was the extent of his living-room furniture.

Remembering the table and chairs she'd seen in his kitchen yesterday, Tracy wandered in there. She sat down at the table and smiled at the cookie jar in the middle. When she lifted the lid, the jar mooed. Tracy didn't laugh until she saw the contents. Instead of cookies, the jar held a miscellany of condiment packages, plastic utensils and business cards. She wasn't surprised.

Smiling, she took out one of the cards and read the information for a local construction company. She dropped that one back in and pulled out another. This one had a California address, for a place called Oakland U-Stor-It. Tracy turned the card over. Riley had printed a few words—*ten-by-ten unit, rent due fifteenth*—then a series of numbers and letters that must be a security code.

She dropped the card back into the jar and quickly replaced the lid, as if the contents would boil over without it. Why would he store his things across the country? It would have been better to haul them here.

If he meant to stay.

Tracy frowned. She knew her worry was illogical. He'd started a business, for heaven's sake. She was being silly.

When Riley arrived in the kitchen, Tracy looked up and smiled brightly. "I'm here to call you to dinner."

"Criminy, it's good to see you." He pulled her up into a hug that progressed into a long kiss that felt good, despite the thousand questions in her mind.

"I missed you, too," she said. "But let's keep it cool around my family." She put a hand on her chest, then moved it across to his. "This feels too new to broadcast to them. Especially Hannah. Okay?"

He frowned. "Do you want me to stay home?"

"No. They're expecting you."

During dinner, Tracy nibbled at her food, listening as her family chattered. Riley seemed to fit right in. Of course, he would. Afterward, he played a few rounds of "Jack-slap" with Hannah while Tracy sat on the sofa near them. When Riley let Hannah win for the third time in a row, the little girl shrieked. Riley glanced across at Tracy, catching her smile.

His gaze grew intense. Interested.

She jumped up and went to the kitchen to start on the pile of dishes. She wanted to be alone with him, desperately so, but at the same time she knew she should be cautious.

She wouldn't be able to date Riley until some personality quirk or inexcusable action allowed her to end the relationship. She already knew his frailties, as well as his strengths. She already cared.

He came into the kitchen and picked up a dish towel.

"What are you doing?" she whispered.

He frowned at plates she'd left in the sink. "Drying. Aren't these clean?"

"They're ready to go in the dishwasher."

"Oh." His chuckle was heartbreakingly sweet as he opened the dishwasher and started stacking plates inside.

"I meant, what are you doing here? In Kirkwood?"

"Fixing up Gran's house. Starting a business." He glanced toward the living room, then reached across to drop a kiss on her neck. "Kissing you. What does it seem like I'm doing?"

"I don't know."

His smile turned slightly cockeyed. "It feels clumsy sometimes, doesn't it? You and me together?"

She sighed. "Lord, yes. I think I'm panicking."

His chuckle was short and rather serious.

"Maybe part of the problem is that our families are around all the time, watching," she said. "Are you in the habit of introducing your girlfriends to your family right away?"

"Nope."

"Me neither. With boyfriends. Not this soon." Tracy sighed, wishing she felt more at ease. "Karen is leaving Sunday evening. Can we leave it alone until then?"

He turned to drop a handful of silverware into the dishwasher. "Maybe that would be best."

Tracy returned to rinsing dishes.

"Can I tell you something before we separate?" he asked.

"Yes?" She held her breath.

"I'll never forget last night," he said. "I've never experienced anything like it."

She knew the feeling. She was saved from admitting that to him, though, when her mother came into the kitchen to shoo them away from the sink.

FOR THE NEXT FEW DAYS, Tracy thought a lot about what Riley had said. It was comforting to know that the physical aspect of their relationship was special to him, too.

Even though she was busy constantly with work and her family, waiting out the week was tough. On Friday, she arranged to take a long, early lunch hour, and went straight to Riley's office. She walked in with two lime-ades and a bag of hot dogs, and grinned at Duncan. "I came to see Riley. Is he back there?"

"Uh, no. He's not."

"Is he out with a client?"

Duncan shook his head. "He's out of town. He said he wouldn't be in the office at all today."

Tracy set the bag down for a moment on a light table. She considered asking Duncan if he knew exactly where Riley had gone, but she knew it was none of her business and she didn't want to embarrass Riley.

"Oh, well. I knew I was taking a chance," she said, still smiling. "Guess I'll catch up with him later."

When she arrived back at Vanderveer's, Tracy dumped the hot dogs into the trash and drank both lime-ades. Then she ran through a list of reasons she shouldn't be upset.

He could be anywhere. She'd asked him to wait until Sunday. She couldn't expect him to wait around in case she decided to drop by.

It had been foolish to drop by.

Still, his unexplained absence brought back a lot of memories. He might not have slept with Karen all those years ago, but he'd left without saying goodbye to her, Tracy. They were supposed to have been good friends, but he hadn't confided in her. He'd abandoned her.

And now she felt the most secure with him when they were involved physically.

Kissing. Hugging. Making love.

During those times, she knew he was occupied with her.

That evening, the Gilbert family met at Tiers, the restaurant on the lake. Tracy forced herself to stay out until Hannah's bedtime. When she turned the corner onto her street, Hannah said, "Your big Wiley's here!"

Tracy looked. Sure enough, Riley's motorcycle was parked beyond the edge of her driveway.

She pulled into her driveway and saw him on her front porch with Nellie beside him, prattling in his ear. He gave Tracy a smile that lit his entire face. It was hard to remember her fears under the warmth of that welcome.

As Tracy approached the front door, Nellie began, "I came out to tell your visitor that you were gone, but he insisted on waiting. I'd have let him inside if I still had the key."

Tracy was glad she'd collected it.

"I was telling him about my friend Ruth," Nellie said. "She moved here from Florida six years ago. She's settled in, but she goes back every year to see the ocean. And to see her nieces and nephews, of course."

Riley raised his eyebrows. "We have been chatting a while," he muttered. And that was all he needed to say. Tracy recognized the appeal for a rescue.

"Good to see you, Mr. Collins," Tracy said, pulling his hand into a handshake. "Did you have a question about the consultation? Let's go inside to discuss it."

Nellie made some sort of clucking noise. "I'd have bet dollars to doughnuts you'd be calling him Riley," she said. "Besides, you told me the job was finished."

"As long as the client has questions, Vanderveer's is willing to answer," Tracy said.

"You aren't sleeping together?"

Tracy looked at Riley, who was looking at her. Then

Hannah's laugh burst out from beside the porch, where she'd been continuing her perpetual quest for pill bugs. "Mama and big Wiley are *fwends*," she said as she bounded onto the porch. "But boys and girls can't sleep over."

Even Nellie wouldn't argue with a four-year-old child. She let the subject rest.

A while later, Tracy had tucked Hannah and Violet Plumtree into bed. She found Riley on her living-room sofa, sipping beer from the can she'd offered him earlier.

"You came by the office?" he asked as soon as she entered the room and sat down in the chair across from him.

She nodded. "Just to say hi."

"Still panicking?"

"Maybe. Our being together on a continual basis is sort of a big deal, isn't it?"

His eyes turned dark. "A very big deal." He paused to take a drink. "I meant to start slow. We slipped, but things don't have to get complicated yet."

"When you weren't at your office today, I worried."

"I went to see Otto."

"At the prison?"

"Yeah. Sunday's Father's Day. Since I'm within a few hours' drive from Leavenworth now, I decided to go see him. I didn't know what time your sister was leaving Sunday, and I thought you might be available, so..." He shrugged.

He'd gone to see his dad a few days early so he might be available for her. Tracy's face felt hot. "Sunday night," she said. "Karen's leaving late Sunday night."

"Oh."

"How is Otto?"

"Fine. Older. Quieter. We had a decent chat."

Tracy nodded, trying to ignore the fullness behind her eyes. Her feelings seemed stronger than they should be. She felt like an idiot for caring so deeply, but Riley made reluctance difficult. She wanted to love him.

He frowned. "I've been thinking about you. About your panic. Why do you always try to figure out every possible failure before you try something?"

Tracy shrugged.

Riley chuckled. "Remember that time we rode our bikes down the big hill in the woods?"

She nodded.

"I didn't have any trouble getting you to the top of the hill with me," he continued, "but you sure didn't want to go down once you got up there."

Tracy took up the telling of the story. "You had to give me a nudge. After we crashed, you consoled me about my skinned knees even though you had a broken arm."

"That's right."

Tracy knew why he had reminded her of the incident. "Don't you feel pain?" she asked.

He shook his head. "That isn't it. You concentrate on the pain. I concentrate on what we've done."

"Which is?"

"Back then, we became legends. All the kids talked about riding down that hill. We were the first to do it."

"And now?"

For a moment, Riley seemed to wrestle with the question. "We deepened the connection with someone we care about," he finally said. "It was a daring move, but a good one."

"Mama, my music stopped," Hannah called out from her bedroom. "I need a dwink."

Tracy stood up and looked at Riley. "I'll be busy with Hannah a while tonight," she explained. "And with my family this weekend. I'll call you Monday, after Karen leaves."

ON MONDAY MORNING, after marking a change to his set of plans, Riley dropped his pencil and strode across to pick up the phone before it rang a second time. "Collins Engineering."

"You're answering your own phone?"

It was Tracy! Blood circulated so furiously through Riley's veins that he felt like some charged-up superhero. "You rang my private line," he said.

"Oh. Well. How are you?"

Criminy. Her voice had a musical tone. He didn't know how to interpret that. "Surviving."

"I can take a long lunch today," she said. "Interested?"

He looked at the clock on his desk. Two hours until lunchtime. He could handle that. "Absolutely."

"Meet me at my apartment. Noon."

The click and buzz of the disconnecting phone line was startling. Riley pulled the receiver away from his ear and stared at it, wondering if they'd been cut off. He didn't know whether he should show up with lunch or expect her to provide it. But he let it go. The ball was in her court.

One hour and fifty-three excruciatingly long minutes later, Riley stepped onto Tracy's front porch, empty-handed and prepared for anything. He rang the doorbell once, but she didn't answer. The inner door was ajar, so he opened the screen and peered inside. "I'm here."

Claus sat up in the windowsill to look at him, but Tracy didn't call out a response.

Riley went on in, wondering if she was in the kitchen making lunch. When the cat jumped to the floor, it pulled Riley's attention to the paprika-colored jacket draped over the back of the rocking chair.

The cat skittered through the living room, drawing Riley's gaze to the matching skirt folded on one end of the sofa. Black heels were lined up neatly against the wall nearby, and a white ruffled shirt dangled from a floor lamp in the hall's entry.

Smiling, Riley followed the trail. He chuckled when he rounded the corner and noted that her coordinating lingerie seemed to have been dropped at even intervals, ending at her bedroom door.

Even when she staged a seduction, Tracy was organized.

He stopped grinning when he rounded the corner and found her waiting in bed wearing nothing but nail polish. With the bend of one orange-tipped finger, she summoned him. And spent the next hour proving that she was incredible, even when she wasn't tidy.

Just before they returned to their respective offices, they ate crackers and sliced cheddar cheese at Tracy's kitchen table. They met there again for dinner with Hannah. Cod fillets and quick-fix biscuits with jam were followed by a game of Candyland with Hannah. A trip to the recreation center for the little girl's gymnastics class rounded out the evening.

Claiming she needed to give Hannah a bath and read her a bedtime story, Tracy said good-night at her front door. Riley gave her one lightning-quick kiss under the porch light and returned to his own house. The long-awaited discussion had never taken place, but since he and Tracy had been naked or busy with Hannah almost every minute, the omission was understandable.

Tracy still had control. He wouldn't push.

On Tuesday, Riley invited Tracy to lunch at a deli near her office. He spent the first minutes alternately smiling and grimacing across the table as Tracy snaked her bare foot up his pant leg. When the food arrived, Tracy dug into her mushroom tart with the same lusty attitude. She jabbered about work and Hannah, and must have repeated at least five times that her food tasted delicious.

Riley agreed. The lunch was great—but the kiss in his car afterward was even better. It went on for half an hour, making both of them late back to work. And making Riley wish he'd arranged for a more private meeting.

This brave new temptress was wonderfully adventurous in the bedroom, but she avoided talking about anything of consequence. Tracy seemed to have compartmentalized herself into a racy lunch date during daytime hours and a devoted mother at night. Neither one seemed quite right.

Sexy phone invitations, decadent lunch hours and busy evenings with Hannah passed the week, and on Friday at noon, they met at Tracy's place. Without ringing the doorbell, Riley let himself in and locked the door behind him. This time, he didn't need the cat to lead the way. Tracy called out to him, loud and clear.

He was surprised when he found her, though. If he'd had thoughts of talking or sitting down to lunch, Tracy's invitation to her shower would have changed his mind.

Friday's lunch meeting was possibly the most erotic. He returned to work with damp hair and a smile on his face, and didn't remember until late afternoon that they'd forgotten about food entirely. An apple took care of his physical hunger, but his gut still felt hollow.

It seemed funny that he could be enjoying the best

sex of his life with a woman he adored and still feel it wasn't enough. He missed the real Tracy. His ex-girlfriends would probably laugh to hear it, but he craved an emotional bond.

The physical relationships of his past had often ended quickly, and with few regrets. He didn't want that to happen this time. If Tracy felt the same lack in their relationship he did, she might assume it wasn't working and give up.

He knew their time together could be more than it was. He didn't want to shove Tracy down the hill, but something needed to change. Instead of heading straight to Tracy's house after work, Riley decided to keep his standing Friday-night date with his grandmother. He figured if he and Tracy spent an evening missing each other, it might encourage a meaningful discussion the next time they met.

Also, he needed to ask Lydia for another baby-sitting favor. Hannah was a great kid, but Riley was beginning to realize that he and Tracy needed to be alone together for more than an hour at a time.

Lydia embraced the idea. Despite her comment about weekend mornings and waffle irons, she seemed genuinely pleased with the prospect of spending more time with Hannah. She offered to take the little girl to the zoo on Saturday morning, said she'd even call Tracy to set it up.

A morning instead of an hour might be a minor change, but it would allow for some time away from the bedroom. He and Tracy should have plenty of time to talk.

Chapter Fourteen

When Tracy answered her door Saturday morning, Riley was encouraged by her long brown skirt and walking shoes. She was dressed to go out. He envisioned a lazy stroll through a park or a mall, perhaps some lighthearted conversation followed by a kiss fit for public viewing. Maybe even a few confessions of tender regard on both sides. Nothing too forward, but progress, nevertheless.

He and Lydia had just stepped through the doorway when Hannah skipped into the room in a yellow sundress. "Hi, Nana Lydia," she said. "Are we goin' to the *Beast?*"

Lydia smiled. "No, but I called your mother to arrange a trip to the zoo. Would you like to see some other kinds of beasts?"

Hannah was ready with her customary pleading, but it wasn't necessary.

Tracy kissed Hannah goodbye, offered Lydia money for souvenirs and snacks, which Lydia refused, and watched them leave. Then she turned to Riley. "When I saw you drive up, I thought you were planning to go to the zoo with them." She smiled teasingly. "I guess not."

Riley had surprised Tracy with this visit because he'd

wanted to put her a little off balance and keep her from donning the role of seductress. He was hoping to get to the real Tracy Gilbert. He smiled back. "I was hoping we could spend the morning together."

"Were you really?" Tracy's glance seemed shrewd.

"I don't see why we shouldn't," he said.

"Okay." She grabbed her purse from a table near the door. "But we ought to get going."

"You have plans?"

"It's Saturday morning. Of course I have plans," Tracy said. "But you're welcome to join me."

Riley followed her out to the porch. "Mind if I ask where we're headed?"

"Not at all. There's a three-bedroom house for sale a couple of blocks over. I've arranged to see it." When she turned around to smile at him, Riley recognized the old Tracy, a woman right on stride and ready to tackle the world.

He was glad. Tracy would be easier to talk to when she was acting normally. And since he was adaptable, it didn't matter where they went. "I'm blocking your car in the garage, aren't I?" he said. "I'll drive if you'll direct."

As if magically summoned, a blue sedan pulled up in the driveway, blocking Riley's car. A well-dressed older woman got out and smiled at Tracy, who was walking toward her.

"I see you're ready," the woman said as they shook hands.

"I am," Tracy said. She turned to introduce Riley as her friend, and the woman as her Realtor. Both women got in the front seat of the sedan, leaving the back to him.

Riley climbed in and kept quiet. His plan for the day

might have changed, but he thought he could nudge the idea around to make it work. And having an extra person around might work to his advantage.

All the way to the house, Tracy and the Realtor discussed the benefits of moving to a place within the same school district. When they arrived, the women got out of the car and stood in the yard talking about the covered porch on a small yellow house with green trim.

Riley got out, too. He noted the nice-sized yard and chimney, which were pluses; and the one-car garage, which wasn't. He wondered if Tracy had ever thought about the two of them sharing a house. He sure had.

But Tracy might consider *his* listing of criteria for a house too pushy. And he knew she wouldn't want him to mention their moving in together in front of the Realtor. He'd have to hint.

The Realtor led them into the house and talked about how the vaulted ceiling opened up the entryway. In the living room, she mentioned new carpeting, big windows and the nice fireplace and mantel. She asked Tracy to meet her in the kitchen next and disappeared through a doorway.

The privacy made Riley's task easier. "This is my favorite feature in this room," he told Tracy as he took her hand and led her toward the fireplace.

"It's mine, too," Tracy said.

"Think of a snowy day with everyone bundled in layers," he said, squeezing her hand. "But the fire's burning hot enough to make clothes optional next to the hearth. Can you picture that?"

Tracy pulled her hand away. "Yes, I can," she said with a sweet smile. "School is canceled because of the snow, and Hannah asks at least a dozen times if we can build a snowman. I take her outside. The fire dies." Before Tracy followed the Realtor, she whispered, "So you see? An absence of clothes was never an option."

Riley frowned at the hearth. He should have thought to include Hannah in the scenario, but the omission would be easy enough to fix.

By the time Riley caught up to Tracy, the Realtor was praising the large kitchen. Tracy made a comment about pantry space, and Riley joined in to point out that there was plenty of room for a family-size table.

"That's good," Tracy said. "Hannah likes to play with clay. She could get out her cookie cutters and have a ball."

There was nothing at all hintable about the first bedroom down the hall—Tracy declared that one perfect for Hannah—but the second room was decorated with blue molding and yellow-chick wallpaper. The implication was obvious.

Tracy squeezed into the small room beside the other woman. Riley squeezed in beside Tracy. "This could be used as an office or playroom," the Realtor said.

"Or a guest bedroom," Tracy added.

Riley frowned. Had they missed the chicks? "Or it could stay intact as a baby's nursery."

The Realtor smiled at him, but Tracy laughed. "Maybe, but I could actually *use* a guest bedroom."

After they'd all trooped down to look at the master bedroom at the end of the hall, Riley heard the older woman say that it was large enough for a king-size bed. Since the Realtor seemed to be taking up his cause on her own, Riley didn't comment. Tracy could make her own inferences about a big bed.

"Are you two engaged?" the Realtor asked.

Tracy turned to look at him.

He looked back at her, rejecting the impulse to drop to one knee and ask. Absolutely too pushy.

Criminy. He couldn't believe he'd even thought it.

"No," Tracy answered in a composed voice.

"Rats! I thought this might be the selling point," the woman said with a chuckle. She opened one of several doors at the north edge of the room and stepped back.

The bathroom was enormous, with a huge whirlpool tub encased in a gray-tiled platform. Riley stood next to Tracy in the doorway and tried not to think what he was thinking.

Tracy was silent.

When Riley realized the Realtor was behind them, he nudged Tracy. They both turned around and listened as the woman suggested visiting other properties.

"Not today," Tracy interjected. "My daughter is due home soon and I need to be there. But I like this house. Would you run the figures for me? Down payment and monthly mortgage amounts?"

"Sure," the Realtor said. "I'll take you home and call you by early afternoon."

Riley frowned. Tracy seemed serious about purchasing this house on her own—another life-changing and deliberate choice made by a woman who was in the habit of thinking things through.

She wasn't dreaming about sharing her life with him for the next fifteen- or thirty-year mortgage term.

She was thinking single, and that hurt.

Riley hadn't figured out every detail, but he knew he wanted more for both of them. He wanted to share a garage, a hearth, even snowman-building duties.

It seemed too late for hints.

"We'll walk," Riley said in a voice so commanding that both women turned to look.

But Tracy waited for the Realtor to get in her car and leave before she complained. "Why did you do that?"

"It's only a mile and the weather is nice," he said as they headed down the sidewalk. "Let's get some exercise."

Tracy didn't argue. She started walking at a brisk pace, her arms pumping and her hair bouncing.

"What are you doing?" he shouted after her as a gap widened between them.

"Getting some exercise," she shouted back.

He caught up to her, but after half a block she plopped down on the sidewalk and started messing with her shoes.

"What are you doing now?"

"Taking off my shoes. My feet hurt."

He knelt beside her and offered a hand to help her up. But when she started to walk away in bare feet, he stopped her. "What I'd really like to know is what you've been doing all week. Why aren't we talking?"

She held his gaze. "I'm doing exactly what you asked."

"Which is?"

"Going down the hill without thinking."

"But you're riding the brakes and your eyes are squeezed shut," he said. "You can't enjoy the ride if you anticipate the crash."

She nodded and started walking at a slower pace.

"Tracy. I—"

"I'm doing my best," Tracy interrupted, already two yards ahead. "We're together, right?"

"Right." Riley caught up to her, but didn't finish what he'd been about to say.

Hinting about a future together was one thing, but he'd been about to tell Tracy he loved her.

Love. The word sounded almost foreign. He'd used it before, on women besides his mom and grandmother, but those women had known what he meant. They'd often repeated it back with the same intent.

I love you, they'd all said. They'd meant, *I like and desire you enough to stick around a while.*

Tracy would perceive the word differently. If he told her he loved her, he needed to mean it in the deepest and most permanent way. He needed to be certain.

For now, he could accept what Tracy offered. She would eventually grow tired of organizing every minute and every response. Hopefully, she'd relax into the relationship and allow him to become more than a lunchtime lover and evening sidekick. Then they could figure out the rest. Together.

INDEPENDENCE DAY could get crazy in Kirkwood. College students, stuck in town for jobs or classes, were anxious for the freedom of summer. In one night of timehonored revelry, they could cause a lot of expensive commotion.

Since her parents had always been active in civic groups, Tracy had grown up hearing the stories. Poorly aimed Roman candles and drunken brawls increased the number of emergency-room visits by half. Police and fire departments grew accustomed to dealing with late-night explosions and the subsequent phone complaints. Even the city and county crews had to devote extra personhours to cleaning up the countless beer cans and blownout firecracker wrappings.

A few parties were to be expected in a college town. Nevertheless, eight years ago, local authorities had banded together to organize a more controlled celebration. The Kirkwood Days festival, held annually now at the lake, had been their solution. Since Tracy was participating as a businesswoman this year, she was privy to the current town leaders' goals: plan creative events that tap into trends; keep booths appropriately patriotic, but make them fun; draw kids of every age out to the lake and keep the risks contained. Tracy hoped the Bachelors Picnic Raffle she'd planned with the help of the sorority girls would be a favorite of the bigwigs and the students.

"Mama, can I get a puwple heart on my face?" Hannah asked as they passed two young boys sporting face paint and toothless smiles.

"You may," Tracy said with a smile, "but I need to get back to the pavilion now. Riley said he'd meet us there. I'm sure he'll take you."

When Tracy had arrived at the park three hours early to set things up, the five young sorority women she'd met at the coffee shop were waiting to sell tickets. At Tracy's suggestion, the girls had dressed in red or blue shorts and tees and tall Uncle Sam hats—a ploy for the attention of passersby. Normally, Tracy would have donned a similar outfit and stuck around to help, but she hadn't liked the thought of abandoning her daughter on a holiday. She couldn't neglect Hannah for her job.

When Riley had offered to care for Hannah during the actual raffle, bringing her along had become workable. So Tracy had charged Jennifer, the most vocal of the sorority girls, with temporary responsibility for the event. Tracy had taken Hannah out to enjoy the carnival rides and games until time for the presentation.

After watching Hannah ride a pony and taste her first mouthful of cotton candy, Tracy knew she'd done the right thing. The buoyant mood of the other festival attendees had been infectious. Upbeat music played by local school bands caused many of the festival-goers to walk in time to the music and smile at strangers who were doing the same thing. From the looks of things, the celebration would be a great success. Tracy was as excited as Hannah.

Nevertheless, as Tracy returned to Pavilion Two and saw the gathering of people who had filled fifty folding chairs and were also milling around the basket tables, her heartbeat seemed to drown out the music. For the first time in a long time, she was tempted to gnaw at her nails.

Although public speaking was an occasional requirement of her job, it wasn't her favorite. She was a nervous speaker.

Riley stepped out of the crowd and walked toward them. "There you two are," he said as he swung Hannah up into one arm and slid the other around Tracy. "Did you have a good time this morning?"

"I wode a horse with a pink heart on its saddle!" Hannah said. "I want a puwple one."

"Let me get this straight," Riley said. "Do you want a purple horse or a purple saddle?"

Hannah rested a palm against each of Riley's cheeks, as if ensuring that he was paying careful attention. "No, silly. I want a puwple heart on my face. Mama said you'd let me."

"I will," he said. Before he left, Riley pulled Tracy closer. "You okay?" he murmured against her ear.

Tracy chuckled at her body's response. After two weeks of kiss-crazed lunch dates, she was growing used to hearing that sexy voice from way up close. It never failed to thrill her. "I'm fine," she said. "Thanks for watching Hannah."

"No problem."

After Tracy gave her daughter a few last-minute reminders about proper public behavior, she watched Riley walk into the throng with Hannah grinning over his shoulder.

Those broad shoulders belonged to the hunkiest bachelor around, and Tracy didn't have to buy a ticket to win a chance for a date. She had one, anytime she wished.

She felt very grown-up. Riley was the first man she'd actually thought of as a lover. Not a boyfriend, but a lover.

But now it was time to do her job. Turning around, Tracy entered the pavilion. This morning, she'd arranged twenty-three picnic baskets on two rows of tables. Near each basket was a slotted box with a bachelor's photograph attached.

The fraternity men had been creative. Their offerings ranged from a humongous insulated basket smelling of fried chicken, to a cute pink Easter bucket containing two peanut-butter-and-jelly sandwiches in plastic bags. Since that one's creator resembled a young Mel Gibson, Tracy suspected the corresponding box would be full of tickets.

Hopeful women had stood in line to buy tickets all morning, and the sorority sisters had taken in more than seven hundred dollars. Tracy accepted the heavy bank bag from Jennifer and stepped up to the front, depositing the bag on the podium shelf as she tested the microphone.

The audience quieted immediately and turned almost as one to face the front. Tracy noted that the bachelors themselves were scattered throughout the tent. She recognized some of them from their pictures, but the anxious looks the men directed out at the women made their identities obvious.

Tracy introduced herself and the college groups, and after a round of polite applause, the fun began. One by one, the sorority women brought a basket and a box to the podium. One by one, Tracy drew a name to send a lucky female winner off for an hour-long picnic with a fraternity man.

The audience laughed when Mrs. Eunice Harris, who looked at least ninety years old, won the romantic wine-and-cheese basket of a young blond swim-team captain with brown bedroom eyes. The young man wore a huge smile as he broke into the crowd of women to take the woman's arm and escort her away. Tracy awarded them the title of Most Odd Couple.

The Couple Most Likely to Extend Lunch designation went to a voluptuous redhead and a curly-haired linebacker. The redhead jumped up and batted her eyes as her guy approached; the bachelor's grin made his delight obvious.

By the time Tracy had doled out the twenty-three baskets on her list, her mouth was dry and she'd stuttered a few times, but the audience had seemed interested and amused all the way through. Things had gone well.

"There's one left," someone hollered as Tracy began to thank the college students again. Tracy glanced at the bottom entry on her list to make sure she hadn't missed one, and then out at the tables.

A wicker basket lined with red, white and blue tissue paper was perched prettily at the edge of the last table. It looked legitimate, but there was no slotted box nearby. "I don't know about that one," Tracy said. "Anyone claim it?"

No one answered, so Tracy asked Jennifer to bring it to the front. Frowning when she read the note taped to one side, Tracy said, "This is *my* name."

Laughter rippled through the audience.

As Tracy examined the box, she noticed a string of tickets tucked along the edge. "There must be fifty dollars' worth of tickets here," she said, pulling them out.

"Draw one!" someone shouted from the back.

The voice sounded familiar. Glancing out at the audience, Tracy noticed Lydia standing in the back sporting a big smile. Riley stood empty-shouldered beside her. Tracy squinted toward him, searching for Hannah, and decided her daughter must be between him and his grandmother but hidden behind the crowd.

"Draw a ticket!" a bald man in front repeated.

"I'm willing to do my part for the Family Aid Center," Tracy said, smiling as she named the sororities' and fraternities' chosen charity, "but someone else should draw the winner."

The bald man stepped forward and made a show of spreading the tickets print down on a table. He plucked one from the bunch and read, "Riley Collins." Tracy squinted out toward Lydia again. She'd bet every one of those tickets had Riley's name printed on it, in his grandmother's handwriting.

Riley leaned down to say something to Lydia, then walked up the center aisle to the podium. With an apologetic smile, he took the microphone from its stand. "My grandmother has a great sense of humor," he said to the audience. "If no one minds, I'd like to speak with your announcer."

He turned to Tracy and said, "I know this wasn't planned, but I'll donate an extra three hundred dollars if you'll share a picnic with me."

Several gasps sounded from the audience.

Since Tracy had shared lunch with Riley every day for two weeks, his contribution was generous. Between grandson and grandmother, Tracy never knew what to expect.

Smiling into Riley's eyes, Tracy took the microphone and allowed her hand to rest against his long enough to communicate her thanks.

She turned toward the front, but before she could speak, someone hollered that she and Riley were the Couple Most Likely to Cause a Small Grassfire on the festival grounds. Another voice said they were the Couple Most Likely to Push a Baby Stroller through next year's carnival tents.

After that comment, people actually clapped. "It's settled," Tracy said, ignoring the hecklers. "I'm having lunch with Mr. Collins, and his contribution will bring the amount donated to over a thousand dollars! Thanks for attending, and enjoy the rest of the festival."

As the audience filed out of the tent, Tracy was glad the event was over. The ending might have been a crowd pleaser, but it had frazzled her nerves considerably.

"You did a great job," Riley said from beside her.

Tracy shook her head. "Booker lectured me about representing Vanderveer's in a businesslike manner."

"You were very professional," Riley said. "Don't worry."

Tracy told the sorority girls she could handle cleanup after her picnic and sent them off to enjoy the afternoon. Seconds later, Tracy and Riley sat in two of the empty folding chairs with the wicker basket on the ground between them. "Looks like some kind of sandwiches," Riley muttered as he handed Tracy one of two foil-wrapped packages.

Tracy unfolded a corner and wrinkled her nose at the contents. The stench was horrendous.

"Don't eat that!" Riley said abruptly. He grabbed her

package and tossed both into a trash can a couple of yards away.

"What were they?" Tracy asked.

"Sardines on pumpernickel," Riley said. "Gran loves them, but the heat must have got to them today."

Tracy tittered. "Remember when Lydia sent you on a field trip with a can of meat and her homemade applesauce?"

"I do," Riley said. "On the way home that day, you gave me your leftover cookie and your sister donated an orange."

Nodding, Tracy realized the competition for Riley's attention might have started early, although she hadn't been aware of it then. She'd never have dreamed she'd someday be Riley's lover.

"What else is there?" Tracy asked, peering at the basket curiously. Lydia's meals could be an adventure.

Riley pulled out a glass drink container and unscrewed the lid to smell the contents. "Good for her," he said.

"What is it?"

He handed the container across. "Wine, I think."

Tracy took a sip and grimaced. "She might have been trying to make a spritzer. I'm not sure."

After scrounging some dried apricots from a mixture also including stale peanuts and melted chocolate chips, Tracy and Riley were both chuckling again. "Gran might be the worst cook in a hundred miles," Riley said, "but her heart's in the right place."

Tracy smiled as she bit into an apricot. Lydia's intentions were always big-hearted. Despite the often strange results, Tracy appreciated that the lady made an effort. She even took Hannah when—

Hannah. Where was Hannah? Tracy focused on the vanishing crowd. Lydia was walking toward the carnival area behind the sorority girls—and she was very much alone.

Chapter Fifteen

"Oh! I meant to tell you," Riley said when Tracy turned a panicked gaze to him and asked if he knew where her daughter was. "Remember Duncan, from my office?"

Tracy swallowed a heavy lump of the fruit and shook her head in confusion. "Of course."

"I ran into him at the face-painting booth," Riley said calmly. "His wife and kids were with him, and Hannah knew the youngest boy from day care. Joshua invited Hannah to his grandparents' house on the other side of the lake."

Tracy frowned. "What for?"

"To play." Riley's smile was teasing.

Tracy looked sharply at him. "And you let her go?"

Riley shrugged. "Hannah had already seen most of the festival booths and was begging to go," he said. "I didn't think it would hurt to allow it."

"But I don't really know Duncan or his family!"

"Sorry," Riley said. "Lydia had asked me to meet her here at one-thirty, so it seemed like a good solution."

Tracy stood up and tossed her handful of apricots into the trash can. Slapping her hands together to brush away the crumbs, she said, "Where's the house? I'll go now."

"I don't have the address," Riley said, stretching his

hand across the space to grasp hers. "She's okay, Tracy."

Tracy pulled her hand away. "What's the last name?"

Riley stood, too. "I don't know," he said as he began to gather trash. "It's Duncan's wife's parents."

Tracy knew she shouldn't be surprised. Riley had always been a risk taker. "Hannah is four years old," she said. "I can't believe you didn't think to ask her mother if she could go to a stranger's house."

"Duncan isn't a stranger to me, and he said he would return Hannah to this pavilion in two hours," Riley explained. "I figured you would be busy finishing the event and packing up. I was planning to help you, and I knew Hannah would have more fun with her friend."

"She's *my* daughter," Tracy said hotly. "She means little to you. You should have asked."

"She means the world to me. I'm falling more in love with both of you every day." Riley paused as if astonished by his own statement, but added softly, "You know that."

Tracy thought his choice to tell her that now was almost as audacious as his choice to let Hannah go. She couldn't respond to a man's romantic claims when her daughter was missing due to the same man's negligence.

When she scowled at him, he frowned and shook his head. She realized his admission couldn't have been easy, but she had more important things to worry about.

Figuring it would be best to ignore him, Tracy folded two chairs, slipped them under her arms and started across the grass toward the van she'd rented. Her stomach felt like a massive tangle of worry, anger, embarrassment and guilt, and she knew she wouldn't feel all right until Hannah's return.

Soon Tracy became aware of Riley passing her on the

path to and from the van. He was helping her load. Since he was making an effort to stay out of her way, she didn't stop him or acknowledge him. And as they worked in silence, the bands played on. Each new song upset Tracy more. The drumbeat kept knocking away pieces of the afternoon, and her daughter wasn't back.

"I'll vouch for Duncan and his family," Riley said once when Tracy jumped down from the van and he was nearby.

"It's obvious you aren't a dad," Tracy said.

With his arms full of chairs, Riley stepped in front of her. "Maybe not," he said somberly, "but I'd never put Hannah in jeopardy."

When Riley loaded the last item, though, Hannah was still missing. Tracy stood behind him, seething even as she watched his muscles bulge from the weight of the podium. "My daughter is not here yet," she said.

Riley jumped down and closed the van's doors. "I know."

Tracy crossed her arms in front of her. "I'd hoped to return the van by three," she said. "And Hannah needs a nap if she's going to stay up and watch the fireworks tonight."

"Sorry," Riley repeated as they made their way back to the pavilion. "I'm sure they'll be here any minute."

"You shouldn't have made that decision."

"Believe me, I know that now." Riley's clear enunciation indicated his patience was wearing thin, but he softened his comment by adding, "If it helps, Duncan's wife seems very caring."

"I'm glad you think so. *I've* never met her," Tracy said as she sat at one of the picnic tables to wait.

Riley sat down across from her. "Trust me, Hannah

is okay. Duncan's the kind of dad who thinks the world of his kids. He talks about them every day.''

''I'm glad you think so,'' Tracy repeated.

''Criminy, I don't think I've ever seen you this upset.''

''You've never lost my daughter before.''

''Tracy—''

''Hi, Mama! Hi, big Wiley!'' Tugging at the sleeve of a freckle-faced boy, Hannah weaved through the crowd toward them. ''I jumped on a twampline and petted a belly-pot pig!''

''You did?'' Tracy swung Hannah up into a hug. Since she'd read newspaper reports about trampoline injuries, she felt slightly justified in her worry. She moved Hannah to one hip and smiled at Joshua and Duncan, thanking them both for inviting her daughter to visit.

She didn't look at Riley, and she couldn't bring herself to speak to him. After she'd talked to Duncan and his son for a few minutes, Tracy said goodbye and left with Hannah. She felt strange as she walked away, as if she'd discovered herself naked in front of an audience and was trying to hold her head high and pretend she was clothed.

It was her job to protect her daughter, but today's events had disturbed her deeply. And she wasn't relieved now that Hannah was safe.

Thinking her sense of unrest might stem from an accumulation of unfinished chores, Tracy got on with her plans for the afternoon. She returned the chairs and podium to Matthew's department at the university, then drove out to the airport to return the van. By the time she got Hannah home, it was late afternoon and the little girl seemed too excited to settle down for a nap. Tracy allowed her to stretch out on the sofa to watch a favorite video.

She still didn't feel ready to talk to Riley, but she wondered what he was doing. This was the first non-working afternoon they would spend apart since they'd gotten together.

And maybe that was the problem. She'd let the relationship go too far, too fast. As much as she cared about him, Riley didn't fit her life. He was impetuous and wild, and he encouraged Tracy to do things a single mother shouldn't do. Today he'd even put Hannah at risk.

Maybe it was time for Tracy to open her eyes to see whether she'd reached the bottom of the hill.

In the next two hours, she finished four loads of laundry and all her evening paperwork. She even scrubbed the kitchen floor, usually a failproof mood lifter. But the uneasy feeling had settled around her. By the time Hannah's movie had reached its happy conclusion, Tracy knew she was going to have to get on with her evening, too.

The festival's grand finale included fireworks, and Tracy's parents had a clear view of the aerial displays from their patio. Weeks ago, they'd asked Tracy and Hannah to join them. Tracy had subsequently invited Riley, and it seemed too late to cancel. Since she hadn't heard from him, she didn't know if he would show up, anyway.

After a hamburger dinner with Hannah, Tracy had cleaned up the kitchen and looked at the clock, knowing it would seem like a long wait until dusk. She'd given Hannah a pail of water and an old paintbrush to pretend-paint the backyard fence. As Tracy'd watched from the back-porch stoop, she'd pretended, too. That she wasn't listening for the doorbell chime or the phone's ring or

Riley's voice from around the corner of the house. That she didn't miss him.

Now she was alone in her parents' backyard garden while her family played cards inside. Hannah didn't like the cannonball explosions signaling the beginning of the fireworks display, so Tracy had promised to wait until the aerial show began to get her family.

But instead of watching the sky over the lake, she watched Riley's doors and windows. Three successive booms signaled the start of the show, and Tracy's heart sank deeper with each one.

Apparently, Riley wasn't coming.

Dutifully, she got up and padded into the house to get her family. But her parents were playing cards at their dining-room table, alone. "Where's Hannah?" Tracy asked.

"She fell asleep on the sofa," her mother said. "We thought it'd be best to leave her."

"Right," Tracy said. "I'll take her home now."

"Don't run off," Matthew said. "Hannah can sleep and you can celebrate with us."

"I'm not in the mood," Tracy said. When her parents frowned, she picked up her shoes from near the patio door. "There'll be fireworks next year. I'm going out to start the car. I'll come back to get Hannah."

Her mother flipped on the front-porch light and followed Tracy out. "Are you okay, love?"

Tracy faked a yawn as she opened her car door. "It's been a long day and I'm tired," she said. Tossing her shoes in the passenger seat, she couldn't help stealing a glance at Riley's front windows.

Her mother looked over there, too. "Go talk to him."

Tracy frowned, ready to deny any genuine interest in Riley or his whereabouts. But two blasts interrupted, and were followed by twin sprays of blue and silver that lit the northern sky. As the ashes drifted down, Tracy finally said, "I need to get Hannah home to bed."

"She'll be cranky if you wake her," her mother warned. "Didn't you say you have a day off work tomorrow?"

"Yes, in compensation for working on the holiday."

"It won't hurt to let her stay."

Tracy was tempted. "Are you sure?"

"I'm sure," her mother said, smiling. "I'm going to go inside and beat my guy at gin rummy while we watch fireworks through the patio door. You can make amends with your guy or go on home. I'll see you tomorrow morning."

Tracy watched her mother disappear inside. The porch light extinguished, then a series of bursts fired in quick succession between the two houses. If some cosmic force was trying to help Tracy decide what to do, she wasn't understanding the message. She tossed her keys from hand to hand and looked at the windows next door. Riley's living room was dark, but his bedroom was lit. He must be there.

Since he hadn't come over, it should be a cannonball signal for Tracy to go home.

But with Hannah asleep, tonight would provide a good opportunity to talk to him. She owed him that, didn't she? Except she wasn't in the mood to talk. It occurred to Tracy that she'd never spent a night alone with Riley. And that one more night couldn't change much in the scheme of things.

Finally, while the night sky was illuminated by a brilliant gold display, Tracy slammed the car door, shoved her keys into her pocket and headed across the lawn.

CRIMINY. Tracy was at the door. Her silhouette was unmistakable through the peephole, and she was waving as if she knew he was watching. Much to his disgust, he'd been watching all night. She'd sat out in her parents' dark yard facing his house, then she'd gone inside and back out the front with her mother.

He'd let go of the window slat he'd been peeking through, thinking she'd go home. After today, it seemed apparent that he and Tracy weren't aiming for the same goal. She didn't want a deeper connection.

At least, not with him.

He'd been certain she would avoid him until she found the courage to end the whole shebang, but she was here now and he wasn't ready. He should have headed for the back roads on his bike tonight. Or turned out all the lights and stuffed cotton in his ears. Or talked to Tracy earlier, when daylight would have made things easier.

Flipping on the porch light, he yanked open the door and was stunned by the flirty tilt of her head. She didn't seem ready to call things off. Hers was the look of a woman who wanted—

"Hi there," she said, sweeping her gaze from his bare chest to his cotton sleep shorts. "Did you know it's a special day in Kirkwood?"

He scowled.

She smiled. "In fact, there are parties going on all across America. Why are you in bed?"

"It seemed as good a place as any."

"It does," she agreed, sliding past him and through the door. She tossed her keys on the cushion of his brand-new recliner and walked toward his bedroom, removing her top on the way.

He followed her, but stopped in the hallway and

watched as she sat on the end of his bed—he'd finally bought a frame and headboard. "Where's Hannah?" he asked, trying to ignore the radiance of Tracy's breasts when she dropped her bra on the floor.

"Asleep next door," she said with a soft smile. "Have we ever spent a whole night alone together in your bed?"

"Not since you were about five," he said, and practically choked when she summoned him by crooking her finger.

He walked into the room, thinking he really should throw a blanket over Tracy and send her away. She was back to the vamp act.

He still couldn't believe he was thinking that way. He also couldn't believe Tracy was wiggling out of her shorts and tugging at the drawstring on his pants. Her fingers were warm and firm against his flesh, but her mouth was hot. He clenched his hands into fists and closed his eyes, catching his breath at her boldness. "This isn't a good idea, Tracy."

She moved closer and cupped his bare buttocks with her hands to pull him onto the bed. A muffled blast sounded beyond Riley's window, reminding him that it was late night, that he and Tracy were in his bedroom, and that there was no need for hurry. The idea seemed smarter.

Her fingers and lips continued their quest, making him feel manly and powerful and out of control, all at once. He would have paid the devil for another night with this woman, and she was here on her own and clearly feeling adventurous.

The idea now seemed brilliant.

He let go of a caution he'd never been comfortable

with, anyway, and allowed Tracy to do things she confessed she'd never done before.

Later, when he pleasured her the same way and turned her startled gasps into satisfied cries, he was reminded of her sweetness.

By the time he thought to turn out the bedroom light, the sounds of the lake celebration had ceased. Most of America was quiet and still.

But in Riley's bedroom, the fireworks raged on. He was constantly aware of the fact that this time might be the last. Tracy seemed just as insatiable. Riley felt as if they were both storing reserves of touches and kisses. Of completion.

And for him, of love.

When Tracy fell asleep a few hours before dawn, Riley watched her for a while. He loved the guileless look of her face in sleep. Without a flirty smile or pensive frown to change her features, it was the face of the woman he loved.

The wild woman of the past few hours was as amazing as any woman he'd been with—but she wasn't enough for him. The mother Tracy became around Hannah was very caring; the businesswoman was wonderfully efficient.

But they weren't enough, either.

He needed the whole woman, the *real* woman.

Riley touched her cheek gently, then rolled out of bed. Pulling on his pajama bottoms and a T-shirt, he went to the kitchen to start a pot of coffee. He pulled a chair through the house and left it next to his bed. Then he turned on the bedroom light and immediately turned it off again. He walked out to turn on the hallway light and left it on. He wanted the softest light possible.

The gentlest ending.

Going back to the kitchen, he poured two cups of coffee, returned to the bedroom and sat down with a cup in each hand. And watched Tracy again for a minute. He'd give anything to see her eyes open and look at him in love. To see her mouth smile and say the words he needed to hear.

Unless she could offer that kind of honest emotion, things would never be right between them. "Tracy, wake up," he said, his voice loud against the quiet of deep night.

Her languid movements against his sheets made him want to join her there, and reminded him why this was necessary. "Wake up," he repeated.

She opened her eyes, and closed them again.

"You can go home to sleep and we can talk in the morning, or we can talk now."

"You're kidding," she said, smiling as she opened her eyes again.

"No."

As Tracy sat up, she seemed to notice that he was clothed and she wasn't. She pulled the sheet up and tucked it under her arms, accepting the cup he held out to her. "What's wrong?" she asked after she'd taken a sip. "Is Hannah okay?"

He drank from his cup, too. "As far as I know, she's still asleep next door."

"Didn't I just go to sleep?"

"Yes." He offered a quick grin that felt painful. "But if we don't talk, the cycle will keep repeating."

"Cycle?"

"We'll go to work tomorrow, meet for lunch and spend the evening with Hannah. The days will pass and we won't ever talk about what's bothering both of us."

She handed him her coffee cup and wriggled out of the bed to snatch her clothes off the floor. "Which is?"

He got up and set both cups on the dresser, keeping his back to her to allow her some privacy to dress. "That we're together, but we're not. That you have to put on an act to feel comfortable alone with me. That you don't believe we can work as a couple."

She was quiet, so he turned his gaze to hers long enough to read the truth in her eyes. Then he turned around and stared at his fingers, gripping against the edge of his dresser. "I love you," he said quietly, finally admitting to himself that he needed her to return those words to him as much as he needed the breath he was holding.

"You said that earlier."

It was all he needed to hear.

Or not hear.

She was obviously interested enough to sleep with him, but not interested enough to take that last step. He didn't blame her, really. He'd always been the troubled boy next door. Who would choose Otto and Vanessa as their child's grandparents? Tracy knew exactly what she wanted from life and it wasn't him.

"Go home," he said, turning around without caring whether she was finished dressing or not. "We'll say hello if we bump into each other, but that's all. I'll move away as soon as I can sell the business and convince Lydia to come away with me."

Tracy seemed shaky as she pulled on her shorts. Even though she was dressed in patriotic red, white and blue from neck to thighs, she looked fragile.

And he felt horrible. He didn't want to care.

She fastened the button at her waist before she looked

up at him. "A gold-star girl knows what to do in every situation. Why do I feel like such a dork?"

He shrugged. "I guess because you're looking for someone else. Isn't that it?"

She gathered his sheet in a ball and tossed it on his bed. "I don't know," she finally said, almost whispering.

"I do."

She frowned as she glanced around his floor.

"Need something?"

"My shoes?"

"You were barefoot when you got here," he said, and bit his cheek at the stricken look on her face as she walked out of his bedroom, then his front door. His life.

He wished he could make this easier for her or take consolation from her tears, but he could do neither. The way he saw it, it didn't matter how much either one of them hurt. Ending things was the only way to preserve his dignity. He couldn't keep loving a woman who saw him as the pitiable little boy next door.

He wasn't that little boy anymore.

AFTER SHE'D STARTED her car, Tracy looked at the clock on the dashboard. A three and a colon, and seventeen. Three-seventeen in black on gray. Three-seventeen on the steering wheel. On the lawn. On Riley's bedroom window.

The numbers were superimposed on her brain, making her think this might be a nightmare. She couldn't decide if the time was very late or very early, and finally concluded that it didn't matter. She was too upset to sleep.

Riley was right. If the relationship wasn't going anywhere, it should end. Sooner was better than later. He had only been strong enough to do what she couldn't. Why didn't she feel relieved?

The streets were empty as she headed toward the duplex, yet the drive seemed difficult. She didn't like the thought of being home alone before dawn. She wanted the sounds and motions of daytime. To exert herself in the activities of caring for a child and living in a world of Internet mail, drive-thru dining and credit cards. No one knew how to wait anymore, and for once, Tracy was glad. If she kept busy enough, this deep sadness couldn't overrun her heart.

That was her wish for today—to be too busy to think.

At four in the morning, Tracy vacuumed every room of the apartment. At five, she cleaned the bathroom. At six, she sat on her exercise bike and pedaled furiously for nearly an hour. When she finally sat down in her rocker to rest, Claus came out from hiding. He walked to the middle of the living-room floor and stared warily at her, as if he wasn't sure he recognized her. Tracy called to him and patted her lap, but he scampered off toward the laundry room.

Just as abruptly, Tracy bounced up and went to Hannah's room to sort through the closet for outgrown clothes. When the phone rang a while later, Tracy dashed down the hall to her own bedroom and grabbed the receiver off the stand, thinking it might be her mother calling about Hannah.

"I trust I'm not calling too early," Booker said in a cool tone that did nothing to soothe Tracy's nerves.

"Of course not," she snapped. "I'd normally be reporting to your office about now." It *was* the middle of the week.

"That's what I thought," Booker said. "I called to ask about your big day."

"Big day?"

"The raffle," he reminded. "How did things go yesterday? I trust you didn't hit any snags."

Was that yesterday? It seemed like aeons ago. "Of course not," Tracy said. "It went fine, and we earned over a thousand…er, over seven hundred dollars."

"Which was it? Three hundred dollars would buy several weeks' worth of groceries for a needy family."

Riley hadn't given her the money he'd offered, and Tracy didn't have the heart to call and remind him. "A thousand," she said, figuring she could write a personal check and no one would know the difference.

"And you have the money?"

"Of course," Tracy said, realizing immediately that she didn't. Her horrendous morning had just become worse.

"Excellent," Booker said. "I'll come by to get it around eleven. Did you ask the sorority women to meet me at the Family Aid Center?"

"Yes." That had been the plan. Since the banks had been closed for the holiday yesterday, Tracy was supposed to have brought the money home. Booker was supposed to convert it to a cashier's check today, then meet Jennifer and the others at noon to make the donation.

If Tracy didn't find the money, a lot of people were going to be disappointed. She tried to imagine where it might be. The last time she'd touched the blue bank bag, she'd put it on the podium shelf. It could still be there. It could have been stolen. It could have dropped out.

When she heard the dial tone, Tracy realized Booker had hung up. She hoped he'd only said goodbye, because she hadn't heard him. She hung up and stood in the middle of her bedroom. Slipping her pinkie finger be-

tween her teeth, she ran her tongue over the sharp round-
ness of her nail. Over the past few weeks, she'd been
too relaxed to bite her fingernails. Or too happy.

Things had certainly changed, but she'd gotten her
wish. She should be too busy to think.

Stripping out of yesterday's clothes, Tracy pulled on
jeans and a T-shirt. She was in a rush, and there was no
reason to dress up. She didn't want people to associate
her with Vanderveer's, anyway.

She grabbed her cell phone, slipped on her sandals
and headed out the door. Before she pulled out of the
garage, she called her mother and explained the situation, asking her to watch Hannah for a while longer.

She sped toward the lake, only slowing when she traveled the stretch of highway behind Riley's house. She
wondered if he was awake. He might remember if he'd
seen the money when he'd loaded the podium. Even if
he didn't, he'd find a way to make the situation easier,
she knew. He'd help her in her search, and probably get
her to laugh about the situation.

It was hard to believe she couldn't call him.

Tracy looked in every trash can around the pavilion
and even asked the cleanup volunteers. No one had
found the money. Leaving her telephone number at the
lake office, she took off toward town. As she passed
Riley's backyard again, she held off a strong impulse to
forget everything else and stop by his house.

The car-rental agency hadn't found the bag, but they
let Tracy check the van. It wasn't there, so she left her
number there, too. Finally, Matthew helped Tracy search
the empty lecture hall where the chairs and podium were
stored. The money was truly lost. Tracy asked her stepdad to dial her cell number if it turned up, but she knew
it didn't matter.

In the middle of a morning when she'd been too busy to think, she'd kept thinking. She'd discovered she wasn't particularly bothered about the possibility of losing her job, the money or her status as full consultant.

She was upset about losing Riley.

She recognized how much she missed his help and advice, and knew he'd become her best friend again. She remembered the hours they'd spent alone and knew she'd never find a more creative lover. She acknowledged how well he'd reconnected with her family, and knew she couldn't find another man who fit her life so well.

He was a good friend. A strong man.

And the love of her life.

For the first time in a long time, Tracy knew what to do. She drove to Vanderveer's, parked in her usual spot and surprised Booker by walking straight into his office and sitting down in the client's chair. "I have a confession to make," she announced.

Booker leaned back in his chair and frowned.

"I lost the money."

"The thousand dollars?" Booker asked, turning pale.

"Yes." Tracy plopped her checkbook down on the cherry-wood desk and wrote a check to the Family Aid Center. "I looked for that blue bag all morning and couldn't find it," she said calmly as she slid the check toward Booker.

Booker looked at it. "But why is it made out for thirteen hundred dollars?"

Tracy stood up and started backing toward the door. "A dear friend donated three hundred dollars just to split a few apricots with me yesterday. I'm adding the same amount and replacing the rest."

Booker tapped his index finger on the check. "Thanks for this, but sit back down. We have things to discuss."

"I realize I made a huge mistake," Tracy said. "I'm willing to listen to whatever you have to say, but not right now. I have somewhere to go."

Booker's mouth dropped opened.

"I'm sorry," Tracy said, starting to smile as she left.

And all the way to Riley's office, Tracy couldn't stop smiling. She might have confessed herself out of a job and she'd given away a big chunk of her down payment money, but she knew she and Hannah would survive.

It was time to adapt her goals to a new situation.

After parking in the alley beside the purple door, Tracy went inside and listened to Duncan tell her Riley wasn't there. He'd called this morning to say he had things to do.

He wasn't at home, either. Tracy rang the doorbell a few times, knocked a while and finally stepped off the porch to peek in his garage windows. His car was inside, but his motorcycle was gone.

She called her mother to explain that she was next door but not ready to pick up Hannah yet. Then she went through Riley's gate and across to the swing set. Facing his house this time, she sat down to think about where to look next.

When she heard his motorcycle a few minutes later, she laughed and started swinging. Sure enough, within a minute he stepped outside the back door with his helmet in his hand. "Tracy? What are you doing?"

She jumped out of the swing and started toward him, smiling all the way. "Waiting for you. Where've you been?"

He stepped out of the way when she nudged past him into his kitchen. "I was at the duplex listening to Nellie," he said after he'd followed her in. "She was worried because she heard you vacuuming in the middle of the night."

Tracy chuckled. "What did you want?"

"I remembered that I owed you some money," he said, pulling a check out of his wallet and handing it to her. "I also regretted sending you away so late."

Tracy stuck his check in her back pocket. "I couldn't decide if three-seventeen was late or early, but I knew you were right to do what you did."

Smiling in the cocky way that turned her insides to mush, Riley leaned on the door frame between his kitchen and living room. "Why are you here, then?"

She stepped toward him. "I came to apologize for the way I treated you yesterday at the festival."

He shook his head and started to speak, but she put her index finger over his mouth. "I'm not done," she said. "I also came to tell you that I love you and I'm extremely glad you love me back."

He swept her into a gigantic hug that turned into a soulful kiss and then back into a hug. When he finally let go, he moved his mouth tiny inches away and kept his eyes closed. "You've covered every base again," he whispered. "Or almost, anyway."

He kissed her again, and Tracy was too lost to talk for a while. But when he finally moved back to smile at her, she asked, "Almost? What did I miss?"

"I knew that would draw a response," he said with a chuckle. "I was wondering if you'd help me put a stop to those damn quickie lunches."

She laughed. "How?"

Taking both of her hands, Riley dropped down on one knee. His eyes were bright yet earnest. "Tracy Gilbert, will you marry me?" he asked.

Tracy knew she'd remember this moment forever. Riley's strong, sure voice. His sweet expression. Her own joyful reaction. She knelt down, too, wanting to look in those sexy eyes so that he could see the certainty in hers.

"I'd be honored," was her answer.

Epilogue

Closing her eyes, Tracy inhaled the salty air and smiled when the water lapped her toes. It was hard to believe the folks in Kirkwood were digging out from under a foot of snow. Nellie had called this morning to ask whether Claus would survive after munching down half a fruitcake. When she was satisfied with the affirmative answer, she'd kept talking. Tracy had never considered that asking her neighbor to cat-sit would lead to daily gossip reports from over two thousand miles away.

Today's news was that Nellie had seen Booker trudging through the downtown snow on his way from one errand to the next. Tracy hoped he would realize he should hire help soon. She'd left the job amicably a few weeks after she married Riley, when she realized she was no longer willing to give up her evenings for paperwork.

Besides, Riley truly needed her help, and the fringe benefits were wonderful. Taking the month off, for example.

Riley had said that since his gold-star office manager was vacationing during December, he might as well close up shop. He'd given Duncan the entire month off with pay, then he and Tracy had spent the first two weeks up at the lake. They were building a house there that would be big enough for Hannah, any future siblings and as many guinea pigs as Claus would tolerate.

And now they were on Antigua.

Tracy extended her left hand to watch her diamond catch fire in the sun. "I hope you don't mind a hand-me-down wedding ring," Riley had said when he slipped it on her finger six months ago. "I'll get rid of it and buy you something new, if you'd like."

"No!" Tracy had dropped her hand and frowned at him, then chuckled at his teasing smile. She loved the character of this ring. Designed for Lydia in 1954, it had been worn throughout a passionate and loving marriage. Riley's grandmother had offered it to Riley to give Tracy as soon as she'd heard of their plans, and Tracy had cherished it—and the man who'd slipped it on her finger—every day since.

Over the past six months, she'd caught her breath at the beauty of her ring at least twice a day. Today it seemed to hold a special brilliance that had little to do with the backdrop of the white sands and turquoise waters, and everything to do with the significance of the day. For today, although they'd been legally married since four days after Riley had proposed, they would repeat their vows in front of those dearest to them.

Riley stepped up behind her and wrapped an arm around her waist. Turning to face him, Tracy stepped back to admire his suit. "I love the way you look in that shade of gray." Her eyes moved down, and she squealed, "And your feet are bare!"

He grinned. "I couldn't let my bride be the only one sensible enough to leave her shoes in the cottage." Pausing, Riley let his eyes travel slowly from her head to her toes. "You are stunning," he said quietly.

Tracy spun a slow circle in the sand. The cream dress she'd chosen was simple and elegant. "This dress makes me feel like an island princess," she said. "And the ring and dress are my something old and something new."

"What about the next line—something borrowed?"

Tracy showed him her hand. "Karen painted my nails this morning using her bottle of polish."

"Don't tell me," Riley said. He took her hand and made a show of examining her nails. "It has to be Princess Pink."

"No."

"Bridal Blush?"

She laughed. "Try Caribbean Champagne."

"Mama! Daddy!" Hannah flew across the beach and jumped to a stop in front of both of them. She frowned, looking from Tracy to Riley and back, then finally threw her arms around Riley. "Nana Lydia took me on a boat. We saw thwee doll-fish!"

"Dolphins, Bean. That's wonderful," Tracy said as she hugged her little girl. "You and your nana have been like two peas in a pod ever since you got off the plane."

"The others are coming," Karen said as she approached with an armful of blue-crystal headdresses. "They were meeting the minister in the lobby to lead him out here." Karen positioned one headdress on Tracy's head, one on Hannah's and one on her own. Then she led Hannah ten feet up the beach to wait.

Tracy noted her parents' linked hands as they approached. She smiled at Alan and Karen's greeting kiss, and chuckled when Lydia bent down to kiss Hannah's nose.

There were no chairs for this audience. She and Riley hadn't planned a promenade and there wasn't a fresh flower in sight. Just the two of them, six beloved family members, the minister, the sky and the sea.

It couldn't be more beautiful.

Two remaining headdresses were put into place on her mother's and Lydia's heads as the minister walked across the beach toward Tracy and Riley.

"Your something blue is very becoming, and it was a nice touch to have all the women wearing them," Riley whispered. "As usual, you've thought of everything."

"'Something old, something new, something borrowed, something blue,'" Tracy chanted, smiling. "But the rhyme has another line. It ends with, 'And a silver sixpence in your shoe.'"

"You aren't wearing shoes," Riley reminded her as the minister positioned himself in front of them.

"I got around that technicality," she said. Glancing shyly at the minister, Tracy lifted the hem of her gown to show off a silver ankle bracelet with coin-shaped charms.

Riley grinned.

And they began again.

HARLEQUIN®

AMERICAN *Romance*®

proudly presents a captivating new
miniseries by bestselling author

Cathy Gillen Thacker

THE BRIDES OF HOLLY SPRINGS

Weddings are serious business in the picturesque town of
Holly Springs! The sumptuous Wedding Inn—the only place
to go for the splashiest nuptials in this neck of the woods—
is owned and operated by matriarch Helen Hart. This no-
nonsense Steel Magnolia has also single-handedly raised
five studly sons and one feisty daughter, so now all that's
left is whipping up weddings for her beloved offspring….

Don't miss the first four installments:

THE VIRGIN'S SECRET MARRIAGE
December 2003

THE SECRET WEDDING WISH
April 2004

THE SECRET SEDUCTION
June 2004

PLAIN JANE'S SECRET LIFE
August 2004

Available at your favorite retail outlet.

HARLEQUIN®
Live the emotion™

Visit us at www.eHarlequin.com

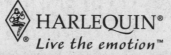

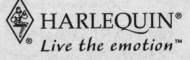

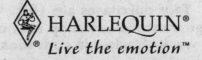

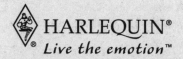